D0648413

THE
Shark Club

Also by Ann Kidd Taylor

Traveling with Pomegranates: A Mother-Daughter Story (coauthor)

THE

Shark Club

Ann Kidd Taylor

VIKING

VIKING
An imprint of Penguin Random House LLC
375 Hudson Street
New York, New York 10014
penguin.com

ISBN 9780735221475 (hardcover)
ISBN 9780735221499 (e-book)

Printed in the United States of America
1   3   5   7   9   10   8   6   4   2

Set in Fairfield LT Std
Designed by Cassandra Garruzzo

For my parents, Sue and Sanford, who are also my friends,
with love and gratitude

There is, one knows not what sweet mystery about this sea, whose gently awful stirrings seem to speak of some hidden soul beneath . . .

—Herman Melville

THE
Shark Club

One

*T*ucking away a long strand of hair that floated in front of my scuba mask, I kicked through the blue-green waters of Bimini on the last day of my research term, keeping watch for Sylvia, a five-foot, four-year-old lemon shark I'd named for oceanographer Sylvia Earle. The shards of sunlight that pierced the water earlier had started to wane, leaving the surface brushed with shadows, and I glanced nervously at Nicholas, my dive partner, then checked my watch. We should have seen her by now. Just beyond her juvenile years, Sylvia had begun venturing outside the protective nursery mangroves where she was born, a habit that worried me, but one I also admired.

Back on the small island off southwest Florida where I lived and worked as a marine scientist, they called me Maeve, the shark whisperer. It implied I could somehow get close to these apex predators, even tame them, which was, of course, a fatal kind of lunacy. The nickname had caught on even here at the Marine Field Lab in Bimini, where I'd spent the last six months tagging lemon sharks with passive integrated transponders, then tracking, collecting DNA on, photographing, and cataloguing them morning, noon, and night. I'd monitored close to a hundred of them, but Sylvia was the one I'd grown fond of.

She had a funny habit of scooping up small bits of fish left behind after she'd bitten and gulped them down, as if she couldn't stand for anything to go to waste. Her frugality not only amused me, it endeared her to me. I liked the way she rested on the bottom after the other lemons swam off, claiming a little extra lounge time for herself. Lazy girl. I could usually identify her before I found the scar on her second dorsal, shaped like an upside-down checkmark. She had often swum closer to me than was comfortable, though I knew that theoretically lemons were generally nonaggressive, and it was probably my imagination and not my science that gave me the odd feeling she recognized me as well.

"You two are simpatico," Nicholas had once remarked. He was only half joking.

It was June 12, 2006, my thirtieth birthday. I should have been back in my small room packing or cooking one of those god-awful cake mixes in the communal kitchen to pass around to the other scientists after dinner to at least acknowledge the occasion, but I hadn't wanted to leave Bimini without a farewell dive. Tomorrow morning, Nicholas and I would be on a short, chartered flight to Miami. From there, he would head to Sarasota and his stingrays. Originally from Twickenham, England, he'd come to the United States as a student fifteen years ago and, after a stint in London, ended up in Sarasota at the prestigious Southwest Florida Aquarium. He'd recently become their youngest director of Ray Research at thirty-five. He'd been here at the Field Lab for a ten-month sabbatical—longer than any of us; I could only imagine how eager the aquarium would be to have him back. Me, I would go back to the Gulf Marine Conservancy on Palermo and to my grandmother Perri's hotel, perched beside the Gulf of Mexico.

The Hotel of the Muses, where I'd grown up and where I still lived, was not your typical hotel on Palermo. While the rest of them were predictably nautical—seascapes over the beds, captain's wheels in the restaurants, aquariums in the lobbies—my grandmother's high-brow resort was overrun with books. Her hotel held readings and book talks in the lobby and had its own lending-library system with a trolley that went room to room along with the housekeeping cart. Every one of the eighty-two rooms was dedicated to an author whose work Perri admired—Charlotte Brontë, Jane Austen, Gwendolyn Brooks, Octavio Paz, Edna St. Vincent Millay, Henry David Thoreau . . . The *Tampa Bay Times* had called it "the real buried treasure on the Gulf coast, a library hotel on Ecstasy." By summer's end I would leave all that "ecstasy" once again for whale shark research in Mozambique.

Whenever my research terms ended, everything I'd put aside and ignored—especially Daniel—inevitably returned, rushing in like tidewater to retake the shore. Already I could feel the past washing up: the last, stubborn image of Daniel the day we'd said good-bye, his back framed by the glare of Miami sun on the window, and then all the silence that followed. The memory returned more mercilessly this time. *Thirty.* What was it about that age? All the clocks ticked louder.

Swimming farther from the cobalt-blue bottom of our boat, Nicholas and I came upon a shower of tiny silver minnows glinting like nickels as they darted in unison. Earlier, a redmouth grouper had found Nicholas and me to be objects of fascination, drawn by the bubbles drifting from our tanks, coming so close I could see the inside of its mouth glowing orange. Among fish, as among humans, there seemed to be two basic schools: the venturesome and the cautious.

Nicholas pointed to a pair of southern stingrays sailing by like a scene from *Swan Lake.* The vibration of their wings rushed toward me, reverberating the way all sounds did beneath the sea, blurred and muffled, a strange, slow-motion percussion. Nicholas felt about rays, especially spotted eagle and giant mantas, the way I felt about sharks, and he snapped a picture just before they vanished.

Holding up his palm, he motioned for me to stop, and I thought for a moment he'd spotted the lemons, but he shook his head and shrugged, a signal for "the sharks aren't coming, our air is running out." After working together the last six months, we'd become adept at one another's body cues. I cocked my head to the side and held up five fingers. *Another few minutes?*

He gave me a thumbs-up and pointed to a crop of sea fans on the ocean floor. *Okay, but let's hang here.*

I nodded. I was going to miss him, and that was a surprise. It was always a surprise to miss someone other than Daniel.

As I drifted over the waving garden of fuchsia and pink fans, I watched a green moray eel partially lured out of its rocky home, while a diligent cleaner shrimp worked its magic on the eel's head. The eel looked ancient—wrinkled, scarred, and oddly serene. It was possible the two of us were the same age. Its mouth gaped open, then closed, over and over. "Ommms" only the sea creatures could hear.

When I used to imagine my life at thirty, I envisioned myself doing just what I was doing now, studying sharks. But I'd pictured myself as a mother, too, teaching my child to swim in the Gulf. Buckled up to his chin inside a life vest, my little boy would frogkick beneath clear, spearmint water. Sometimes the child was a girl, locks of wet, dark hair stuck to her cheeks. After swimming I imagined we would walk back to a small house with an orange tree in front, the branches drooping with fat, ripe fruit. I would shake the branches, then poke my thumb into the top of an orange like my dad had done for me. Sometimes he would carve out the top of it with his pocketknife, then etch an *M* for Maeve on the side. I always thought I would do the same for my little girl. She would drink from the orange like a cup. Daniel would be waiting for us in the kitchen, shuffling a pan of porcini mushrooms on the stove.

So far that dreamed-of future hadn't arrived. Maybe it still would—it's not like my thirties put me out of the running to be a mother. But at some point, if it was still just me and the sharks (thank God for the sharks), perhaps I would put the whole family thing to rest. I could be

Aunt Maeve to any children my twin brother, Robin, might one day have, and I would marry the sea. A lot of people, including Robin, would say I already had.

If Sylvia was anywhere around she already knew Nicholas and I were here. In limited light, her eyes became stronger, and her sense of smell was ten thousand times better than mine. Rows of sensory cells running along each side of her body would already have detected changes in water pressure and sent the message to her brain. As she drew closer, she would use receptors around her head and snout to pick up the electrical field emitted from my heartbeat and brain activity, a kind of GPS that allowed sharks to cross oceans by following the Earth's magnetic field. Whereas Nicholas and I were reduced to hand signals and air tanks, Sylvia was magnificently equipped.

Suddenly the eel withdrew into its nook, jerking quickly like a snapped rubber band. I tensed, alert to the fish darting frantically upward. I turned a slow pirouette, noticing Nicholas doing the same, aware of how small we seemed in the vastness of the Atlantic. Taking a few measured breaths, I listened to the crackle in my regulator and stared into the distance, where the water settled into a trio of shades like a Rothko painting—indigo, violet, and near the surface, pale green.

The shark emerged through the swathes of color, its tail waving back and forth with the hypnotic swing of a pocket watch. I placed a vertical hand atop my head, our signal for shark, doing so almost simultaneously with Nicholas.

As the shark neared, I spotted the scar on its second dorsal fin, the scuffed-up snout. Sylvia.

She wasn't alone. A second, then a third shark appeared behind her—Captain and Jacques, two other lemons in my research.

Nicholas and I watched them without moving. How many times had I been suspended beneath the water just like this as a shark approached? But it always felt like the first time. Sylvia swam toward me, part ballerina, part stealth missile. My adrenaline spiked, and I caught myself holding my breath. It had only been for a second, but even rookies knew that departing from the steady rhythm of inhaling and exhaling was a bad idea and could cause a dangerous expansion of air pressure in the lungs while ascending. Unraveling the knot of air in my throat, I slowly exhaled and began to photograph her long, elegant body, her skin the color of sandpaper. As she passed me, though, the hand holding my camera fell to my side, and I did something I'd never done before. I swam alongside her.

Trailing a respectful distance beside her pectoral fins, I could feel the sheer force of her in the water. The sound her movement made was like thunder coming from far away, yet I felt it shuddering against me. I swam instinctively, not thinking, floating in a half-dreamed place, and what came to me was the quote stenciled on the wall in room 202 of my grandmother's hotel—the Keats Room: "Love is my religion. I could die for that." The sea, its creatures, its sharks—they were my religion. I could die for that.

Sylvia turned and seemed to regard me with interest, and observing her sudden awareness of me was like waking. Though I felt a kinship with her, I couldn't forget for a second she could be provoked into aggression. I drew up, letting her swim away, flattening a hand over my breastbone as she was swallowed into the blue-gray gloom.

Electrified, I kicked my fins.

When I turned toward Nicholas, he was clasping the handles of his camera, and his face mirrored my own. The way his lips stretched into a smile around his regulator reflected my own exuberance.

Two

When people ask me why I love sharks I tell them it's because I was bitten by one when I was twelve. Statistically speaking, the coconut palms around the hotel had posed more of a danger to me than the sharks cruising the Gulf. Coconuts dropped like torpedoes around there, so it was stranger than strange that I was not concussed by a coconut, but instead, bitten by a shark—a species over four hundred million years old, older than humans, dinosaurs, and trees. It was a blacktip, *Carcharhinus limbatus,* the shark known for breaching out of the water and spinning in midair while feeding on fish near the surface. The bite resulted in a thirteen-inch scar, thirty-three stitches, and an obsession with sharks.

Robin, responding in true twin fashion, became the counterbalance to my morbid fascination, developing a fear of sharks bordering on revilement. I didn't begrudge Perri sending me back to Dr. Marion, a child psychiatrist over in Naples, I still don't, but I did wonder how Robin's hating sharks was viewed as perfectly normal and my loving them was considered detrimental.

If you were hit by a car, would you become a mechanic? Robin used to ask. If you were struck on the head with a rock, would you become a geologist? What about falling off a roof? Would that turn you into a roofer? If you were trampled by a horse, would you become a jockey? His list of catastrophes and careers became an ongoing joke, the kind that weren't really jokes at all. He'd never gotten over almost losing me, and after what had happened to our parents, I couldn't blame him.

I used to fantasize that if Mom and Dad had been alive, they would've downplayed Perri's and Robin's worries over my becoming a sharkophile.

My English professor father, Perri's son through and through, had loved books more than Perri did, if such a thing was possible, and two small volumes of his poetry had been published. He had been the opposite of our sky-minded, engineer mother, whose head had been firmly planted in the clouds, while his had been perpetually bent over books by Keats, Shelley, and Byron.

Mom had had her private pilot's license for two years when the accident happened. Surprising Dad with a weekend in Key West for his birthday, she'd chartered a 1980 Piper, filing a flight plan and arranging for Perri to pick up six-year-old Robin and me at our house in Jupiter, Florida. Their plane had crashed into the Everglades before we'd even arrived at the hotel, before we'd raced through the lobby, up the stairs, arguing over who got the bed by the window, before we'd yanked on our bathing suits and tore down to the beach, giddy over the hundreds of Florida fighting conchs that had washed ashore overnight, squealing whenever some gooey part of the snail oozed onto our palms.

It had taken an airboat to reach their bodies. The National Transportation Safety Board reported Mom had encountered a thunderstorm wind shear. For a while, the sight of a small plane droning overhead, even the mention of an airboat would summon the scene of my parents strapped in their seats, dead, stuck in the muck with the alligators. Gradually, the image stopped haunting me. I can picture them now as they'd been before the accident: Dad, reading poems to us at the kitchen table that were fathoms over our heads. And

Mom, routinely dragging us outside on clear nights in a semifailed effort to teach us the constellations, lying beside us on the lanai by the pool calling out Big Dipper, Little Dipper, Orion's Belt.

After their funerals, Perri had sold our Jupiter house with the lanai where we'd named Mom's stars and the kitchen table where we'd listened to Dad's poetry, and she'd brought us to Palermo to live with her in the Hotel of the Muses. Perri commandeered four rooms on the second floor, knocked out the walls, and reconstructed it into an apartment for the three of us. "It will be an adventure. Like the Swiss Family Robinson," she'd said, rousing herself for the sake of two sad little kids. Night after night, we crawled into her bed, where she read us the Johann David Wyss story, followed by *Peter Pan, Alice's Adventures in Wonderland, The Secret Garden*, and a trove of other classics.

Losing Mom and Dad devastated both of us, but we had grieved very differently. Robin's grief had been quiet and hidden, only screaming out of him unconsciously in his sleep, while mine had been open and expressive. In over her head and desperate to help us, Perri had put us into the capable hands of Dr. Marion. That was my first go-round with therapy; years later when I found myself back in his office after the shark bite, I already knew the drill.

Robin and I spent hours sitting side by side on Dr. Marion's green sofa, Robin in silence, refusing to draw the pictures that were supposed to help us express our feelings. The more he withdrew, the more I talked of alligators circling our parents' plane, of their caskets closed tight. And the more elaborate my drawings became. Sometimes it seemed everything that would go wrong with Robin began with those drawings. One in particular roiled up from a dark corner inside of me. While Robin watched, I had pulled crayons from the jumbo box and begun by creating the same horror scene as usual—a tangle of green jungle, black sky, brown water streaked with red, a gray airplane half immersed, and beneath the water, two broken stick figures.

"You sure you don't want to draw, too?" Dr. Marion asked Robin, holding out a blue crayon. "It can be anything you want. How about your room? What does that look like?"

Robin glared at him, arms folded over his six-year-old chest, then took the crayon. He might have actually drawn something that day—the stuffed frog on his bed, the *Empire Strikes Back* poster on the wall, the baseball cards on the bulletin board—but he was distracted by the surprising addition of a third tiny stick figure I was drawing beside the other two.

"Who's that?" he asked.

I scribbled a mess of red on the little body.

"*Who is it?*" Robin said, and I heard the frantic tone, but still, I didn't answer him.

"Do you want to tell us?" Dr. Marion asked me. "You don't have to, but your brother . . . he's interested."

"It's me," I said, the picture starting to distort through my tears. "I don't want to be here if they're not here."

"You want to die, too?" Robin's voice sounded small and faraway, and then he began to cry, terrible gulping sobs, the first tears he'd shed since our parents' deaths. His whole body shook, and seeing what I'd caused, I began to sob with him. I knew even then, I didn't mean what I'd said. I didn't *really* wish I'd been in the plane, but wishing it seemed the only way to convey the power of my distress, to communicate how much I missed Mom and Dad.

Dr. Marion told us it was okay to cry, but that seemed to backfire on him as the tears and wails went on and on. In the end he summoned Perri from the waiting room. She squeezed between us on the sofa, gathering us against her. When the outburst was finally over, Dr. Marion tried to help Robin understand what I'd meant, but I don't think Robin ever understood. My confession landed on him like a betrayal, like a brutal rejection. After that we saw Dr. Marion separately. I never knew what happened in Robin's sessions. Revealing my awful wish that day was the beginning of mending myself. My grief morphed from excruciating sadness into a kind of resignation, and finally into peace. Perri became my greatest solace and closest confidante. But the plummeting planes in Robin's nightmares continued, though our parents were no longer in them; now, it was only me. He would bolt awake shrieking my name, once so loudly a hotel guest called the front desk. Terrified by his screams, I would crawl into bed with him and grip his hand beneath the covers. "I thought you were dead, too," he would whimper.

The following year his night terrors ceased, giving way to all sorts of misbehavior and acting out—biting and shoving classmates at our new elementary school, mouthing off to the teacher, and once lashing out at Perri when she ordered him to clean his room, yelling, "Don't tell me what to do. You're not my mother."

In time, he returned to something resembling normalcy. He, Daniel, and I formed our alliance, hanging out on the beach and roaming the hotel. I have a memory of Robin doing his Rocky Balboa impression for hotel guests, one of his many budding charismas, but his grief never seemed to heal, not really, and he never became comfortable talking about Mom and Dad, as if his mind just couldn't go there.

Troublemaking would be his go-to method of expressing his grief, and I believe writing must have been an outlet for it, too. He did both, on and off, with great aptitude.

I'd never stopped feeling bad about that drawing, never stopped feeling responsible.

Perri liked to say that some kids just had swing sets in their backyards, but we had the Gulf of Mexico. The island and every living thing swimming in the Gulf became my Eden. And Daniel, he became my Eden, too.

Daniel's mother, Van, worked at the hotel reception desk when she wasn't teaching ballet. Daniel was always at loose ends in the hotel, lugging his skateboard around, occasionally rolling across the marble floors in the lobby. Almost a full year older than Robin and I, Daniel was the first friend we made on Palermo. It didn't take long for the three of us to become inseparable. His father had been the high school baseball coach on the island, and from all appearances, a reasonably good father. Until he left one day, simply disappearing from Daniel's life, a cataclysm that he rarely talked about. Robin, Daniel, and I shared fatherlessness—whether from abandonment or death—like some tragic glue that cemented us in ways none of us really understood. Constantly mistaken for our older sibling, he had a mess of dark hair like us that the sun leached to golden brown. Robin liked being confused for Daniel's brother, but I never wanted to be Daniel's sister.

~

The shark attacked on July 30, 1988, early in the morning, when the air was hazed with mist and the beach deserted. Daniel and I had wandered to the water's edge to investigate a washed-up horseshoe crab, when I spotted a brown-and-white-striped osprey feather nearly a foot long floating on the waves ten or so yards out. Maybe I wanted to impress Daniel with how audacious and unfettered I could be; maybe I just wanted that magnificent feather; but I waded out in my shorts and T-shirt until the water lapped a cold circle around my waist.

"What are you doing?" said Daniel, gaping at me from the shoreline.

"Are you worried about getting a little water on your shorts?" I teased, plucking the feather off the surface and using it to wave him in.

Grinning, he treaded out to where I stood, lifting his arms and bare shoulders to stave off the chill. He swiped the feather from my hand and stuck it in the band of my ponytail. "There," he said.

I reached back, feeling for it, aware of how close he stood to me, his shoulders peppered with freckles, his skin caramelized brown, his eyes the color of a blue tang fish. Leaning up, I kissed him, jolted at how he kissed me back, at the salt air on his lips. For a moment I felt dizzy, like the world I'd wakened in had fallen away, and I had become someone else. It thrilled me and it scared me.

"I think I'll love you forever," I said.

Daniel glanced back toward the beach, where Robin and Perri were beginning to set up lounge chairs beneath the chickee huts that studded the sand in front of the hotel. "Me, too," he said.

Suddenly, he pitched forward in the water like he'd been struck behind the knees. "What was *that*?" he said. I thought he was trying to scare me, but whatever had bumped into Daniel then collided into me. I lost my balance and dropped beneath the water as an unfathomable force attached to my leg. I held my breath and flapped my arms, trying to fly right out of the water like the diving seabirds I often watched splash up into the air. I could see it very clearly, the top of the shark's gray head, its teeth clamped into my leg, the fin's black tip, the tail ruddering back and forth.

It was noisy under the water, sounds and vibrations whipping off both our bodies. Blood coursed from my leg like a can of teargas going off. Nothing at all went through my head, only a primal, ferocious instinct to live.

Stretching my neck toward the surface, I glimpsed one of the shark's eyes—a small, black, unblinking night. I felt certain the shark regretted sinking its teeth into me, or did that thought come later? Its eye disappeared under a lid that closed from the bottom up, and then as suddenly as the commotion had begun, it all ceased.

The shark let go of my leg and swam off. I had no idea why. Now I know it was exhibiting classic hit-and-run behavior: a bump, a single bite, and then a retreat when it realizes its prey is not food, but a case of mistaken identity.

The bite had been oddly painless at first, but then a searing sensation ripped through my leg. I wanted air. I needed air. Breaking the surface, I gasped and tried to stand, but my right leg was useless. I floated on my back using my left foot to push against the ocean floor.

Panting frantically, I couldn't raise a single sound from my throat. Water sealed my ears. I thought I heard someone yell, "Maeve! Maeve!" Daniel grabbed me under my arms and began pulling me to shore, running backward.

"A shark bit me and swam away," I said as calmly as if I'd suffered a jellyfish sting.

Daniel shouted for Perri, his voice hoarse with terror. Water rushed into my nostrils, filling them with salt sting, causing me to choke, but the pain in my leg had dwindled to a strange burning sensation from my hip to my toes.

Daniel laid me on the sand. I gazed at him bent over at the waist with his hands on his knees, his eyes filmed with water. "A shark bit me and swam away," I said again.

Struggling onto my elbows, I stared at my leg. The back of my calf was ripped open, ragged and bloody like a science class dissection gone horribly wrong. I flopped back onto the beach as Perri reached us, morphing into one of those women you hear about who become superhero strong and unflinchingly clearheaded in times of crisis, lifting cars off children and barking orders like General Patton. "Robin, run to the hotel. Call 911. Daniel, get towels!"

A little border of darkness began to close in around everything. I shut my eyes to make it go away. Perri pushed a web of hair off my face. "Maeve, honey, open your eyes."

I concentrated on a V of pelicans that glided across the high blue dome of sky overhead, their wings unmoving, all of them ready to turn at once if their leader changed course.

Daniel dropped a stack of towels in the sand, and Perri twisted one and tied it tightly around my thigh. Her bobbed hair was swinging across her face in a white blur. "We've got to stop this bleeding," she said, her voice starting to take on more urgency.

As Perri applied pressure against the wound, the dull burn in my leg erupted again into a blaze of exquisite pain. I rolled my head to the side as a terrible keening sound filled my throat. I began to flail.

Robin dropped beside me, his face blanched and terrified. He put his mouth by my ear. "You're okay." He went on repeating it. "You're okay. You're okay."

Perri hovered over me, blocking out the sun. She shouted at the crowd that was beginning to gather, "Somebody give me a belt!" She lashed it above my knee. "You're going to be all right," she said. "Take a deep breath. Come on." She nodded at me and I sucked the air like I was drowning. "There you go. Slow down. That's good."

Perri placed her hand on my chest, and something inside of me unclenched. I felt safe.

"Let's get her warm," she said, and instantly a coral-colored canopy snapped open above me and the hotel emblem, an oyster shell with a small pearlish-looking book inside stitched in navy, fluttered down.

Searching for Daniel, I pressed my cheek against the sand and saw him a few feet away. "The shark pulled her under," he was saying to Perri. "I tried to get to her. It was all so fast. I—I couldn't get to her."

"How long was she under the water?" Perri asked.

"I don't know. Five seconds? Ten?"

It had felt so much longer.

Much later, Daniel and I would talk about what that day was like for him, how the Gulf had never felt as deep or endless as when I vanished beneath it, how he'd looked underwater for me, afraid of what he might see in the water muddled with a storm of blood and upturned sand.

In the seconds before I lost consciousness, he turned and looked at me, and I saw he was holding the osprey feather that had come loose from my hair.

～

I think Perri feared I'd become infatuated with my attacker, the black-tip, but Dr. Marion assured her that while what I was experiencing was unusual, it was harmless. I sat beside her in his office one day, staring into my lap, looking up to see her gazing at me sympathetically. She decided right then to no longer worry about the jars of saltwater I hoarded under my bed, the medicine cups I filled with shark teeth, the pictures of shark eyes I drew and tacked to the wall. That same evening, I overheard her explaining to Robin that the doctor wasn't worried about me and he shouldn't be either. He tried, eventually venturing into the Gulf with me, but he kept inventing reasons we should cut it short. He never lost his dread that something in the water would take away what was left of his family.

Perri would continue to send me to Dr. Marion. At twelve, I had a million hashed and unhashed thoughts. Flashbacks about my parents' crashed plane. Ambivalence about Robin and me living in a hotel, which really was like the Swiss Family Robinson, and which my friends thought strange, how I wished sometimes for a normal house. I confided that I hated the scar that jagged across my calf, but I forgave the shark, who was just being a shark. I told him about Daniel, who saved me. Daniel, whom I loved.

I was fourteen when I visited Dr. Marion for the last time. We were having one of those August tropical storms that blows up quickly around Palermo. Rain was slashing sideways against the windows of his office with flashes of lightning in the distance. When I jumped at a sudden clap of thunder, he asked if I was afraid of storms.

"No, not storms," I said.

He laid his pen down on his tablet. "What then?" he asked.

"Everyone already thinks I'm crazy. I don't want you to think I'm crazy, too."

"I won't think you're crazy, Maeve. I've never thought you were crazy."

Moments passed while I stayed silent, terrified of saying it. The words were burning a hole in my throat, and for the first time I felt like keeping them in would feel worse than letting them out. "Well," I said. "I—I want to know everything about sharks. I want to study them when I grow up, to really understand them. Know what they're like. I check out books all the time about Jacques Cousteau and being a marine biologist. That's what I want, but I'm afraid my grandmother will tell me I can't. I'm scared it would come between me and Robin. That Daniel and my friends will think . . . you know, that I'm weird or something."

I stopped, feeling like I might cry. I sat there listening to the rain, waiting for Dr. Marion to say something, but he waited, too.

"I'm not stupid," I told him. "I know what the shark could've done to me that day, but it didn't. It let me go. It could've ripped me to shreds, but it let me go. This year I got to be in a play at school, and my class went to the Edison Museum, and I read Anne Frank's diary—all things I loved. But I've never felt about anything the way I feel about sharks."

"And how *do* you feel about sharks?"

My longing to answer this question, to say it out loud, was so intense that a flood of feelings hit me at once and the tears I'd been holding inside let loose.

"I know it's weird," I said, shoving them off my cheeks. "But happy. When I think about sharks, I feel happy."

He leaned back in his chair and smiled. "Jacques Cousteau seems like a happy guy. I bet Eugenie Clark is happy. Have you heard of Eugenie Clark up in Sarasota?"

I shook my head.

"They call her the Shark Lady because of her research with sharks. She trained them. Got them to ring bells. Can you believe that? And then there's Sylvia Earle—she's from Florida, too. Ever heard of her?"

"No."

"She just happens to be the only person ever to walk solo on the ocean floor. A quarter mile down. She's known as Her Deepness. You should look them up."

"I will," I said, and it felt like something in my chest was opening. A clamshell.

"I don't know much more about oceanographers than that, but I do know this. Whatever makes you feel alive, you ought to pay attention to it. If it makes you happy, it's worth following."

Three

Nicholas and I surfaced simultaneously. The sun was lower than I'd expected and the wind had picked up. Our nineteen-foot Twin Vee teetered on the seesawing waves, small swells slapping the sides. As we swam through the ruffling chop, I could hear a Midnight Oil song drifting from the radio on board. We climbed in, stripped off our equipment, and shared a spontaneous, celebratory embrace, wet suit to wet suit.

Simon, the local captain who'd been piloting our boat for the last six months, managed a smile from beneath his oversized straw hat, its cord drawn snug under his chin. "Your lemons showed up, did they?"

"Sylvia, Captain, and Jacques," I told him.

He nodded and cranked the engine, swinging the boat toward the dock at the research lab. Nicholas and I stood in the stern, struggling to peel down to our bathing suits without losing our balance as Simon picked up speed, the noise of the motor drowning out everything else.

Wrapping a towel around my black one-piece, I sat on a cooler and squeezed the water from my hair, then shook it out around my shoulders. As I watched the expanse of ocean open up behind us, I was hit with a small surge of sadness. I despised endings.

I glanced up. Nicholas was watching me.

"Happy birthday," he mouthed.

"Thanks," I mouthed back. I expected him to look away, but he didn't. It was only when Simon asked him to take the wheel that he turned his attention elsewhere.

~

The sadness of my life was losing Daniel. The memories had a belligerent quality, retreating for long lapses only to return, as if from a nice, replenishing rest. He'd proposed to me on the dock behind his childhood home in Palermo on Christmas night, 1998. "Let It Snow" floated out from a neighbor's lanai, a totally incongruous tune in the 68-degree weather. I said yes. Of course, I said yes. Back in Miami, where I was a grad student at the university and Daniel was in culinary school, we rented a stucco house painted an appalling shade of aqua and began planning a beachside wedding at Perri's hotel. We set the date—June 5, 1999.

For a few weeks, our life together seemed perfect and unassailable. But we'd been engaged only briefly when the fault lines began appearing. Coming home from class one day in January, I found Daniel in the kitchen, looking morose and distracted as he scooped the green flesh out of a half dozen avocados.

"What's wrong?" I asked.

He waved it away. *It's nothing*. But it was hardly nothing—he'd turned down a chance to study in Italy for eight weeks in the Spring. He explained he didn't want to be away that long, especially since he wouldn't return until right before the wedding.

"But it's *Italy*," I told him. "You should go. I can handle the wedding plans. Perri will help."

"No, really, it's a done deal. It's fine." He smiled at me, but I felt his disappointment sail across the room and hit me in the face.

Neither of us spoke the word *Italy* until several weeks later, when, by a monumental twist of irony, I was one of two graduate students chosen for a ten-week academic program at the prestigious Shark Behavior and Conservation Reserve in Fiji. The program ran from May 18 to July 27 and would cinch my dissertation work. I swept into the house that evening blinded by euphoria, certain I could make him understand.

He sat on the beaten-up leather sofa we'd bought at a garage sale, his hands dropped between his knees while I did my best to explain and justify. Finally, I knelt in front of him. "We'll have to postpone the wedding till August. Just for two months, Daniel. That's not so bad."

He gazed at me almost expressionless, then stood and walked to the middle of the room, leaving me there on the floor.

"I turned down Italy," he said, his words drenched in hurt and disbelief.

I went to him. I tried to twine my arms around his waist, but he pulled away.

"I would have loved an opportunity like Italy, and I turned it down because . . ."

"Because what, Daniel? Are you saying you turned down Italy because of me?"

"Not because of you. Because of *us*."

"I was the one who told you to *go*," I said.

His face flared with anger. "For Chrissake, Maeve, you want to postpone our wedding so you can take off to Fiji for ten weeks! I put our relationship first. I put our *wedding* first. Would it be so hard for you to do that?"

"You act like I'm going off on vacation. It's for my dissertation. It's the chance of a lifetime."

"Right."

He stormed toward the front door.

"I don't want to hold you back, Daniel," I called after him. "Please don't do it to me."

Daniel came around, and we postponed the wedding until August, but after that night, a strange crevice opened between us, a vague distance that welled up when all the busyness and demands fell away and it was just us. The week before I left for Fiji, he began spending longer hours at school. I told myself he was protecting himself from the pain of me leaving. I know how injured he must have felt. How he believed he wasn't as important to me as the sharks in Fiji or my dissertation. Perhaps he felt I was leaving, the way his father had. Abandoning him. But my leaving could never pardon what he did while I was away.

I returned from that pivotal trip at the end of July, ten days before Daniel and I were to be married. He swooped me into his arms at the airport and held me for so long, I'd finally laughed and said, "Missed me, huh?" He let me go with a wan smile. On the ride home, he seemed oddly quiet.

He made coffee while I walked around the kitchen, noticing how he'd rearranged the countertops. I was woozy with jet lag, woozy with happiness at the sight of him. We took our mugs to the little sunporch, where I plopped onto his lap.

"God, I've missed you," I said.

He'd tapped my leg, signaling me to get up. I slid to my feet and watched him set down his coffee, pace a few feet away, and stand in the arched doorway, his face still and grave. I felt my stomach tip over.

He said, "While you were gone . . . While you were gone, I made a mistake."

Bounced rent checks came to mind. A forgotten deposit to the florist. Perhaps he was going to Italy after all and we would postpone the wedding till December.

"What kind of mistake?" I asked. He looked away, toward the window, at the thick, graying clouds. "Daniel, what is it?"

"I'm sorry," he said. "This isn't easy to say to you." His eyes suddenly grew shiny, filling with tears. "I'm going to be a father."

I stood there motionless and confused.

"She's in culinary school," he said. "I didn't mean for it to happen. Any of it. I just found out two days ago."

Daniel, a father. With another woman.

For a long, shocked moment, I didn't feel anything, and then a crushing sensation like I couldn't breathe. He stepped toward me, but I held up my hand. *Don't.*

"I'm sorry. God, Maeve, I'm so sorry."

I dragged myself to a chair and sat. He was talking, begging me to forgive him, but I could barely hear what he was saying.

I didn't feel anger—that would come later—only a gut-wrenching anguish, the bottom dropping out of everything. I tried to right myself by asking calm, rational questions.

"Are you sure about the baby?" I said. "I mean that it's yours?"

He nodded. "It's mine."

"What's her name?"

"It doesn't matter," he said.

"It matters to *me*."

"Holly."

Holly.

"How many times?" I asked.

"Maeve . . ."

"How many times?" I repeated. "Were you with her the whole time I was gone?"

"No," he said, coming toward me again.

I picked up his mug of coffee and threw it across the room. The ceramic shattered and the smell of coffee rose up, enveloping us. "Just long enough to get her pregnant," I said. "Well done."

I walked to the front door, where my bags still sat packed. I picked up my car keys from the wooden bowl on the side table and dropped my engagement ring into it.

Cheating is so mundane until it happens to you. Then it's the first time such deceit has ever happened.

The same week he broke the news to me, I sent a card to every invited guest, regretfully informing them that there would be no wedding. I retrieved the deposit for the small band we'd reserved for the reception, a calypso trio; let go of the block of rooms at the hotel Perri had set aside for out-of-town guests; informed the minister; and terminated the gift registry. Then I went underwater in more ways than one.

Daniel escaped to northern Italy, and despite the fact that he was alive and well, practicing techniques for grilling plums and asparagus, sampling Parmesan polentas, and curing meats, I experienced his loss like an actual death. One day he existed. The next day he did not.

Not only did I let him go, I let go of everything we'd planned. We would not get married at the hotel under a chickee hut on the beach. We would not have a child who might inherit the flat bridge of his nose. We would not housetrain a puppy, or talk about my work with sharks or his work with risotto.

I threw myself into finishing my dissertation and found a job at the Conservancy that put me in the water with sharks, and the sharks saved my life. I was too busy during the day to grieve; it was nights that were a torment. I imagined a time in the future in which Daniel would be assembling a crib or viewing an ultrasound image. He would be reading *What to Expect When You're Expecting,* saying things like, "Has the baby kicked yet? It happens around five months, doesn't it?" The worst agony, though, was not Daniel raising a child with another woman, it was realizing I couldn't trust the person I'd known and loved since childhood.

Although it sounded good and noble when Keats said it, maybe I *could* die for love; it might truly be the death of me.

It took two solid years, but in the interest of saving a life—mine—

I moved on the best I could. There are places in the sea deeper than Everest is high, places that light cannot reach. That is where I placed Daniel.

～

After Simon docked the boat and Nicholas and I unloaded scuba gear, coolers, and cameras into the equipment shed at the dive station, we stood side by side at the large outdoor sink, sloshing our masks with fresh water, presumably for the next batch of scientists who would no doubt be struck with our same clownish smiles at the sight of one magnificent creature or another, a spiny lobster, a sea horse with its tail spiraled around a thin blade of feather grass.

We hung our wet suits to dry. I pulled a pair of shorts over my suit and wriggled my feet into flip-flops. Nicholas went barefoot, always barefoot—I wasn't sure I'd ever seen him wear shoes. He picked up a large white bucket stuffed with a muddy cast net that he and Simon had tossed around in the shallows near the mangroves. A pump in the desalinator shed kicked on with a low hum, as he spread the net across the concrete, clattering the lead weights around the edges. "We must leave no footprint. Or dirty cast nets," he said, turning the hose on it.

I stood beside him watching the mud wash away. When the net was clean, Nicholas nudged me with his hip.

"You looked a little depressed back there on the boat," he said. "Come on, cheer up, it's your birthday."

"I'm fine. I'm going to miss Sylvia. All of them, actually. That's all."

"So, on to Africa?" he asked. His nose was pink with sun, and his short dark hair glistened with sand and the first traces of silver. Above his right knee, his skin was still inflamed from a jellyfish sting a few days earlier.

"Mozambique by way of Palermo," I told him. "First, I'll go back to the Conservancy and try to compile all the data I've collected here into something publishable. What about you?" I asked. "I guess you'll be glad to see your ray buddies?"

Nicholas laughed. "Yeah. I plan on teaching them some new tricks. Sit. Stay. Roll over."

A rainbow spectrum appeared in the mix of sun and spray, then evaporated abruptly as he cut off the water and knelt down to peer closer at the net. "Look at that. A juvenile stone crab. Still alive."

I stooped beside him. "Where?"

"There," Nicholas said, and pointed.

"Oh my God, it's . . ."

"Impossibly small." It was no bigger than a plum pit, its minuscule pincers locked onto the nylon threads.

"And purple," I added.

He pulled on a gray T-shirt. "Let's take him to the beach and let him go."

He gently gathered up the net and lowered it back into the bucket. We slung our bags over our shoulders like we'd done every week for the last six months and headed down the path toward the beach, bypassing the living quarters and the lab, Nicholas toting the bucket with the tiny stone crab inside. The solar lamps had already popped on along the path, glowing yellow around our ankles as fiddler crabs and tiny geckos darted in front of us.

Out on the beach the sky had that faded, stonewashed look, the sun hovering just on the horizon, engorged, ready to spill its colors. Nicholas fished up the net from the bucket and spread it over the sand. Poring over it on our hands and knees, we searched for the infinitesimal crab, our fingers passing over the net like we'd discovered a washed-up harp.

After a few minutes, I spotted its royal purple carapace dotted with white flecks. "There you are."

Nicholas tenderly pried it free and held it up between his index finger and thumb.

"The little prince," he said, and that made me smile. His eyes were a funny hybrid of light brown and deep green. Under his jaw, a streak of mud I hadn't noticed back at the sink smudged the side of his neck. His hair had been blown straight up by the wind.

For the entirety of my six-month term, we'd kept it professional. Friendly, maybe a little flirtatious. But definitely professional. Nicholas was my dive partner—there were rules of conduct here between scientists, and I hadn't allowed myself to consider anything more. He was separated from his wife and soon to be divorced. They'd been married four years and separated for one. No kids. He'd divulged all this one day while we were cutting bait, not long after we'd begun working together. I can't remember now how the conversation turned personal, only that he'd brought it up. I had the feeling he wanted me to know. There'd been just one moment after I'd first arrived—New Year's Eve, in a fog of champagne—when we'd almost broken the rule.

"You better let the little guy go before he freaks out and autotomizes a claw," I said.

"That happened to me in Curaçao," he said. "I picked up a hermit crab on the beach and it self-amputated a claw right in my hand. So badass."

He stepped into the water, then turned around. "You want to do the honors?"

"It's all yours."

As he released the crab into the waves, I thought of Daniel, and it angered me that I'd let him insinuate himself into the moment. *This* moment. For a while after our breakup, Robin was so furious at him I thought he might get on a plane, go to Italy, and beat the shit out of Daniel. Eventually they'd mended their relationship, but Daniel and I, we hadn't spoken since the day I broke the engagement. Now and then Robin and Perri had passed on bits of news. The mother of his child lived somewhere in Florida. Daniel visited regularly, but the prevailing opinion was that Daniel never pursued a romantic relationship with her. He was head chef of a restaurant in Miami that I wished I didn't know the name of. I knew too much. Before I'd left for Bimini, I'd asked Robin and Perri to stop with the updates. Keeping him out of my head was another matter.

After several seconds of watching the spot where the crab had disappeared, Nicholas walked out of the water and straight up to me. Without saying anything, he studied my face the way I'd studied the crab.

I looked away toward the wild peach stains the sun had left in the sky. "We missed the sun go down."

"Let's sit," Nicholas said, and we settled onto the sand where the tide stopped just short of our feet, depositing miniature flotillas of foam.

"You remember when we met?" he asked.

"It was in the hallway of the dorm, the day I got here. You said, 'You're the shark person,' and then you eyeballed my scar and used it as a quasi scale to estimate the force of the shark's bite."

"Right. I calculated the shark that bit you did so very, very hard."

I laughed.

He went on. "I went to my room after that and thought: *she was literally bitten by the object of her obsession.* That made you the single most fascinating person I'd ever met."

"Or the craziest," I said.

"Plus you live in a hotel—who lives in a hotel?"

"Who doesn't live in a hotel with a book-obsessed grandmother and a ne'er-do-well twin brother?"

"So, do you two share that psychic twin connection? Is he into sharks, too?"

"Hardly. Robin manages the hotel, but he's been working on a novel for a while," I said.

"Oh yeah? That doesn't sound like a ne'er-do-well."

"It's just, for years Robin couldn't exactly keep a job. He had his share of trouble, and I made a habit of rescuing him. Maybe that *is* a psychic twin thing."

When his car was impounded, I paid the parking tickets. When he partied too much and was in danger of failing a class, I wrote his papers. Whenever he woke up hung over on a fraternity sofa, I drove him home and put him to bed.

"I'm simpatico with sharks," I told Nicholas. "Not always so simpatico with my twin." For a second, I felt I was being too hard on Robin. "I've made it sound like he's a bad guy," I added, "but he's not. He's done a good job managing the hotel. The last few years he's really settled down; he gave up being the life of the party, but he's still the most magnetic guy in the room. I admit, he can be self-centered, but he's my brother and I love him."

I looked at Nicholas, self-conscious that I'd divulged all those family details. "So after all that, am I still the single most fascinating person you've ever met?"

"I'm definitely rethinking my earlier statement," he teased.

"That day we met I asked you what your field was—remember?—and you said you were a ray person, but you never told me why."

"Here it is, short and sweet. My mother took me to the aquarium when I was a kid—maybe eight. It had a touch tank full of stingrays and they were looping around and around. I put my hand in the water, a bit nervous—I didn't know if they would sting, but then I touched one. Its skin was like velvet. Nothing like I thought it would be."

I liked listening to him, liked watching him as he told his story, the way he stared straight ahead as if he were talking to the water. "There was this one ray that repeatedly broke ranks to flutter under my hand. It was like a cocker spaniel wanting to be scratched. It was seeking me out on purpose, and I knew there was more to these animals than I could imagine. That was it. I was a goner for rays."

"Sounds like a true religious experience."

"It was, sort of. My father was religious. He used to take my brother and me to church—the good ole Church of England. I didn't mind; I liked it well enough. Then, one Sunday the rector gets up and reads some Scripture about man having dominion over the fish of the sea and every living thing on the earth, and I thought uh-oh, here's where it went wrong. Not to second-guess God or anything, but the next thing you know the ocean is full of junk, we've got trawling, gillnetting, oil spills, whole species disappearing, and half the coral reefs are gone."

The whirring of waves rose, fell, rose again. Imperceptibly, the sky had darkened, and turning, I glimpsed a faint wedge of moon rising behind us. I reached over and touched the place beneath his jaw where the mud had splattered and dried, then dragged my thumb down his neck.

An S-hook crease furrowed around his left brow. "Sarasota is only two hours from Palermo," he said.

"Are you saying you're going to miss me?"

He kissed me then. He smelled like saltwater and sunblock. Like fish and mud and stone crabs.

He said, "I've wanted to do that since . . ."

"Since I got here?"

"Well, for sure since the second week."

"You could come to Mozambique," I told him, and then feeling the gravity and implication of what I'd said to a man who was separated and not yet divorced, added, "The Indian Ocean is prime territory for mantas. Anyway, you might think about it."

"I don't need to think about it," he said.

Four

*A*rctic-like air broke across my face, carrying the familiar scents of the hotel. Stargazer lilies, coffee beans, pineapple, coconut-scented sunscreen. Light poured through the bank of windows along the back of the lobby, showing off the bright curve of a pool, and beyond that a prairie of sand and infinite green Gulf.

Pulling my suitcase behind me, I stopped in the middle of the lobby before a four-foot twisting glass sculpture that sat on a pedestal, glowing blue from the lapis ceiling tiles. It was new, Chihuly-like, something Perri had added while I was away. It looked like radioactive seaweed.

I smiled. I couldn't leave for a minute without some new spectacle appearing in the Hotel of the Muses. A couple of years ago, I'd returned from a term in Australia to find she'd redone the section of the lobby known as the Library with love seats arranged around ottomans the size of tidal pools and loaded them with tangerine and steely blue pillows. At the moment, the sofas were unoccupied, but a few guests perused the bookshelves that encompassed the wall behind them. Two women in swim sarongs had paused to read a sign propped on a brass easel.

~June 13~
Happy Birthday, William Butler Yeats
Join us in the Library at 7:00 P.M. for
An Evening with Yeats.
Complimentary cake, wine & poetry.

The author birthday parties had started when I was a kid. Perri had gotten a whim to celebrate Virginia Woolf the whole month of her birth. Poaching the menu display case from Botticelli's, the hotel restaurant, she'd showcased *Mrs. Dalloway, To the Lighthouse*, and *A Room of One's Own*, and roped a local actress into doing a dramatic reading from each, dressed in period costume. A tradition was born, and over the years, book clubs poured into the hotel to celebrate their favorite authors.

I looked around for Perri, and spotted Robin behind the reception desk, busy with a guest. As I strode toward him, he caught sight of me and handed off the guest to one of the staff, who, I noticed, was now dressed in a shirt the same tangerine color as the pillows. Another innovation in my absence. I hadn't seen Robin since Christmas, and we'd not kept up with each other very well while I was in Bimini. As he swung around the desk, I wished I'd been better about e-mailing him.

"Well, if it isn't Dr. Donnelly, returned from the sea." He pulled me into his arms, and I squeezed him, then leaned back to look at his face. His dark hair was longer, curling on his neck, the front pushed to the side like he'd worn it in college. He was starting to resemble Dad more—the sideburns, his chin, the light brown eyes. At thirty, Robin and I had almost lived longer than Dad, who'd been thirty-two when the accident happened. The thought was surrounded by a tiny corona of ache, and I reached for Robin again, holding on a moment longer.

"You shaved your beard," I said.

"It wasn't much of a beard to start with." He rubbed the back of his hand across his cheek. "Besides, it was hot."

"I like being able to see your face."

"All you have to do is look in the mirror," he said. It was true. Our features were nearly identical, except perhaps for my skin, which, unlike his, was pale like Mom's. It didn't seem fair that Robin, who hardly ever ventured in the sun, bronzed like some Greek god while I, who practically lived beneath the sun, pinked and freckled.

"Thirty suits you," I told him.

"You, too."

We wandered over to one of the love seats, and I drew my feet up under me, dismantling the assembly of pillows.

"Yeats, huh?" I said to Robin.

"Yep. I just hope we don't have a repeat of April. The Shakespeare crowd can put away some wine." He broke into his famous smile. No one could resist Robin when he flashed that smile. He said, "No new scars from Bimini, I hope."

"I'm unscathed," I said, holding out my arms as proof. "Where's Perri?"

"You haven't seen her?"

"Not yet, just walked in the door."

"Your coming home is all she's talked about."

"What'd you do on our birthday?" I asked.

"Drank too much. What about you?"

"Swam with sharks. Packed." I kept the evening with Nicholas to myself. I pointed to the glass sculpture. "Where'd that come from?"

"It's awful, isn't it?"

"I don't know. I kind of like it."

He stared at it a moment, his face growing serious, then slid up to the edge of the sofa. "Look, there's something I need to tell you."

I studied him, suddenly worried as he pressed his hands together, then rested his elbows on his knees. "What?" I asked. "Are you okay?"

"I'm fine. Sorry. I guess when I say it like that it sounds bad. No, it's good, actually. A publisher accepted my book."

I put my hands on top of my head. "Oh my God, Robin, that's great! When?"

"This week."

I gave his knee a shake, genuinely bowled over. There was never any doubt he'd gotten Dad's creative genes and talent for writing. In high school Robin had won a partial scholarship from the Naples newspaper after placing first in its yearly short-story contest. Then at college, he'd majored in English, announcing his aspiration to be a novelist—assuming it gave him license to act the part of the hard-drinking, free-spirited writer. To his surprise, the college literary journal, *The Lyceum*, turned down every short story he submitted. The rejections soured him, but didn't put a dent in his confidence. He promptly set out to write the Great American Novel. Though he seemed largely motivated by a need to prove *The Lyceum* wrong, he threw himself into the writing—skipping classes, flunking a couple of courses, and working through the summers. It became an obsession—a book about a boy whose parents died in a plane crash.

Shortly before graduation, he let his English professor take a look at it. I think he expected a coronation. Instead the professor gave him a long list of the novel's flaws, pronouncing it not ready for publication, but urging Robin to keep working. Devastated, Robin snatched the manuscript from the professor's desk and walked out. He got his English degree, though barely, and moved back home to the hotel, where I watched him turn into the Ernest Hemingway of Palermo—not on the page, just the boisterous, fraternizing part: fishing, partying, betting on greyhound races, and generally charming his way across the island. He became that strange commodity—a writer who didn't write. His aspirations, however, never left him. He made a painful, repetitive ritual of sending his novel out to a publisher and receiving, in turn, a rejection. After sixteen of them, I lost count.

It was during this time that Robin began bouncing from job to job. A clerk at a scuba shop, an island tour guide, a property manager, a limo driver. He had less problem getting jobs than keeping them. Following a spate of firings and preemptive resignations, I got him a job at the Conservancy writing marketing material for the brochures, only to have him quit a month later. He claimed the work was menial and boring.

It was Perri's turn next. She trained him to be the manager of the hotel. Soon after, he began writing again. He'd been at work on his novel for the last three years, going about it with determination, writing in the evenings, often taking his laptop to Spoonbills Bar and running up a tab. He'd given up on the book at one point, only to return to it a month later, unable to abandon this thing he seemed consumed with but would never discuss. Had he returned to that old college manuscript, finally rewriting it? Whenever I asked about it, he was vague: it was either too early or too difficult to talk about; he needed to incubate the idea in silence; he wanted to contain the energy of it. All he ever revealed was that it was set in a hotel exactly like this one.

"It's autobiographical, then?" I'd asked. "A little," he'd said.

I'd wondered then if it was about the moderately famous Rachel Gregory. Three years ago, at the height of success with her second novel, she arrived at the hotel for the summer as writer in residence, a new program Perri had added. A celebrated writer stayed free of charge and wrote undistracted, and in exchange she or he offered lectures and book signings. Robin, recently employed at the hotel, was infatuated from the moment he picked her up at the airport.

The first hint I'd gotten that something unusual was going on between them came the day I got on the hotel elevator and found the two of them standing exceptionally close, arms-touching close, and the air thick with awkwardness.

Two nights later while reading in bed I heard the unmistakable sound of a woman's laughter in Robin's bedroom. Peering into the living room, I glimpsed the red leather tote bag I'd seen Rachel with since she'd arrived.

I was curious about her. The next time she held a reading in the hotel I sat in the back row. Every chair was taken, not just by hotel guests but by residents of the island. According to the jacket flap on her book, the story explored a family's resilience through crisis. It also noted that she lived in Vermont with her husband and Saint Bernard.

Later Robin would call their meeting seismic, and in truth, it did seem like his world opened, and for the first time he fell in love, but I worried that it was one sided. I worried he would get hurt. He seemed unphased that the thirty-eight-year-old author had a husband. The pair became inseparable. They were discreet, setting up shop in the family apartment that Robin and I shared on the hotel's second floor, reading one another's work for hours. Occasionally they disappeared for the day, once returning from the Dalí Museum wearing fake Salvador Dalí mustaches from the gift shop and laughing hysterically. Robin believed she would make a clean break from the marriage, but at the end of the summer she went back home.

I looked at him now sitting beside me, remembering the wreckage she'd left in his life.

"Wow, my brother, the author. Perri must be ecstatic."

Robin, however, looked like someone who'd written his own eulogy. "Why don't you look happy?" I asked.

"I'm happy." He smiled, but there was no life in it this time.

"You have to let me read it," I said.

"I want you to, but I don't want to tell you anything about it beforehand."

"I can't believe you're still being secretive about it. You do realize it's going to be in bookstores, right?"

He laughed. "I know. I care more about you reading it than any-one, that's all."

"I suppose Perri is already plotting the party. An Evening with Robin Donnelly."

"I told her not to plan anything until I talked to you," he said.

That should have been my first clue, but I let it pass. "Has she read the manuscript?" I asked.

"Yes. And Daniel read it, too."

The mention of Daniel caught me off guard, and I flinched slightly as a familiar reflex of hurt and longing recoiled through my body.

Seeing my reaction, Robin said, "We're friends, Maeve."

I nodded. "Yeah, I know."

"I'll get you a copy of the manuscript tonight."

"Can't wait," I said, trying hard to seem delighted, proud, beam-ing, but there was something off about the way he was behaving. As I pulled my suitcase to the elevator, I felt a thump of trepidation in the middle of my chest.

Turning the key, I stepped into our apartment and paused a moment, taking it in. Needing her own quarters, Perri had moved out around the time Robin and I left high school, leaving the entire suite of rooms to us. He took over her spacious bedroom with the sitting area, while I kept my small childhood room with its separate entrance and inher-ited Robin's old room, too. That was the deal we made. I turned his room into a workspace, or as Robin called it, the Twenty Thousand Leagues Under the Sea Room. I'd attached underwater photos to ev-ery wall, images of the sharks I'd tagged and surveyed.

The apartment was neater than I'd expected. Robin had picked up the living room. There wasn't a single stray dish lying around with food stuck to it. No messy piles of mail, papers, or clothes. Magazines were straightened on the coffee table. In the compact kitchen, dishes had dried in a rack beside the sink. I opened the refrigerator. Brown mustard, soy sauce, American cheese, a variety of microbrews from Ybor City, not much else. Peering into his room, I saw a stack of towels folded and placed on the edge of his bed. I was starting to think Robin had made the extra effort on my behalf when I spied a pair of turquoise flats by the balcony door. *So, who was the girl?*

I wandered into my bedroom and was greeted by the oversized blue shark photograph that hung above the rattan headboard. I'd spotted this migratory queen in the deep open waters of the Caribbean Sea at the beginning of her journey, one that would take her as far as Europe. She was still the rarest shark sighting I'd ever had, and probably the most dangerous. I'd snapped the photo quickly, but perfectly, capturing the big black pupil and a knockout mouth parted into an almost-smile. I named her Mona Lisa.

Everything was just as I'd left it. My terry-cloth robe slung across the bed. On the floor, photographs from Christmas I'd forgotten to pack. A bowl on the bedside table heaped with shells—pear whelks, banded tulips, augers, iridescent jingles—covered in a veil of dust. The osprey feather that lured me into the water the day the shark bit, still stuck in a green bud vase on my dresser, looking lonely and rather pathetic. I should have tossed it out long ago, but I could never quite bring myself to do it. Once, I'd planned to stick it into my bridal bouquet.

I opened my suitcase on the bed and began making a laundry pile on the floor when a knock sent me leaping over the clothes, expecting to see Perri. Instead, I found Marco. He was wearing his usual fishing guide uniform and short gray beard. He liked to joke that we shared a common wardrobe: pants that zipped off at the knees, UV-protected shirts, and polarized Costa Del Mars.

He gave me a bear hug and my feet came off the ground. His neck was sticky with sunscreen and his shirt damp with sweat.

"Aren't you a sight for sore eyes?" he said.

"Sore eyes? What, are the fish not biting?"

"I've been trapped on my boat since dawn with a rich, entitled New Englander and his snotty kid."

"This is why I work with sharks," I said. "They're nicer."

I got him a glass of water in the kitchen sink, watching his Adam's apple slide up and down as he drank. "If I'm not mistaken," I said, "you were once a rich, entitled New Englander."

"That's true," he said. "It's also why I'm an expert at detecting them."

At fifty-eight, divorced and unhappy, he'd walked away from a career in investment banking in Boston to become a fishing guide on Palermo.

Marco and I had never spoken outright about our relationship, but as I had no father or grandfather, I think we both saw him as filling the role, at least partially. He'd taught Robin and me how to tie a double fisherman's knot, cast a rod, drive a boat, and had turned us into Red Sox fans.

He sat on a barstool, filling up the little galley kitchen. "Perri has me doing a third sunset cruise," he said.

Marco had been taking guests out on the hotel's pontoon two evenings a week ever since I could remember. The boat departed from the landing in front of the hotel where Perri kept it docked, the cruises timed to the minute to be in the Gulf when the sky went psychedelic.

"So you finally caved in."

"Yeah, never mind that I have my own charter business—anything for Perri."

The two of them had met the summer of my shark bite and become more than just friends. A year later, on Perri's sixtieth birthday, he proposed. To everyone's shock, she turned him down. Anyone could see she loved the man, but she insisted she didn't want to be a wife again. My grandfather had died before Robin and I were born, and eventually Perri had fallen in love with being on her own. She'd bought the hotel.

She'd started painting. She'd begun orchestrating birthday bashes for dead authors. Though Marco was bruised at first, he accepted her decision remarkably well and never pressured her. As he told me once, he wanted Perri more than he wanted a wife. Now Perri was seventy-eight, and her relationship with Marco was approaching its eighteenth year.

He fell silent, toying with his empty water glass. "I— Look, I do have some news. I hate to welcome you home with this, but I thought you should know. In case you haven't heard."

It was the second time in half an hour I'd been told there was something I needed to know. Marco hesitated, sitting down the glass, clearing his throat, then staring a moment through the sliding-glass doors that opened onto the balcony, and I was seized with impatience to have it over with, whatever it was. Homecomings never went off the way you imagined. I thought of Robin letting Daniel read this mysterious book of his. And where was Perri?

"A guy was caught on Bonnethead Key with close to a hundred shark fins drying in his backyard. The Fish and Wildlife people are saying a shark-finning operation may have moved into the area."

I sank onto the stool next to him. An acute feeling of nausea started high in my stomach. I closed my eyes, picturing the graveyard of fins . . . "A *hundred?* At one time?" I said. "*My God.*"

Once, at a conference, I'd watched a video about shark finning that had been secretly filmed on a boat off the coast of Costa Rica. One hammerhead after another was caught, had its fins hacked off, and was then tossed overboard, where it drowned and hemorrhaged in a slow, torturous death. The finnings had been more gruesome than anything I was prepared for. Horror-struck, I'd covered my mouth as gasps and groans from the audience filled the dark auditorium. I'd been hit then by the same groundswell of nausea I felt now.

I wrapped my arms around my middle. "There are a hundred dead sharks on the bottom of the Gulf and those are just ones we know of," I said more to myself than to Marco, as if repeating it aloud would make it possible to believe. "Some of them are bound to be part of my Conservancy research." My eyes burned, then beaded with tears.

Marco gave my shoulder a squeeze. "Goddamned finners," he said.

The way he said it, hissing the words, abruptly halted my tears and ignited my anger. "They're wiping the sharks right out of the ocean—some estimate that eighty million were slaughtered last year. *Eighty million*, Marco, and for what? Shark fin soup! *Jesus Christ!* There's nothing in that soup but a lot of gelatinous goo and it's thought of as a delicacy." I paced into the living room, too irate to sit. "And you know the worst of it? Nobody cares!"

"I know," he said, trailing behind me. "I know—people see them as monsters."

"It makes me crazy! I follow the Shark Attack File like a bible. Do you know how many people were bitten by sharks last year?"

"Two hundred?" he guessed.

"Fifty-eight bites and four deaths. Probably all cases of mistaken identity."

Marco had seen me rant about shark endangerment before. He stood there, nodding, waiting for me to get it out of my system.

"Sorry," I said, and took a deep breath. "So, when did this happen?"

"Two weeks ago. It was on the local news, but I haven't seen anything else about it."

I was surprised that Russell, my boss at the Conservancy, hadn't e-mailed me about it.

Marco said, "You remember Troy Fuller?"

Of course, I remembered him. Like Marco, he was a fishing guide around the Ten Thousand Islands. From time to time, when I saw him in Spoonbills, I said hello.

"Troy is over at Bonnethead Key a good bit," he said. "He knew the guy caught with the fins. According to Troy, this guy was just a small cog in the operation, just a middleman. He hasn't given up the ringleaders."

The sliding doors were open and I could hear the waves, the endless rhythm. I yearned to disappear beneath them. "The man was arrested, right? I mean, he's in violation of the Lacey Act at the very least."

"Yeah, he was arrested," Marco said. "Out on bail now."

He stood. "I hate to run, but I've got a customer and the tide is right for going out. If I hear anything more from Troy about the finnings I'll let you know," he said.

He pecked my cheek. "Don't be a stranger."

"I won't."

I closed the door behind him. The apartment filled with silence, the kind that almost hurt my ears. Retuning to my bedroom, I mechanically picked up the laundry, then dropped it back onto the floor. What was my work for? What difference did it make? *Eighty million dead sharks.* I would never be able to save them. What I was doing was a drop in the bucket.

I sat on the side of the bed overcome with sadness, unable to look at the photo over the headboard. The black shark eye that had seen more of the earth's depths than I could ever hope to see. The Mona Lisa smile.

Five

I wandered past the pool, through the coral umbrellas at the Courtyard Café, then took the steps down onto the beach in front of the hotel, hoping to take a swim before Perri turned up. The south end was breezy, blowing my hair into Medusa-like strands. Even the flock of seagulls resting near the shoreline fell victim to the wind, their white feathers ruffling up into Mohawks. Except for a few tourists who were shelling or fishing off the rock jetty, most of the beachgoers reclined with their books beneath the hotel's chickee huts, shielded from the fierce afternoon sun. The pontoon rocked on the water, empty.

As I pulled my snorkeling gear from my bag and fixed the mask over my nose and eyes, a little girl in a yellow sundress—a first grader, I guessed—ran full steam toward the gulls, causing them to lift off and flap away like little ghosts fleeing an exorcism, their squawking carrying down the beach until they circled around and resumed their resting positions.

I turned to look at the girl who'd caused the maelstrom. She stared out at the Gulf, hands on hips, elbows cocked, looking like a four-foot conqueror.

How many times had I told Perri to post a sign telling people not to chase the gulls? "The birds get tired, Perri. They fly massive distances. They have to recuperate," I'd told her.

Perri reminded me that I'd done it as a child. "But that was before I knew," I said, and she'd declared me a killer of fun.

Aware of how serious I could be about saving the world and how the lightheartedness sometimes drained out of me, Perri made attempts to keep me balanced, teasing me in an exaggerated way that only she could get away with.

Wading into the surf, I shuffled my feet along the bottom to shoo away burrowing stingrays and thought of Nicholas returning to a generic house to unpack his shorts and T-shirts before heading to the aquarium to check on his rays. "We should spend time together above the water," he'd said when we'd parted at the airport.

"Oh, you mean you actually want to talk to me instead of just making underwater hand gestures?" I'd replied.

I wished I could tell him that I'd come home to the calamity of finned sharks. Nicholas would understand the ruin and distress of that more than most. My colleagues were passionate and devoted about their work, but the sea was a religion for Nicholas, like it was for me. He would never give up on rays just like he hadn't given up on the crab caught in the net. I told myself I would call him. Right then what I wanted was to hear his voice.

Slipping the snorkel into my mouth, I floated facedown, my ears filling with water, turning the sounds of wind, gulls, and boat engines into muffled notes. I listened to my breath whoosh through the snorkel. I watched for everything and nothing, afraid that many of the sharks I'd tagged and photographed in these waters had been finned.

The queasiness in my stomach had nearly gone. Flipping onto my back, I closed my eyes against the sun, seeing phosphorescent splotches on the inside of my lids, and forced myself to think about something besides *drowned sharks*. The words didn't belong together. I tried to picture Mozambique instead, a place I'd seen only in pictures. Snap-shots floated into my head of the whale sharks there, *Rhincodon typus,* of Nicholas in bare feet, the first person since Daniel to actually make me feel something.

I floated for a while, glancing over my toes now and then for the clay-colored roof tiles of the hotel, to be sure I wasn't drifting off to Cuba. Thirty yards out, halfway to the channel marker, I swam back to the beach, where I dug my cell phone out of my bag. After a few rings, Perri's voice mail picked up. "Hey, I'm home!" I said, chirp-ier than I felt. "Just had a swim and heading inside now to track you down."

A caravan of Jet Skis sped by, sending wakes onto the rock jetty, and for a moment I watched the pelicans bob on the water like rub-ber ducks, thinking how melancholy they looked, and then suddenly there she was again, the girl who'd disturbed the birds. The mini conqueror in yellow.

She stood at the water's edge, holding a glass bottle. I waited to see what havoc she would wreak next. Twice she lobbed the bottle into the water, but each time it washed back to her feet. The third time she threw it underhand, catapulting it in a high, useless arc. Again, the tide boomeranged it right back at her. This went on for several more tries, until I began to feel sorry for her. Why didn't the girl's mother step in and help? Or better yet, tell her not to throw trash into the ocean.

As I pulled on my cover-up and adjusted it around my waist, the girl raced over to me, halting inches from my toes.

"Can you throw this for me?" She thrust out the bottle, and for the first time I noticed the scroll of paper inside.

Before I could answer, she pointed the bottle at the jagged scar on my leg. "How did you get *that*?"

"A shark bit me," I said. Maybe I should've lied, told her it was a bicycle accident, and not given her a reason to fear the water.

"Was it a big one?"

"Not really. Bites don't happen that often."

"A megalodon would have taken off your whole leg. *Or your whole body.*"

I stopped worrying about scaring this girl.

"I wouldn't have stood much chance against a megalodon," I said.

"Or a plesiosaur. They had, like, four hundred teeth. I've seen their teeth in a museum."

"That's cool. You know a lot about prehistoric stuff."

"Well, sea creatures I do," she said, smoothing pieces of her short, wheat-colored hair behind her ears. She reminded me of someone. I wondered if it was me as a child.

"Are plesiosaurs your favorite prehistoric animal?" I asked.

"Yeah, and liopleurdons. Have you seen *Swimming with Sea Monsters?*"

"I haven't seen that one." I loved that she'd asked. I said, "What I'm really crazy about are sharks."

Her mouth parted. "But one bit you."

"I know, but he was just testing me out. Trying to find out if I was food or not."

She laughed. "You're not food."

"I have one of the teeth from the shark that bit me."

She jutted out her neck, her eyes big.

"The doctor found it stuck in my leg. It's in my jewelry box. I find shark teeth out here all the time."

"Can you help me find one?"

"I suppose I could do that one day," I said, worried suddenly what I was getting into.

"You promise?"

"Okay, I promise." Chances were I would never see her again. "Where are you from?" I asked.

"I used to live in St. Petersburg. I was in *Beauty and the Beast.*"

"Were you Beauty?"

"I was a spoon," she said. "All the little kids had to be forks and spoons."

"I bet you were good."

"Yeah, so will you throw my bottle?"

Technically, it was a bad idea. The ocean didn't need another piece of garbage, but the bottle had a message in it, and she was a child, and I didn't want to be a killer of fun.

"Okay," I told her. I thought of Perri. She would be proud.

We walked a few feet into the water and I took the bottle, turning it over, feeling flecks of the wet, crackled *Giacomo's Olive Oil, Extra Virgin* label peel off in my fingers. A glob of dark yellow oil clung to the paper inside. I swung my arm back and pitched the bottle as far as I could.

When I turned around, the girl was studying the ripples where the bottle landed. "Look, it's not coming back!" She let out a squeal, a battle cry of exuberance and victory, and though I knew nothing about children really, there was something about this one that seemed distinct.

We stood there gazing at the bottle that was starting to miraculously glide south with the undertow. "My dad gave me the idea to throw it," she said. "It has a message in it. Dad said it would help me."

She squinted up at me, waiting to see if I would ask, *Help with what?* She had pixels of gold in her brown eyes, and they reminded me of the beads of olive oil inside the bottle.

I bit. "Help with what?"

"My mom died."

"Oh. I'm very sorry." I instantly felt out of my depth. I scanned the beach for the inventive father she mentioned. The shell seekers were gone, and while a couple of men still fished, there wasn't a single person around who seemed to be looking for a wandering child.

She was small and trusting, and that worried me, her being on the beach by herself.

"Where do you think the bottle will go?" she asked.

It would probably land on the first barrier island past Palermo—Shell Point Key, I guessed, a small island known for the abundant variety of shells that washed up there, but also for the trash. In high school, instead of adopting a highway, we'd adopted Shell Point.

"I think it'll go all the way to Mozambique," I said.

This made her smile. She seemed to consider this place with the unusual name, satisfied with my exotic answer. Or perhaps she was just tolerating me.

"Do you feel better?" I asked.

She shrugged. "Where's *your* mom?"

I paused. "She died, too. A long time ago, when I was a kid like you."

"Oh," she said, and made a tiny twist with her mouth that suggested the two of us were cut from the same cloth.

"Is there a grown-up with you?" I asked.

"My dad's waiting for me inside. He told me I could throw the bottle, but then I had to come right back."

"Then you should probably get back. It was nice to meet you. I'm Maeve. What's your name?"

"Hazel."

"You're the only Hazel I've ever met," I said. But then my breath stuck in my ribs. It took me only a second to realize I already knew this child. I had imagined her many times before.

A voice called from far across the beach. "Hazel! Hazel!"

Both of us turned toward the source. He was standing at the end of the hotel access path.

Daniel.

"You're gonna help me find shark teeth," she said. "Remember? You promised."

I halfway nodded and watched her scamper off. White tan lines from her bathing suit straps crisscrossed between her shoulder blades. Daniel scooped her up, and they spoke nose to nose. By the time Hazel pointed in my direction, I was already disappearing beneath the water.

Six

I left a trail of sandy footprints that stopped at Perri's door. I knocked hard, and waited for her to answer, glancing at my reflection in the mirror at the end of the hall. Wet, openmouthed, and a little stunned, I resembled a bulgy-eyed goby fish.

Perri swung open the door, her fine hair shorter than I remembered, blunt cut at her chin.

"*There you are*," she said. "And you're sopping."

Once Daniel and Hazel had left the beach, I'd dashed out of the water and back to the hotel after a feeble toweling off. Perri put her arms around me anyway, her silver bangles clinking, and pulled me inside her suite, where I stood barefoot and shivering on her cherry-red Turkish rug. She fetched a towel from the bathroom, while I rubbed my arms and glanced around. I'd always loved this room best: a wall-to-wall holy sanctum of books. They were crammed on floor-to-ceiling shelves, heaped on the round pedestal table in front of the window, and assembled in short stacks on the floor by her comfy armchair. If it weren't for the sketch pad on the coffee table and the easel in the corner, you might've thought reading comprised her entire life.

I thought of the mural she'd painted in the tiny alcove off the lobby. The spot had once been a utility closet, but Perri had turned it into a quiet spot where guests could read or simply sit and stare at the mural. She had painted Charlotte Brontë standing on a clam-shell, the hem of her blue dress dampened by emerald waves. Around her, fat swirls of wind created a tempest, causing pages, books, feather quills, and inkpots to fly about in the air.

"I called your room earlier and just tried your cell," Perri said as she returned, handing me a thick, white towel—only Egyptian cotton for Perri. I blotted my face, arms, and hair before wrapping the towel around my shoulders and dropping onto a wooden chair.

"I was on the beach," I said.

One of her Polynesian drumming CDs played in the background. Perri sank into her armchair and took off her slender black glasses. "I'm so glad you're back. When you're not here . . . well, I miss you, is all."

"I missed you, too. And not that I expect nothing to change in my absence, I mean life goes on, but I've come back and suddenly Robin is getting his book published, my sharks are being destroyed, and—" I broke off, my face contorting in an effort not to cry.

"Daniel is here," Perri said, finishing my sentence. "The minute I saw your face I knew you knew."

"I just met Daniel's daughter."

"So you met Hazel."

"Not only that. I threw a bottle into the Gulf of Mexico for her with a message in it to her dead mother." I took a breath. Then quietly, "She looks like him."

More than that, she was the manifestation of Daniel's betrayal.

I lifted my eyes to the ceiling as they started to fill, feeling Perri study me. When I finally looked back at her, she wore the smile you see at funerals, not pity, but a mix of compassion and sadness.

"She seems like such a great kid," I said. "She talks to strangers, but . . . really great."

Perri scooted forward in her chair so our knees almost touched.

"I'm okay," I told her.

"You don't seem okay."

I rested my fingertips against my eyes for a moment, realizing how useless it was to pretend, that I didn't want to pretend. In the lull, the South Pacific drumming grew deafening, and Perri got up and turned it off, then sat back down and placed her hands on my knees.

"I feel twenty-three again," I said. "Back on that day Daniel told me about . . ."

"Holly," Perri said.

Holly. I think I'd hated her right up until I found out she was dead. I'd never met her, never even seen her, but I'd imagined her as some great beauty, possessing qualities I didn't have. She probably didn't grind her teeth at night and need a mouth guard. She understood the necessity of adding tiny edible flowers and wild raspberry coulis to the edge of a plate. Yet she'd been responsible for that adorable little girl on the beach, and I saw her suddenly as the best kind of mother, the kind who wanted them both to have botanical names—holly and hazel—and the same first initials; the kind who dressed her daughter up like a spoon for *Beauty and the Beast*; the kind who bought her books on prehistoric sea creatures and sundresses the color of marigolds.

"What happened to her?" I asked.

"She had an asthma attack," Perri said.

"*Asthma?* I didn't know you could die from that."

"Apparently it was some really severe kind."

"How terrible," I said, relieved that my tears were slipping back into the dark, nonsensical place they'd come from.

Perri said, "Hazel was the one who found her. She was unconscious in the house. She had her inhaler in her hand. The child dialed 911 herself. It was just too late for anything to be done. She died before they got there."

"*God.* Poor Hazel," I said. She would be around six now—I knew that without having to calculate it in my head. The same age I was when I lost my mom and dad.

"When did all this happen?" I asked.

"Five months ago, not long after you left for Bimini. I think it's been really hard for her, but she seems to be coping pretty well now. Daniel has been great. Right after it happened, he took a leave of absence from the restaurant in Miami and went to stay with her in St. Petersburg. After a few weeks, though, he brought her back to Miami."

Hazel and Daniel together in Miami—I tried to take it in, unsure how he managed it on a chef's schedule.

Perri paused, sliding back in the chair and running her fingers through the little cowlick that sprang off center in her hairline. She seemed to be holding back.

"What aren't you telling me?"

"They're here now. Daniel and Hazel."

"I know. Visiting Aunt Van." Daniel's mom had always been Aunt Van to me.

When Perri spoke, her voice was gentle, a kind of whisper. "No, not visiting. They live here now. They moved in with Van three weeks ago." She closed her eyes, then opened them. "This is my fault, Maeve. I gave him a job—he's the new chef here at Botticelli's."

"He *works* here?"

"Not long after Daniel took Hazel to Miami, his restaurant closed. The owner just shut it down. Daniel felt like they couldn't stay in Miami anyway, not without help. He needed his mom, and God knows Hazel needed her. And me, I needed a chef."

"Why didn't you tell me?" I said, not meaning for it to come out so angry.

Perri put her glasses back on. "I hate making excuses," she said. "First, I told myself you put a moratorium on talking about Daniel and I was honoring it, and then I told myself Daniel coming back here wasn't the kind of thing I should dash off in an e-mail. Maybe I should have. I just convinced myself it would be better if I told you in person, and frankly, I worried if you knew ahead of time you might not come home."

She was right about the last part. If I'd known Daniel had brought his daughter to live in Palermo, I'd still be in Bimini, trying to negotiate an extension so I could stay there instead of coming home.

"Robin kept it from me, too," I said.

"Blame me for that as well. I told him I'd tell you as soon as you got back. It didn't work out as I'd hoped. I'm sorry. I'm sorry you were blindsided on the beach."

I wanted to tell her it was all right, but I couldn't.

She said, "I guess I didn't have to give him a job, but he was desperate. And it's not bad for us to have him here. The name Daniel Wakefield is well known among Florida foodies now."

"I get it," I snapped, not wanting her to justify it.

All this talk about him—Daniel did *this*, Daniel decided *that*. He was someone I didn't know anymore. Why did I care so much? Daniel was like a wound I carried that wouldn't heal.

I looked past Perri at the framed pencil sketch she'd made of my grandfather. It hung slightly crooked on the wall behind her. He stared at me with graphite eyes. I didn't know how she'd endured the death of him, and then later, of Dad. It was too much, but Perri had borne it with the help of books. Books had saved her the way sharks had saved me.

It was cooking that had saved Daniel. Once a year his dad had made spaghetti sauce—marinara, puttanesca, Bolognese. It had been the one domestic thing he'd done, and then, only on Van's birthday— a hard-and-fast tradition right up there with turkey at Thanksgiving. When his mom's birthday rolled around the year after his dad left, twelve-year-old Daniel found a recipe in one of Van's cookbooks and made the sauce for her himself. He was trying to comfort her and carry on the tradition, of course, and perhaps that's when he began to fill his dad's shoes, a job he took on dutifully. He gave up junior varsity baseball that season. He said it was so he could be home more and help out, but I suspected it was also a way to defy his baseball-coach father. He began preparing dinner most every night, and cooking became an escape, a place to disappear, a place the hurt couldn't find him. The surprise was how much he loved the mystery of chopping, measuring, and stirring—creating from scratch. By the time he was in high school, Perri had given him a job in the hotel kitchen, and he worked his way from dishwasher to busboy to steward. It must've meant a lot to him to be back in the place where it all started.

"I *do* get it," I said softly to Perri. "I'm not upset with you—it's just coming back and finding him here. I still think about him. I don't want to, but I do."

She reached for my hand and I smelled her signature cherry blossom hand cream. What came to me was the day we'd spent together before I left for Bimini, when she'd treated me and Robin to the hotel's sunset cruise. The cherry scent had mixed with the wind and spray coming off the wake as we'd leaned over the side of the boat to watch dolphins scudding in the waves.

Perri's bedroom opened directly off the living room, and glancing through the doorway, I could make out the first part of a quote stenciled on the wall over her bed. Every room but mine had a literary quote. I could never settle on a single set of words that seemed adequately self-defining. Perri's quote was from Charlotte Brontë, and it was so Perri: "I would always rather be happy than dignified."

"I didn't just see Hazel," I told her. "I saw Daniel, too. He was at the top of the beach, waiting for her. I didn't want him to see me so I jumped back into the water." I laughed, a bitter sound. "I'm ridiculous."

"You're not ridiculous. You're not the first person to avoid seeing an ex-fiancé."

Perri was being kind. I was good at escaping. Even right now part of me was plotting to fly off somewhere. Somewhere like Africa. Maybe I could convince the center in Mozambique to let me start my research earlier than August.

"It's not like you were expecting to see Daniel," Perri was saying. "Or Hazel, for that matter."

I'd read an article last winter in the waiting room at the dentist's office called "The Science of Love." I'd read it slowly, as if it contained the secret for my happiness or, at the very least, an answer. I'd ripped out the pages and stuffed them into my purse, hoping that whatever I felt for Daniel came down to a couple of haywire neurotransmitters or an overproduction of oxytocin. Was there something wrong with my brain—did my tegmentum regularly misfire dopamine? Was my caudate nucleus, otherwise known as the reward center, stuck in the year 1999?

I *still* wanted a way to explain Daniel. I said, "That's why I declared the moratorium on mentioning Daniel. I don't want to be stuck."

"*Are* you stuck?" Perri asked.

"I met someone in Bimini, so that's something."

I watched Perri's eyes widen behind her lenses, how she seemed to lift up in the chair a little. "Someone?" she said.

"He's a biologist. Nicholas. He's British."

"And you two were a thing in Bimini?" I wished she didn't seem quite so dumbfounded, but why wouldn't she be? You could probably count on one hand the guys I'd been out with in the last seven years, but dating them had not amounted to anything serious.

"We were just dive partners until the last night . . . when we weren't."

She pressed her lips into a suppressed smile.

"Well, technically he's married," I said. "He's in the middle of a divorce. Proceedings are so much quicker in England."

"Still," she said, "it sounds vaguely promising."

"Maybe. Yesterday I asked him to go to Mozambique. Today Daniel pops up and I'm . . . I'm stuck again."

"Maeve, can I tell you what I think?"

Before I could nod, she said, "Clearly it's not all water under the bridge with you and Daniel. You've been avoiding this for years, and yes, maybe you two could be a little less Cathy and Heathcliff, but his being here on the island could be a good thing. You can't avoid him any longer. You can't hide from him, and you can't hide from yourself."

I hated the obvious truth in her words, but there was a strange relief in them, that first sighing moment when I accepted what was. There was nowhere to hide. I couldn't dive into some other world. I couldn't make Daniel disappear. I couldn't make his daughter disappear. I'd come up for air and here we were. Me and Daniel on the same island. That was that.

Perri stood and brushed at her black pants. "Come on," she said, and pulled me out of the chair to the table by the window. "I've got something for you, a birthday present."

She handed me a small package wrapped in brown paper. Inside, I found a portrait of myself. Perri had painted me at the edge of the Gulf, standing atop a loggerhead turtle shell wearing my company uniform, a black one-piece swimsuit. My body was angled to the side just enough to reveal a shining silver shark fin growing out of my back. A jagged scar blazed lava-red on my calf. My hair was blown to the side. Waves splashed around the shell onto my scarred leg in foamy, white curls. On the sand before me, horse conchs, lightning whelks, and one rare junonia glistened. Behind me, the water fanned out to the horizon the color of topaz. Hovering over my head was an osprey, its wings open like two arms.

I stared at it, speechless. Perri had a benign obsession with Botticelli's *Birth of Venus*—the curvaceous goddess of love standing on a shell, arriving on shore. She'd painted her own versions of it over the

years, like the Charlotte Brontë opus in the alcove, along with numerous paintings of herself standing on the shell holding an open
book or sometimes a paintbrush, but she'd never painted me.

"I can't believe you did this," I said, running my finger over the
shark fin.

"You like it, I hope."

"I love it! You made me part shark."

"Aren't you?" she said. "Turn it over."

"The Birth of Maeve (on her 30th birthday)" was scrawled in Perri's handwriting on the back.

"Thank you," I said, throwing my arms around her, letting the towel
around my shoulders fall to the floor.

"Go get changed," she said.

In the corridor, I pressed the elevator button and when it didn't
immediately pop open, I pushed it again and again. Maybe it was
seeing the shark fin on my back, the osprey floating over my head . . .
the Botticelli image of Maeve arriving slowly on the shell of a turtle,
finally showing up after seven years of self-exile. *You can't hide from
him, you can't hide from yourself.*

I made up my mind. I wouldn't wait around for Daniel to find me.
I would change out of my wet clothes and go down to the kitchen. I
would figure out what to say.

Reaching the second floor, I began to walk faster until I was lop-
ing along the hallway. Turning a corner, I saw him, standing beside
my door.

I halted abruptly, my chest filling with sound, a furious thudding.

He turned toward me, and I thought I saw him take a long breath.

Seven

"Sorry to just show up like this," Daniel said.

"You saved me a trip. I was about to come find you," I told him, trying to sound impassive. I didn't know if I should behave friendly or coolly unaffected. Was there a statute of limitations on how to feel about betrayal? How was it possible to feel the pull and force of him again after all this time?

He ran a hand over the short, sandy-brown waves in his hair as if trying to brush away his own uncertainty about what he was feeling, then jammed his hands in the pockets of his work khakis. He was wearing a short-sleeved chef's jacket with BOTTICELLI's stitched in small, navy lettering on the front, partially unbuttoned and flapped open, showing a wedge of gray T-shirt underneath. He smelled like seafood primavera and Parmesan, like an oven of baking bread.

He looked older, of course. Any remaining boyish features Daniel had had were gone. His jaw was more angled. There were tiny lines beginning around his eyes. But then, there was the flat place on the bridge of his nose, and his eyes were as I'd always thought of them. The electric blue of a tang fish.

"Would you, um . . ." I handed Daniel the painting while I dug my key out of my bag. There were little crescents of sand under my nails, my eyes were red, and I reeked of heat and Gulf water. I had pulled my wet hair back into a ponytail while in Perri's room, which made my freckles look more pronounced, and I wished I wasn't seeing him for the first time in seven years looking a little bedraggled.

The tremulous feeling along my ribs had moved into my hands. They quivered visibly, and I fumbled the key in the lock, dropping it onto the blue-and-brown lattice-print carpet. Damn.

I bent over quickly to retrieve it before he could, and unlocked the door.

He followed me inside, and I immediately wished I could retrace my steps and bring him in through the main door that opened into the living room instead of the private entrance into my bedroom, which seemed to suggest the old intimacy between us was unchanged. How many times had we come in just like this? Hundreds? I flushed, berating myself.

My suitcase was spread open on the bed and dirty clothes were separated into three piles on the floor. Whites, colors, bathing suits. He stepped around them as I stuffed down the urge to apologize for the mess.

I watched as he propped the small painting against the mirror on my dresser, then folded his arms over his white jacket and stared at it.

"Perri at work," I said.

"Only Perri," he replied. "It's something else—Maeve, the shark."

"It's a birthday present."

I wanted to undo that, too—to unmention my birthday, take away the reminder that birthdays were things we used to do together. We used to celebrate with ice cream cake from Baskin-Robbins. There were so many little things I hadn't forgotten about Daniel. That he considered "Ring of Fire" the best love song ever written; that he could perfectly produce any recipe he laid his hands on, but couldn't bake a cake to save his life. It was possible neither of those things was still true. Did he still hate fondue, had he overcome his aversion to circuses, taken the trip to France he'd always wanted to take?

"Happy birthday," he said. "Thirty, huh?"

"Yeah, all grown up now."

He wandered from the dresser to the bedside table, then over to the glass doors that led to the balcony, as if remembering the spot where his photo had been, the lounge chair where we used to curl up and fall asleep. I imagined the black eye of the Mona Lisa blue shark following him. Finally, he pulled the desk chair out and sat, so I took a seat on the bed.

"Can you believe Robin finished the book?" I said, desperately wanting to keep it casual. "He said you've read it."

"I read it in one night."

He smiled and I had to glance away. For what felt like an eon, but was probably only seconds, neither of us spoke.

"I think you met Hazel today," he said, plunging in, and I had the sensation of falling through some strange wormhole into a place where events were happening, words were being spoken, but I was far away underwater, watching it through goggles.

"She's beautiful," I managed to say. *She looks like you.*

"Yeah, she is, isn't she? And really precocious."

"I could tell. She knows more about prehistoric sea creatures than your average thirty-year-old."

"You made quite an impression on her."

I could have made a joke. Something about how tremendously impressive I was, something about dropping the key earlier. I sensed how easy it would be to return to the way we used to talk, back when being with Daniel was effortless. But how could we go back? I decided to get through this with detachment, ignoring how entirely unnatural it felt to do so.

He said, "I know it must have been a surprise running into her."

And you. It was a surprise running into you.

"You could say that. I didn't exactly know you were back."

He drew another long breath, and I could see how excruciating this was for him. "I guess I wanted to come up and say that I'm here, that Hazel and I are here." He forced himself to laugh. "Which seems pointless now because it's all pretty obvious. I mean, I'm sitting in your room, and you and Hazel played together on the beach."

"Played? No, not really. I mean, we talked. I threw a bottle."

"She hasn't stopped talking about 'the shark lady with the scar.' I knew it was you before she mentioned your name. You should have seen her face when I told her I knew you."

That's one way of putting it.

"She told me about her mother. I'm really sorry," I said.

At the mention of Holly, Daniel gazed across the tan carpet, at the hills of clothes, as if carefully mulling over his words. "It was awful for Hazel at first. Now, I guess it's . . . less awful. Mom is really helping."

"I bet Van is crazy about her."

"It's mutual. She'd love to see you, you know."

"Yeah, me, too."

Beyond the window, fishing boats popped up along the horizon, each one trying to outrun the setting sun. Pink light was sticking to the bottom of clouds and the tips of waves.

Suddenly Daniel rose to his feet, and I did the same. It seemed he'd said what he'd come to say.

But he hadn't. He went on standing there, gazing at me, shifting his eyes toward the window and back. It felt odd and uneasy, being in the same room with him, seeing his chef's jacket with its two neat rows of buttons.

"Since I work here now, we might see a lot of each other, and the way we left things . . ."

"I know." I wasn't sure I wanted to go down this road. The *us* road.

"I tried getting in touch with you several times after . . ." He broke off. "I finally asked Robin to help me, but you probably know that."

No, I didn't know that.

"I just couldn't, back then," I said.

He walked to my dresser and stood in front of the little painting—Maeve, the Shark. I stared at him, hoping he would let it go now, and from inside the silence came a flood of memories more personal than birthdays. I was suddenly awash in old feelings. That sharp, sweet, first love.

~

At twelve, recovering from the shark bite, I was forbidden by my doctor to go into the ocean for six weeks, what seemed like a lifetime. Daniel, knowing this must have felt like a death sentence to me, brought me a jar of saltwater. He set it beside my bed, and soon we were joking around like always. As for the kiss and the declarations of love we'd exchanged in the water before the bite, I think we were both a little embarrassed. We were kids. We pretended it never happened.

I went on loving him quietly and to myself, certain he'd forgotten, or worse, that he'd dismissed it as a moment of childishness. Throughout high school, though, he sometimes made me wonder. Like when he designed ways for just the two of us to pick up the Friday night pizzas or when he sat beside me on the sofa so that our legs touched while we watched movies. Once, when Robin left the room, he slowly pulled his fingers through my long ponytail, not letting go when I turned to look at him, but slowly twirling his hand, dropping it only when Robin returned. I'd raked my fingers through my hair countless times after that, unable to reproduce the feeling I'd gotten in the pit of my stomach. Despite all this, I watched him take a very nice girl to prom, and he watched me go with a boy from the baseball team. On the outside, we were buddies, friends, pals. On the inside we were filled with hidden compartments of confusion, awkwardness, longing, and fear.

The first time we spent the night together I was eighteen and about to start my freshman year at the University of Miami. He was home for the summer, headed back to UM as a sophomore. One night, when he'd come by to see Robin, we'd gotten into the hotel elevator together, and astonishingly, he'd brought it up. "What you said that day in the water when we were kids, that you'd always love me, is it still true?" For a moment, I thought he was teasing me but he'd looked so hopelessly unguarded and serious, so defenseless.

"It's always been true," I told him, and he was on my side of the elevator before I could go on. The way he kissed me—I'd not wanted it to end.

We swiped the key to the E. M. Forster Room. If I had been nervous about my first time, I would've been comforted by the words from Forster that Perri had stenciled on the wall—"The poets are right: love is eternal"—but I wasn't nervous. As Daniel kissed my scar, the quote arranged itself permanently in my head. We left the room exactly as we'd found it, except for borrowing *A Room with a View*, which I took to read.

We went to enormous lengths to hide our relationship from Robin. Daniel had insisted on it, thinking Robin would be overly protective of me, that it would change things between the two of them, but it became a secret impossible to keep. Before the Thanksgiving break, when it seemed clear and irrevocable to me that Daniel and I would stick, I sat Robin down and told him the whole story, everything, starting when we were kids. I left out the part about the Forster Room. There were some things I would not divulge even to Robin.

"I love him. I want you to be okay with it," I told him.

A look of short-lived confusion swept across his face. He said, "I think I knew this."

I chalked it up to our twin-ness.

⌒

Now, in my room, Daniel studied something on the dresser with great intensity, what I imagined to be the painting, but then I saw him lift the brown-and-white osprey feather from the green bud vase. A feather that had changed my life.

Holding the quill, he turned it over in his hand, inspecting it like he would the quality of a tomato. He couldn't be sure this was the same feather, and I hardly knew what I'd tell him if he asked, but he knew—didn't he?—that I'd saved it. No, *displayed* it. When I was twelve, it was more articulate than any diary. It held the memory of my first kiss and my first love, of the shark's bite and the beginning of my inexplicable enthrallment with the creatures. I kept the feather because how could I not keep it, because so much of what mattered in my life, so much of what made me who I was had converged around it.

Did it also suggest that I had never let him go? As he returned the feather to the vase, I watched his reflection in the mirror, but he gave nothing away.

"I should get back to the kitchen," he said.

When I opened the door, Daniel stopped on the threshold.

"Hazel said you promised to take her to look for shark teeth. If you'd rather not, I'd understand."

I'd made the promise to Hazel without really meaning to, but I wasn't backing out. Somewhere in the hotel, hidden in storage, my wedding dress was yellowing like old, discarded newspaper.

"I'll take her," I said. "A promise is a promise."

Eight

A few days later, I sat on the ledge of the fountain in the outdoor Courtyard Café and waited for Hazel the Conqueror. I was fairly certain the discomfort of spending time with Daniel's child was going to do me in. The sculpture at the fountain's center was composed of the upper half of a horse and the lower half of a dolphin—the hor-phin, as Daniel, Robin, and I used to call it. It spewed a canopy of water into the air, and I leaned my head back and tried to absorb the sedative sound of the spray.

When Daniel had called to arrange the shark tooth expedition, he'd joked that I'd cleared a background check. Oh, we're making jokes now, I'd thought.

"Hazel is really excited," he'd said.

"Great," I told him, determined to stick to my promise. "I'll meet her at the hor-phin at low tide."

In hindsight, sticking to my promise felt a lot like chumming the water. I was angry at myself for getting into such a complicated predicament. When Perri learned of the outing, she'd pointed out that I'd succeeded in facing reality, but perhaps this was too big a dose of it. "Do you know what you're doing?" she asked.

"Not at all," I told her.

The Courtyard Café was akin to a rainforest. The coral umbrellas over black wrought-iron tables were flanked by a profusion of potted Arecas, date palms, bougainvillea, and lemon trees, creating a playground for the lizards that zipped around in alarming numbers. By now, the lunch crowd had abandoned the tables for lounge chairs at the pool, where most of them pummeled the tiny keyboards on their BlackBerrys, read business reports, made to-do lists, firmly believing that if they could just get caught up, *then* they could relax.

Mist from the fountain had dampened the back of my shirt, but I didn't move. I crossed and uncrossed my legs, watching the double glass doors that lead into Botticelli's.

When Daniel stepped into the courtyard, he paused to slide on his sunglasses, while Hazel squinted into the brightness, then skipped ahead of him. She wore a pair of white knee-length shorts over a hot pink bathing suit. A khaki field bag with a dinosaur on the front was strapped across her body. She stopped before me at the fountain and gave me a closed-lipped grin. Her bathing suit was covered in little black polka dots.

"Hi, there," I said.

She rested one hand on her field bag. "We have a playdate."

"Yep."

Daniel walked over, his surf shop T-shirt partially tucked into his jeans.

"Hey," he said.

"Hey, Dad," Hazel answered, giggling, aware his greeting was for me.

"You monkey," he said.

Hazel leaned over the fountain, peering in like a cat staring into a fishbowl, then walked around it, lifting her hand out behind her, reminding me of the leotard-clad women who lead horses around circus rings.

Daniel motioned me to a nearby table. "She had a rough night last night."

I watched as she plunged her hands into the water. "Cold!" she yelled.

"Oh? Is she okay?" I asked. Whatever the events of the night before, her upset seemed untraceable now. She wiped her hands on her shorts, a silver coin pinched between her fingers. She mumbled something—a wish?—and threw the coin back in.

"She misses Holly most at night," Daniel said.

He'd said her name to me only one time before.

"When Hazel is upset, she gets quiet," he said. "When I got home last night, Mom had been sitting with her for hours. She wouldn't sleep, wouldn't talk, wouldn't eat. She even refused to watch TV, and she loves TV." He gazed at her as he spoke, his voice soft and tinged with sadness. "I got her to eat a hot dog and tried telling her a story. That usually works, but around midnight, we ended up scrambling a carton of eggs just for fun, putting food coloring in them. I slid plate after plate of them in the trash. Blue eggs, pink eggs, green eggs. A total waste, but it made her laugh, and after that, we fell asleep on the sofa watching *Prehistoric Park*."

"Does she get like that a lot?"

"Every once in a while. It's gotten better."

Daniel cooking pink eggs in order to bring Hazel around filled me with an irrational pang. I remembered Robin during those excruciating weeks after our parents died, the nightmares that haunted him, the terror that he would lose me, too, waking sometimes to find him asleep on the floor beside my bed. My grief had been less complicated, but it was no less profound. When it overtook me, I would rush to Perri and cling to her, not wanting her out of my sight.

He took off his sunglasses and rubbed his eyes. They looked tired. The skin underneath was tinted purple. "I told Hazel we've been friends a long time. That's all. I thought it was best if she didn't know the whole thing."

"Agreed."

"If you need to cut this short, call me," he said, handing me a piece of paper with his number on it.

I stuffed it in the pocket of my cover-up. "Don't worry. We'll be fine."

He called her over, bent down on one knee, and lightly held her wrists. "Be a good listener for Maeve, okay?" She began to twist at the waist. "She's going to drop you off in the kitchen in an hour." He glanced at me like a good parent might, seeking confirmation that I understood when to deliver her back. My first inclination was to salute. Our history was full of footnotes like that. I nodded instead.

"Can I call her Maeve, or do I have to call her Miss Maeve?" she asked.

"Why don't you ask?" he said.

Hazel looked at me and waited for an answer.

"Maeve is fine with me."

Daniel waved to us when he got to the door. I couldn't help but wonder if he found the sight of me and Hazel together unbelievable.

Once he'd disappeared, Hazel looked at me like I possessed a starting pistol.

"I guess we can go," I told her, and she set off, speed walking past the café tables, her arms swinging back and forth, her hands balled into fists. Her feet came off the ground when a lizard ran in front of her with a French fry in its mouth. Once we reached the beach, she took off running, me chasing after her.

Crouching where the sand was soft and dry, she pulled a plastic shovel out of her field bag.

"Hold this," she said, handing it to me, then riffled through the bag, producing a purple headband, red wide-lense safety goggles, and several Ziploc bags labeled TEETH in big chunky letters. She'd thought of everything.

She pushed the headband onto her forehead. Her face was framed with pale wisps of hair, much lighter and finer than Daniel's. "You have to wear these on digs," she said, putting on the safety goggles. Sitting on her cheeks, they covered half her face. "But I only have one." She waited to hear if this was okay. I assured her I'd be careful.

"We don't need these yet," she said, stuffing the Ziplocs back in her bag and pulling out two paper circles. She handed one to me. "I used a cup to trace these. They're shark badges," she said with such sincerity it did away with every bit of resistance I'd felt about getting involved with Daniel's child.

Hazel had drawn a shark on each circle. Black body, triangle for a fin, dot for an eye. The shark's belly rested on three multicolored squiggles. The shark was either swimming in colorful ocean water or jumping over a rainbow. With Hazel it could have been either way.

"I love them," I told her, and realized that I actually did.

She produced two paper clips and told me I could wear the badge if I wanted.

"Of course I do," I said, and fastened it to my shirt, then helped Hazel with hers.

When she hopped up, my God—she was a sight. The enormous goggles, her yellow hair floating like spun thread, the dinosaur field bag, and the shark badge clipped to her hot pink bathing suit. A mini–Margaret Mead convinced there were things in the world worth finding and that they were hers to find. If she were mine, I thought, I would move heaven and earth to ensure she stayed just like this. Where had she gotten her unselfconsciousness? Daniel was never quite like this. Did it come from Holly? Maybe it was uniquely Hazel. I didn't know, but her earnestness broke me open.

"I guess we're a club now," I said.

"That's what I was thinking," she said. "The Shark Club."

I led her down near the water where the sand was wet and where teeth were more likely to wash up. We sat down beside a little armada of sea foam. "Keep your eyes open for small black triangles," I said.

"Or big ones. You never know."

"You're right," I conceded.

Please. One shark tooth is all we need.

As she chopped with her shovel, sand flew, hitting her glasses, and she tapped satisfactorily on the plastic lenses. I dug up a handful of mushy silt filled with crushed shells and who knows what—particles of mollusks, mangrove pods, driftwood, whelk egg cases, sand dollars. I sieved through it, practically grain by grain.

Hazel announced ten or fifteen times that she had a tooth, only to discover it wasn't one. We tried different spots, picking and preening our way down the shoreline like hungry ibises. My shoulders began to sting from the sun.

"Are you wearing sunscreen?" I asked, feeling protective of her shoulders.

"Dad doesn't allow me on the beach without it."

Of course, he doesn't.

Behind us, pelicans dive-bombed the water and gulped their catches. The waves carried on their drowsy music, while Hazel dug determinedly, leaving a string of potholes in her wake.

Suddenly she stopped and looked out at the water. "Do you think my bottle is still out there?"

"I bet so," I said.

It was either stuck on Shell Point Key or caught in the Loop Current headed south to the Keys. I was curious about what she'd put inside the bottle, but I didn't ask. I didn't want to risk her shutting down. I had no bag of tricks. No eggs and no food coloring.

"I didn't know you and my dad are friends," she said.

"He was my best friend when we were younger. My brother's, too." I told her I'd known him since we were seven, and this beach had been our playground. "Have you met my brother, Robin?" I asked.

"Oh, Uncle Robin. He's your brother? We have a special handshake."

Uncle Robin. I tried to let that sink in.

"Were you friends with my mom, too?"

I looked at her hands, busy digging and sifting. "I never met your mom."

"Are you married?"

"Nope."

"My parents weren't married either," she said. "Who do you live with?"

"Your Uncle Robin is my roommate. We live here in the hotel where your dad works."

She laughed. "That's weird."

"It is kind of weird, isn't it?"

"Dad and I live with my grandma, but he wants to get a house for me and him," she said.

"Oh yeah?"

"Yeah. He said I could get a cat."

"I like your grandma," I said.

"She's a dancer."

"I know," I told her. "She used to teach me ballet."

Hazel peeled off her goggles. "How old are you?"

"Thirty. How old are you?"

"Six."

She got up on her knees and piled sand into a tower, then dug out a moat. I hoped she wasn't too disappointed that so far we'd failed in our mission. There had been discoveries, but they'd all been mine, all unexpected, and nothing to do with shark teeth. I was stunned by my fondness for her. She was more herself than anyone I'd ever met, so bright and curious and funny, and I could've talked to her for well over our allotted hour.

"Did my dad cook back then?" she asked.

"You mean when he was a kid?"

Hazel nodded.

"No, but he ate a lot," I said.

She laughed again. "He still eats *a lot*." She bugged out her eyes incredulously. "And he cooks stuff I don't like."

"Like *what*?"

"Eggs."

"You don't like eggs?"

"I like cracking them," she said, smoothing the sides of her tower. "Dad likes coloring them."

"What are your favorite foods?"

"Chicken nuggets. Dad says I'm going to turn into one. Cake is better."

"Okay, I'll make you a chocolate cake," I said.

Abandoning her castle, she watched as I shaped a sand cake and pressed shimmering translucent jingles and coquinas on the top.

"There. It's ready," I said.

"It doesn't look like a cake. It looks like a turtle wearing jewelry," she said with her palms up. Then, she sang the words *fancy turtle* three times. She wasn't wrong, and I liked that she'd said so.

"You know, I used to make necklaces from the teeth I found," I said, leveling the fancy turtle.

She raked her fingers through the demolition. Holding yet another lump of sand, she swirled her finger through it until there was nothing left but a shiny, black splinter. "What's this?" she asked.

The tooth was half an inch long, shaped like a tiny T-bone steak. The knob at the top was only as wide as my pinky nail.

"You found one!"

Hazel leaped up, her feet smashing into her tower. She held the tooth up to her gums, her elbows sticking out like wings. "What do I look like?"

"Hmmm, like a tiger shark."

She handed me the tooth. "*Is* it from a tiger shark?"

I studied it. "I think it's from a lemon shark," I said, giving it back to her. "Or it could be millions of years old. Practically every shark tooth out here is a fossil."

Suddenly she seemed overcome by her find. She sucked in her breath and blinked, cradling it in the cup of her hands as if it were a baby bird that had fallen from its nest, and for a moment I thought she was going to cry out of sheer awe. I remembered the day we'd met, how she talked about megalodons and plesiosaurs and asked if I'd seen some DVD she had . . . what was it called? *Swimming with Sea Monsters.* That was what she loved, not so much dinosaurs like the one on her bag, but the preposterous ancient ocean dwellers.

I said, "Maybe this tooth came from a shark species that has died out, like one you saw on your DVD."

"I need to watch it again," she said in a resolute way, and carefully placed the tooth inside one of her labeled Ziplocs, then inspected it through the plastic.

"Score one for the Shark Club," I said.

Hazel gave me a funny look, and I thought I was getting my first taste of being an uncool grown-up, but then she darted into the waves, kicking wildly at the water, yelling "Shark Club!"

⌣

Before we reached the kitchen, the potent smell of garlic caused Hazel to pinch her nose. I pushed open the swinging door and let her walk ahead. Daniel stood at the stove with his back to us, shuffling a pan back and forth over a burner. The garlic culprit. Hazel tiptoed up behind him, squeezing the shark tooth between her fingers while I hung back, holding her field bag, watching as she tugged on his white jacket.

Turning, he took her in, smiling, and then, spying the tiny fang, he gave her exactly what she wanted: shock and amazement. "Wow, Little Bug, you found this?"

Hazel nodded four times at least, and Daniel looked over at me. "Good day, huh?"

"Very good. She waited until the last minute to find it, though. It was a nail-biter."

Daniel removed the pan from the heat and asked a woman in an apron to take over, rattling off instructions and pointing to a bowl of thinly sliced prosciutto.

"We're in a club, Dad," Hazel said.

"A club?"

"Yeah, the Shark Club. I want you to be in it. Maeve's in it."

She grabbed his hand and led him over to me, where she opened her field bag and pulled out a third badge. Daniel spied the circle clipped to my shirt, then met my eyes as if to say apologetically, *It's the first I've heard of this.* Once he'd attached the badge to his jacket, Hazel stepped back like a director taking in the scene she'd created, obviously pleased at her achievement—she'd found a fossilized shark tooth, formed a club, and membership was up.

I took off my badge and offered it back to her. "You keep it," she told me. "Wear it next time."

I hadn't imagined a next time.

There had been little to say when it was only me and Daniel and our history filling up the room, but Hazel's presence required us to be cheery and speak about things like the Shark Club, yet also to be empathetic and commiserate over the child's grief. I couldn't think of another way this sudden alliance with him could have happened.

She peered up at him. "Can Maeve come over and watch my video?"

At the back of the kitchen, a clacking erupted as someone stacked plates for the lunch hour. Daniel hedged. "We'll talk about it, okay?"

"Okay, but it would be for the club," she said.

"I have a book you can borrow, if you want," I said. "It has lots of pictures. I remember one of a prehistoric shark with a protrusion on its back shaped like a small ironing board."

"Oh yeaaaah," she said.

"That's very cool, right?" Daniel said to Hazel, and she nodded as the plate clatter gave way to *chop, chop, chop.* Flames mushroomed up from the garlic pan and turned into a puff of smoke, and the smell of scorched prosciutto wafted up, prompting Hazel to bury her nose in her father's side. He said, "Why don't you wash your hands, and I'll make you a grilled cheese."

As she started to saunter off, Daniel called after her. "Wait. What do you say?"

"Oh, I forgot." She wrapped her arms around my waist. Her small body was sun soaked, and smelled like sea wind. I tried hugging her back, but given our height difference my hug amounted to covering her arms with mine. Letting go, she navigated through the stainless steel surfaces, holding her nose.

Daniel said, "Mom and I have a saying: if you want the truth, ask Hazel."

Yep, fancy turtle. Got it.

"I'll bring the book by later," I told him.

Back in my room, I checked my shelves—no luck—then went to the storage area in the hotel basement, where Perri kept the Christmas decorations. She'd marked off a section for my belongings, basically a heap of cardboard boxes containing everything from childhood puppets and macaroni jewelry boxes to high school yearbooks and college theses.

There was no trace of the box that held my wedding dress. Perri had probably stashed it with her things so I'd never have to stumble upon it. But there was the small white hatbox containing the remnants of Daniel. I hesitated a moment, then wriggled off the lid. Wedding gloves, CDs, R.E.M. concert ticket stubs, a pile of old photos: me in the front yard of the aqua house; our engagement photo; high school graduation; ten-year-old Daniel and his dad at Perri's Fourth of July party, roasting hot dogs on the beach. At the bottom I found a small stack of letters held by a taut rubber band. When I pulled at it, the band crumbled. I took the envelope on the top of the stack and pulled out the letter.

Maeve,

It's been six weeks since I made the biggest mistake of my life. The regret and pain I feel over what I did are with me every day. It was stupid and I'm so sorry. Letting you go is incomprehensible to me. Love like ours doesn't just go away.

You are the first person I ever loved, and I love you still.

Please, let's talk.

Daniel

A little bolt of pain shot through me. I stuffed the letter back into the envelope, quarantined it inside the hatbox, and forced myself to look for a box marked MIDDLE SCHOOL.

Finding the book for Hazel, I sat on the concrete floor and thumbed through the pages until I found the picture of the extinct shark I'd told Hazel about, *Stethacanthus*, "the ironing board" shark. As I sat there with the book open on my lap, I noticed my hair was infused with the scent of garlic-prosciutto. I pulled a lock over my nose and breathed it in.

Nine

*R*eturning to my apartment, I opened my laptop, planning to sort through my field notes from Bimini and begin a catalogue of dorsal fin profiles of the sharks we'd tagged, but my thoughts kept spinning back to Hazel in her hot pink swimsuit and those gigantic safety goggles . . . to Daniel holding the osprey feather, Daniel scrambling pink eggs, Daniel's eyes meeting mine in the kitchen.

I stared over the computer at Hazel's hand-drawn badge with the shark on it with sudden panic churning inside my rib cage, the sensation of diving too deep or swimming too far. *The Shark Club.* How had I let things unspool like this? I'd been an island of my own making, but being with the two of them had unhinged some fixed, unquestioned place inside of me, and as terrifying as that was, the thought of putting everything back the way it was before I'd arrived home scared me more. I told myself that Daniel and I could be in a club together with his daughter, that we could pass one another in the hotel corridors, and run into each other at Spoonbills, our old hangout, and it would be okay. It would become routine, a new normal. Right now I felt unmoored, that's all, but in time, bumping into Daniel and Hazel wouldn't dredge up all these unsettling memories and feelings.

I listened to the air conditioner whining through the vents, to laughter passing in the corridor, then to a weighed-down silence until

I couldn't sit there anymore. I headed for the living room to flip on the TV and stopped abruptly as my eyes fell on a box perched on the coffee table with a pale-green sticky note on top bearing my name. The box was tied with a piece of string and had seen better days. I was sure it hadn't been here earlier.

Knowing suddenly what was inside it, I carried it to my bed, kicked off my sandals, and removed the lid.

The Hotel of the Muses
by
Robin Donnelly

I lifted out the manuscript pages. Three hundred twenty-one of them. Robin's novel. I turned the page to find a dedication.

For Maeve & Daniel

It suggested we were a couple. What was Robin thinking? Couldn't he have put our names on two different lines? Or with a little clarification? Was that so hard?

Any other sister would have felt pride in her brother and recognized that of all the people in the world he could have dedicated the book to—Mom, Dad, Perri—he'd chosen me, his twin, and Daniel, his best friend. *Stop quibbling,* I told myself.

But a kind of foreboding swirled up in me, making me want to slide the lid back on the box. Instead I sat cross-legged on the bed and began to read.

CHAPTER ONE

Moments before Margaret was pulled on shore, bleeding, a breath from unconsciousness, she and Derek stood waist deep in the ocean, water tilting around their waists as Margaret scooped a feather off the surface. At thirteen, she had already loved Derek half her life, and though only slightly older, Derek routinely teased her about his six-month edge over her.

"Osprey," she said, studying the feather.

She was always doing that. Expertly identifying bird feathers, seashells, fishes.

Derek slipped the feather from her hand and tucked it into her ponytail. It stuck up from the crown of her hair, turning her into an exotic bird. Then he kissed her. A one Mississippi, two Mississippi kiss.

"I love you," she said, blurting it out. Then, embarrassed, she dived beneath the shimmering green water, emerging with her dark hair slicked back, tiny sequins of water on the ends of her lashes. She tried not to look at him as he swam toward her, parting the water between them with his arms, causing it to ripple in wide, half circles.

"I love you, too," Derek was saying when suddenly his knees buckled and he lunged forward as if he'd been shoved.

Pain exploded through Margaret's leg as she was jerked violently beneath the water, then whiplashed back and forth. Stinging water rushed into her nostrils as she fought against a monstrous black shape fastened to her calf. A blacktip shark.

Derek grabbed for her, thrusting his arms frantically beneath the water. A plume of blood rose up like a gruesome flower.

"Margaret," he screamed. Over and over.

Seconds later, her face broke the surface, water peeling off her cheeks as she coughed and gasped. "Shark," she cried, her voice chopped up by her breath.

Derek pulled her through the water, leaving a bright red tributary in the waves . . .

I looked up from the page to the other side of the room, my eyes falling on *The Birth of Maeve,* which still sat propped on my dresser. I stared at the painting while pressure built in the back of my throat. I wanted to scream. It was unthinkable. Robin had spent the last few years secretly writing the story of me and Daniel.

Part of me wanted to dump the manuscript into a trash can, but it was like an accident on the side of the road that I couldn't help slowing down to gape at. I read to the end of the chapter, to its last shattering line.

> *The day Margaret was bitten by the blacktip, the two great loves of her life intersected, traversing like lines of latitude and longitude at the place where love saves you and breaks you.*

I slammed the pages onto the bed, where they made a soft, unsatisfying thud on my white comforter. *Is that what Robin thought? That I was broken?*

I stormed into his room without knocking and, finding it empty, grabbed the phone to call him, then put it down.

He'd stolen my life.

My first kiss, my admission of love, the shark bite—those moments belonged to me in the most private way. I'd confided them to Robin, but I'd never imagined he would usurp them from me. Daniel had never been comfortable divulging details about our relationship to Robin, at least back when we were together, but perhaps he'd been more revealing than I'd suspected, and perhaps Robin had been more observant than I'd given him credit for. And he'd been sly. He'd given me the manuscript when it was too late for me to do anything about it.

I returned to my room as the silence in the apartment turned into a headache of white noise. I rubbed my forehead, sickened as I remembered that Daniel had already read this. He'd read it in one night. I pictured him in Van's kitchen, the pages spread across the countertop. *God.*

Gathering up the manuscript, I slid onto the floor and leaned my back against the foot of the bed, where I read until far past midnight.

Robin had written a love story. The shark that bit Margaret ignited a bizarre love of sharks in her, which led her to study marine biology. Derek was a chef who betrayed her on the eve of their wedding. His betrayal, his "mistake," as Robin referred to it, didn't alter his love for Margaret, but she, poor, broken Margaret, rebuffed all his penitent attempts to talk to her and set things right. Crushed, stubborn, and inflexible, she walled herself off. She became completely alone.

Somewhere around 1:00 A.M., I read a sentence that caused me to stop in the middle of the page. For hours I had been reading in a stupor of benumbed disbelief, but there was something different and arresting about this sentence, a kind of genuineness, a kind of truth that left me defenseless. I read it over several times until the tears leaked out.

> *Margaret was a woman racked with regrets. A woman who could have had everything she ever wanted if she'd been able to forgive.*

It split me apart the way magma cracks open rocks. Was Robin right? If I'd been willing to pick up the phone all those times Daniel called, if I'd been willing to write him back, to see him, to listen, could I have moved on and learned to trust him again? Back then, I didn't owe him forgiveness, but maybe I'd owed it to myself. Perhaps we would be together now, married, with a child of our own. And Hazel. In a way, she would be mine, too. Had I stood in my own way? *A woman who could have had everything she ever wanted if she'd been able to forgive.*

The sentence was going to keep me up for the rest of the night. Maybe for the rest of my life.

I shoved the manuscript under the bed, grabbed my car keys, and without any real thought about what I was doing, I careened out the door, unable to bear the years of regret, the thought of Daniel reading that line. I hurried down the hallway, past all the DO NOT DISTURB signs, seized by the need to see him, to look him in the face and know if I could forgive. *Too much had gone unsaid for too long.* I was always so damned rational, so deliberate, so controlled—what if I just knocked on his door?

I paused in the dim, deserted lobby, forgetting for a moment where my car was, then remembering it had been parked in the employees' lot since Christmas.

When I turned the key in the ignition, a twitching sound emanated from under the hood. I looked past the dirty film on the windshield and tried again, hoping the engine would catch life before the battery died completely. I tried again and again, pressing the pedal harder with each effort. *Click. Click. Click.* The lights on the dash went dark.

Back inside the hotel lobby, trembling and agitated, I slipped into the alcove that housed Perri's Charlotte Brontë mural. Overcome with exhaustion, the desperation and impulsiveness starting to slip away, I laid down on the bench, resting my head in the crook of my elbow, unsure whether or not I was relieved that the car stalled. Was I, as Robin had written, a woman racked with regrets? Daniel's betrayal had broken us apart, but I was the one who'd kept us apart. Deep down, I'd wanted to forgive him, but I'd been proud, principled, unrelenting.

It was a relief when sleep came.

When I opened my eyes, the ceiling in the alcove was lit with morning sun. I swung my legs off the bench, recalling my insanity of the night before, almost showing up at Daniel's in the middle of the night.

It came back to me then, my fury with Robin. He'd breached something between us, the sacrosanct thing that bound us, our twin-ness.

Hotel guests, shiny with freshly sprayed sunscreen, mingled just outside the alcove slurping to-go coffees, their noses in maps of Palermo. I felt around for my keys beneath the bench, but ended up retrieving them on my hands and knees. I smoothed my hair, smudging away last night's mascara, and tried to appear as though I'd just slipped into the alcove on my way to breakfast instead of sleeping there half the night.

Speed walking through the lobby, I spotted Robin and Daniel by the radioactive seaweed sculpture.

"Maeve, wait," Robin called, catching up with me.

My face must have said it all.

"You read it," he said. "Please don't look at me like that. I'm sorry."

"I don't know where to start," I said, and gazed past him at Daniel, buttoned up in his chef's jacket.

"Let me explain," Robin said.

"You think I don't want you to explain? You *have* to explain," I told him.

I left him standing there, the whole world off kilter.

Ten

*W*hen the phone rang at 2:00 P.M., I glanced at the caller ID—
Ridley, N.—and hesitated, unable to place the name. I'd
been shut in my room all day working on my lemon shark research,
ignoring the unread half of Robin's manuscript under the bed and the
tap-tap that had come and gone on the door, accompanied by Robin's
voice, "Maeve? Can we talk? You all right?"

I'd demanded an explanation from him, then promptly become
incommunicado. It was unlike me, but I was angry, too angry to be
sensible. I wasn't ready to hear his bullshit explanation.

I had just turned back to my log notebook when the name on the
caller ID finally hit me. Nicholas.

"I'm in the lobby," he said, when I picked up.

"You're *here*? In the hotel?"

"I'm sitting here with your grandmother. I wanted to see you. I hope
it's okay."

In the background, I heard her say, "Call me Perri."

"Of course, it's fine," I told him. "I'll be right down."

Taking a peek at myself in the bathroom mirror, I decided the reflection could've been a whole lot worse. No dark-bluish circles under
the eyes despite sleeping hours on a wooden bench. I dragged a brush
through my hair, glossed my lips, and took a long, steadying breath.

He was sitting beside Perri on one of the coral love seats in the Library section of the lobby, a book upside down on his knee and a backpack slumped at his feet. He looked rested and clean shaven unlike most mornings in Bimini, when he'd turned out of his bunk and headed straight to the lab. The sight of him was a relief. *What had I been thinking last night, tearing off to find Daniel?*

"I wanted to surprise you," he said, getting to his feet and giving me a kiss on each cheek, European style.

"Mission accomplished—I'm *very* surprised," I said. "So, Perri's been keeping you company?"

"Nicholas was just telling me that Alexander Pope lived in his hometown of Twickenham," Perri said.

He gave me an artful twist of a smile, as if caught in the act of trying too hard to make an impression.

Judging from Perri's adoring expression, he'd clearly succeeded. I gestured at the book on his lap. "Considering your connection to Pope, I'm guessing Perri dug one of his books out of the library for you?"

"This? No, this is *Little Birds*," he said, flipping it over. I'd never heard of it.

"I found it on the shelf. It belongs with the room I'm putting Nicholas in," Perri said, standing.

I lifted my brows. "Oh. You're staying the night?"

"The jury is still out on that. It was Perri's idea. I am, however, quite willing to give up a night of my life for the Anaïs Nin Room."

My reading may have consisted almost entirely of science journals, but even I knew Anaïs Nin was a writer of erotica. The Nin Room was typically reserved for honeymooners.

"That's practically the only room left," Perri was saying. Mostly to me.

"If I've got my authors straight, she had an affair with Henry Miller," Nicholas said. "Am I right?" He grinned, and there was all that overpowering British charm.

"You are quite right," Perri said. "Now, I've got to get back to work." She pecked my cheek, giving me a look she barely attempted to hide. "We'll talk later?"

When she was gone, Nicholas held up *Little Birds*, which sported a nude woman curled seductively on the cover. "I do like your grandmother," he said.

"*God*. Sorry about the erotica. Perri's an artist." As if that explained everything. "Come on, I'll take you to your room."

As we moved along the hotel corridor, he read the authors' name plaques on the doors: "William Faulkner . . . Zora Neale Hurston . . . Marjorie Kinnan Rawlings . . . James Baldwin."

"Did you hear about the man who was caught with all the shark fins?" I asked.

"Yeah, it's terrible," he said. He stopped abruptly, placing his hand on my arm. "I'm sorry, Maeve. I know this must hurt."

He understood better than anyone how I felt, how much it mattered, and I had a sudden desire to lean my forehead against his shoulder and cleave to this perfect thing he'd just said.

"It happened near here, didn't it?" he asked.

"Less than ten miles. A hundred sharks were slaughtered for their fins, and I've heard nothing about an investigation and only one news report—a TV reporter asked some guy on the beach about it and he basically said the best shark was a dead one. This is what we're up against."

Nicholas let out a sigh, took my hand, and pulled me along the corridor. "I know a sergeant in the Marine Bureau in the Sheriff's Office here. I'll give her a call and see what I can find out."

I flipped on the light switch in the Nin Room and two mother-of-pearl sconces lit up on each side of the bed. Plum-colored pillows slanted neatly along the headboard with a matching one in the seat of an antique wooden captain's chair that was tucked beneath a small desk. On a wall shelf over the desk, Perry had displayed a small collection of books to carry out the Nin theme: *The Diary of Anaïs Nin*,

Volume One and *Volume Two*; *Delta of Venus*; *Tropic of Cancer*; *Lady Chatterley's Lover.*

One of Nin's tamer quotations was stenciled on the wall: "You don't find love, it finds you."

I watched Nicholas's eyes drift over the words. "Every room has a quote," I said.

He tossed his backpack on the bed, flung open the French doors, and stepped onto the tiny terrace overlooking the beach. A cloud of warm, humid air floated into the room, followed by the *caw-caw* of gulls. Bending over the rail, he scanned the beach. I watched him, his body mounted against sky and water, so much wide open blue, and I let myself feel for a moment what I'd felt on our last night in Bimini—the possibility of him, the possibility of a future—before suddenly remembering Daniel. Daniel, whom I'd loved, who was very much here, and who somehow still possessed a strange sway over me. I wanted to believe that what I was feeling for Daniel was merely ricochets from the past, but I couldn't explain their power. Was what I felt for Nicholas, in fact, more real? I looked at him, aware of how unburdened the two of us were by shared history.

He said, "When I was a kid, the view from my house was an old toilet the neighbors used as a planter in their front yard. Drove my mother mad. She used to say, 'You can put all the petunias you want in it, but it's still a toilet.'"

I laughed.

"You laugh, but that toilet got me a record," he said.

"As in *criminal* record?"

"My brother and I stole it. We loaded it into my father's car and tossed it in the trash bin at our school."

"How'd you get caught?"

"No, we got away with it. But our mother was so delighted over the toilet's disappearance that my imbecile brother told her who to thank. That we were thieves outweighed her delight. She made us apologize to the neighbors."

I groaned. "How old were you?"

"Fifteen. Jake was thirteen."

"So this criminal record . . ."

"It's not a police record, more like crimes against the neighborhood. What about you? Surely you got into trouble living in a hotel."

"Mostly sneaking out to go night swimming, and eavesdropping on the guests. Eating ice cream out of the industrial-size containers in the restaurant, that kind of thing. We left the toilets alone."

"Fire alarm?"

"God, no. But there was the time we lifted a bottle of Crown Royal from the restaurant bar."

"I think you were in deeper than me," he said. "How old were you?"

"Seventeen. Perri had just stenciled the wall quote in the Emily Dickinson Room, so the room was unoccupied while the paint dried. We took it in there and mixed it with ginger ale." Of course, Robin was doing the pouring.

He was the only one of us who'd gotten into real trouble. At sixteen, he'd been arrested one night for indecent exposure. After an evening of drinking with his friends, he'd peed in the parking lot of the Palermo Pub and Brewery and been sentenced to community service. For two weeks, after school, Robin wore an orange vest and picked up trash under the canal bridges and along the roadsides.

The wall quote in the Dickinson Room came back to me suddenly, full blown, and I made a little show of reciting it. "That it will never come again is what makes life so sweet."

"Is that the Dickinson quote?" he asked.

I nodded.

"I'm duly impressed," he said.

"That was the great thing about growing up in this place—I

absorbed the quotes, which makes me seem far more literary than I actually am."

"Your secret is safe with me." He glanced up at Nin's words again. "So, Perri painted the quotations herself?"

I nodded. "Every single one. But this is the only room that has a second hidden quote."

He stepped back inside from the balcony, casting his eyes toward the ceiling, then the closet. "And where exactly would I find this mysterious line?"

"Well, if I told you, there'd be no fun in finding it."

"So you know this room well, do you?"

"I know all the rooms," I told him. "Of course, this one always had the most allure."

He examined the books over the desk. "I can see that," he said, then turned to face me. "I have to take off early tomorrow morning. I thought we could get dinner tonight. I saw there's a restaurant here."

A romantic meal. Cooked by Daniel.

"I have a better idea," I said. "Let's make a picnic and take it to the beach. You won't even have to wear shoes."

"Sold. A picnic then."

He walked over to the bed, pulled a large envelope from his backpack, and held it out to me. "I was going to give this to you tonight, but I guess I can't wait."

I sat on the white duvet and opened it. Inside were a couple of dozen underwater photographs Nicholas had taken during our last dive in Bimini. I spread them across the bed and studied them—me and Sylvia suspended in varying depths of blue shadow and slanted rafters of light. They were beautiful, Sylvia was beautiful, and I felt an abrupt stab of missing her, the hope that she hadn't swum into trouble somewhere. If she hadn't been finned and drowned in the name of soup, diced up for beach-store necklaces and vitamin supplements, had her jaw cut out for a decoration, or mounted full scale on a wall somewhere, then in seven or eight years she would be producing pups.

In the last picture, Nicholas had captured me close up as I'd watched Sylvia swim away for the last time, focusing on my eyes behind the mask. They looked large and sad and ecstatic.

I lowered the photo to my lap and looked at him. "I don't know what to say. Thank you."

"I thought you might be missing her."

—

Nicholas wrestled a grocery cart free from the queue and pushed it into the produce section at Publix.

"They make really good subs here," I said.

"Thank God. I was worried we'd end up with pâté and designer grapes. Water crackers and caviar. Some sort of black olive tapenade."

I liked how he made me laugh. I liked *him*.

We passed over the red plums and nectarines to pick up chips and beer, then made our way to the deli counter.

"Okay, it's your last chance for a real sit-down dinner," he said as the man behind the counter, sporting a hairnet, asked for our order.

"I kind of like sitting on the beach with you," I told him, and I thought he would kiss me right there.

Ten minutes later, as we stood in the express checkout line, I noticed Hazel near the entrance with her arm in one of those grocery store blood pressure machines, and my stomach did a little flip. *Daniel.* I glanced back toward the produce, then along the wine and soft drink aisle just behind us. I didn't see him.

She could be here with Van, I reasoned. *Please. Be here with Van.*

Glancing up, Hazel spotted me and waved with her free hand, and the magnetic thing that had happened to me during our shark tooth excursion happened again, the way she set loose a funny gladness in me. I excused myself while Nicholas paid for the subs and ambled over to her. "Hey, there. How's your blood pressure?"

She giggled and slipped her arm out of the cuff. "I'm just waiting for Dad," she said, leaping up, pointing toward the first register.

He was leaning on his elbows on the cart handle, second in line. As his eyes dutifully scanned for Hazel, he noticed me beside her, straightened, a smile breaking over his face. He held up his forefinger—*Wait up.*

Hazel said, "Dad gave me the shark book you left for me."

"What'd you think of the ironing board shark?"

She rolled her eyes. "*Stethacanthus.* It was crazy." Then, just as Nicholas showed up, she added, "When are you coming over so we can have Shark Club?"

I willed myself not to look back at the checkout lane. "Hazel, this is Nicholas. He's my friend. You know how we know about sharks? Well, he knows tons about rays."

She smiled a little sideways, appearing shy, something I hadn't thought possible with her, and sat back down on the seat, flutter kicking her legs.

He squatted in front of her. "What's Shark Club is what I want to know."

"It's this thing I started," she answered. "Well, we started, me and Maeve. It's for people who love sharks."

"Hazel is a biologist in the making," I said. "Or a paleontologist. She knows more about ancient sea creatures than anybody I know."

At that, Hazel pressed her lips together, causing them to pink like watermelon flesh.

"Well, it's a pleasure to meet you," Nicholas said, extending his hand. "We could use a person like you at the aquarium where I work."

Hazel's cheeks flushed. She looked flattered and smitten all at once as she placed her hand in his. They were in the middle of a handshake when Daniel walked up holding two plastic grocery bags, one filled with nothing but lemons, the other, a large tin of olive oil. Giacomo's. The same brand I'd tossed into the Gulf for Hazel.

Hazel skipped over to his side and slipped her hand over his, the one that gripped the lemons, and we all stood there while the silence seemed to elongate into something that could snap. Later, I would tell Perri it was the intersection of Awkward and Awkward, and we'd laughed, but right now I didn't feel so droll.

Daniel and Nicholas introduced themselves. Nicholas reached out his hand. Daniel took it, the grocery bag with the Giacomo's dangling from his wrist.

"Nicholas and I worked together in Bimini," I said, sounding a little overeager to explain his presence in a casual way.

Daniel looked at me. "Oh, right. Good. Are you visiting?"

"I'm down from Sarasota," Nicholas said.

Hazel twisted at her dad's side. "He works at an aquarium. He knows tons about rays."

For several uncomfortable seconds no one spoke. An elderly woman had taken a seat at the blood pressure machine, and the cuff buzzed as it inflated. Hazel fixated on the woman like she was watching a shuttle launch.

I said, "Daniel is the chef at the hotel."

"I tried to talk her into a proper restaurant meal, but it's sandwiches on the beach for us," Nicholas said, holding up his bag.

"Oh yeah? A picnic?" Daniel said. "If you change your mind you know where to get a good meal."

I moved toward the sliding doors. "We were just on our way to the hotel."

"Us, too," Daniel said, then, turning to Hazel, "Ready to go, monkey?"

The four of us walked to the parking lot together, Hazel singing some jingle from a candy commercial. "Dad, can Maeve come over?" she asked when Nicholas and I stopped at his silver Jetta.

"If Maeve would like that, then I would like that," he said.

Hazel turned to me.

"Well, sure," I said.

As Daniel and Hazel veered off to his car, he turned back. "Maeve, have you finished Robin's novel?"

"Not yet."

"You should. It's a good ending," he said.

I paused, one foot in the car, his words reverberating across the hot, shining asphalt.

~

We spread a blanket on the beach in front of the hotel. The sound of singing and live guitar coasted from the restaurant terrace: The Drifters' "Save the Last Dance for Me." A fixture at the hotel, Billy had been crooning for as long as I could remember. He had to be at least as old as Mick Jagger.

Even though it was after six o'clock, the sun was high and still at work, busy cranking out heat. Nicholas opened a beer and handed it to me as I unloaded the sandwiches and chips, noticing he'd thrown in KitKats for dessert. We sat, arms touching, facing the water just like in Bimini after he'd released the little prince of a stone crab. Along the shoreline, a great blue heron stood like a yard ornament, perfectly stationary, glaring at its next meal.

"I owe you an apology," I said.

"Why? You didn't steal any liquor at the market, did you?"

I laughed. "No."

"Well, if it's about your grandmother putting me in the erotica room," he said, "I forgive her."

"It's about earlier at the grocery store."

He raised his hand. "You don't have to explain anything."

"I want to," I said. "Daniel and I . . . we grew up together, and a long time ago we were engaged." I took a breath. "Up until a few days ago, I hadn't seen him in years, but he just moved back, and I guess I'm getting used to that."

"I figured something was going on with the chef," he said.

"It was a little weird back there. I'm sorry about that."

"Maeve, it's okay. Really. You don't need to apologize."

I unwrapped my sandwich. "Also, I think someone has a crush on you."

"Do you mean you?" he said.

"I mean Hazel."

He swigged his beer and smiled.

We downed our grocery store sandwiches, munched the chips, ate the KitKats, and clinked our bottles together.

"I called the Indian Ocean Center in Mozambique," he announced. "It looks like they have an opening."

"And?"

"And I took it. Well, I told them I would take it . . . hopefully. They're holding the spot for me."

"You think there'll be a problem getting approval from the aquarium?"

Nicholas got off the blanket and took a few steps into the sand, where he stood with his back to me for several strange seconds—so long that a little spiral of dread began inside of me. I watched his shoulders rise, then fall, before he turned around. "I have to go back to London," he said.

I hadn't seen his face like this before, clenched and serious. "Okay," I said, involuntarily bracing. Why did I have the feeling he was about to say he was going for a job interview or a heart transplant?

He turned back now, coming to kneel on the edge of the blanket, putting his hand on mine and trailing his thumb over my knuckles. "Right after I got back from Bimini . . . my wife, Libby, called and asked for a reconciliation. She has stopped the divorce proceedings."

I scanned the water, the beach, then the sky, trying to absorb what he'd said. Did he mean he was going to London to reconcile with her?

"Maeve. Look, I'm sorry. I have to go back and deal with this. I leave in a couple of days."

"Is that what you want, to get back together?"

"No . . . *no*."

The music from the hotel seemed farther away, carried off by the wind and drowned out by the waves.

"What happened? Why the divorce in the first place?" I tried to sound unaffected. My heart was beating against my ribs.

He squinted into the wash of light. "She never wanted to leave London and come over here, but she did it for me. She hated it here. She missed everything. Her parents, her sister, her friends. She resented me for taking the job, for upending a perfectly good life. I didn't understand why I wasn't enough, why she couldn't be happy with me anywhere."

I listened, thinking of us on Bimini, as friends and colleagues all those months, of our last night there and how he'd spoken about his feelings for me, how I'd let myself have feelings for him.

"Libby and I went on like that for years," he was saying. "She finally gave me an ultimatum. She was moving back to London, and if I didn't go with her, she wanted a divorce."

"*She* asked for the divorce?"

He nodded. "So she left, and last summer I went to Bimini and waited for the papers. You were a complete surprise, by the way. You changed everything. I want the divorce. I didn't in the beginning, but I do now. I want us to go to Mozambique."

I looked past Nicholas to where the heron still stalked the shallows and watched it spear a wriggling sliver of a fish. Nicholas was not holding back anything, while I was hiding the fact that last night, I'd run out to find Daniel.

I got to my feet. I said, "I spent the last seven years believing I was one of those people who loves once, and that's it. I told myself that's the kind of person I am. *I work.* That's what I do. Everything else exists on the outside of that. But then, after all those months together we had that single great night, and I realized when I'm with you I don't want to be the kind of person who loves once. Or just works, but . . ."

The inevitability of what I had to do came to me, and it filled me with sadness. "I don't know, Nicholas. I just don't think we should continue with this or think about Mozambique while you're in London."

And I have to protect myself, I thought. Who could say what would happen when he was back home with her? It could all be different for him then. And how could I live knowing I was the one who gave him a reason to end his marriage? Maybe that's all I was, a convenient reason.

"Your wife changed her mind," I said. "How do you know you won't change yours?"

"Because I'm in love with you."

I didn't think I could bear knowing that, not now. I kissed his cheek. "Go to London. See your wife."

Overhead, the wings of the heron snapped like a sheet. It gave two throaty croaks as it flew over the hotel. Then it was gone.

In the morning, Nicholas was gone, too.

Eleven

I stuffed my research material into the green messenger I'd used since college and took the elevator to the lobby, hoping to find some willing soul to jump-start the battery in my car. Catching sight of Robin coming from the office behind the reception desk, I decided now was as good a time as any to stop avoiding him and the grand theft of my life he'd committed for the sake of his novel.

"Hey, the battery in my car is dead," I called. "Can you get it started?"

"You're speaking to me again!" he exclaimed, and jogged over, ignoring the scowl on my face.

"Don't get excited, you're not forgiven. I just need to drive to work."

I headed for the doors, while he hurried to catch up. Stepping into the atomic afternoon light, I paused by the bell captain's stand and popped on my sunglasses, taking in the blood-orange hibiscus and the gardenia bushes curving in thick, manicured rows in front of the hotel. That was the thing about Palermo—everything was eternally, outrageously in bloom. It made it very hard to feel sorry for yourself.

"It's Sunday," Robin said. "Why are you going to the Conservancy? Wait, don't tell me—it's Eco-Sunday." It happened once a month, targeting some aspect of marine life, usually a creature on the endangered list, involving an open house with exhibits, films, and talks, but I had no idea really whether this was Eco-Sunday or not. I wasn't due back at work till Monday.

"I'm going in because I have work to do; because I have to do *something*."

If I gave my mind an inch of room to think about Nicholas, it took over the entire acreage of my frontal lobe. I pictured him standing in the sand yesterday saying he was in love with me, how disconsolate he looked as we walked back to the hotel. After he'd left, I'd formulated a few lines I wanted to say to him, something about timing and patience and letting things play out, but I'd never called. I would think about Libby. He would divorce her or reconcile with her. He had to sort it out. Wasn't it best that he go back to England without my voice in his head? Wasn't it best that I protect myself?

I waited in the driver's seat of my tan Pathfinder trying not to think about Daniel, but it was hopeless. What had sent me out into the night to find him?

Fanning myself with a file folder, I watched Robin pull his car over and clip the pliers onto the battery. At his signal, I tried the engine. It cranked immediately.

Leaving the engines running, he slid into the passenger side. "All right. Let me have it."

"I don't know where to start," I said.

"Did you read the whole thing?"

"Does that matter?" I asked, raising my voice. "How could you work on this book for all that time and not tell me you were writing about my life? It's *my* life, Robin, and I feel like you're parading it out there without thinking how it would affect me."

"I'm sorry, Maeve. I really am. I'm a selfish prick. You know that."

"You don't have enough shit in your own life to write about? Rachel Gregory, for instance, or do you totally lack imagination?"

"You don't think I tried to write about her? It was too devastating to sit with all that every day. I just couldn't relive that pain again, dissecting it, parsing every molecule of misery it caused me. I loved her. The day she left the island, supposedly to ask her husband for a divorce, I found a copy of her novel she'd left on my bed. It was inscribed: *I'm sorry, Robin.* She never returned one of my calls. She was sitting in a house in Vermont with her husband and it tore me apart. Besides, the last time I wrote about my life it was a complete failure. Five hundred forty-three pages about a boy who lost his parents and looked for a family anywhere he could. My great professor proclaimed the boy's struggle 'insipid' and said the story veered off course. When I try to write about myself, I'm too close to the material; I can't see it clearly. It's easier to see someone else's life."

"Well, you could have at least tried to conceal me and Daniel a little better. What the hell were you thinking with these characters?"

He shook his head. "I know, but just hear me out. When I started, yes, I was writing about what happened to you—the shark bite, Daniel—but you have to know, the more I wrote, the more I imagined. Margaret was inspired by you, especially in the beginning, but she became less and less you. If you keep reading, I think you'll see that."

"You know what I resent? You always seem to take Daniel's side. Even back then, after everything he did, you tried to convince me to work things out."

Robin said, "After it happened, the first time I saw him, I punched him in the face."

"You did?" For a fleeting moment, the thought pleased me.

"I damn near broke his nose."

"Then why did you pressure me to give him another chance?"

"I don't know. Because *he* pressured me? Because I love the guy? Because I love you? Daniel was there for me, for us, and after his dad left, we were there for him. Honestly, I felt like you two were supposed to be together. And for what it's worth, when I said you should take him back, you hung up on me, remember? And I never brought it up again."

I stared straight ahead through the grime on the windshield, pressing on the accelerator to give the battery some juice. The noise and vibration of the engine filled the car.

"How did you know all that personal stuff you put in the novel?" I asked.

"I was there, Maeve. For all of it. I'm very observant."

"But some of the things you wrote were just between me and Daniel. You couldn't have observed them."

"He told me blow by blow what had happened. There was one time—" He stopped.

"What?" I asked.

"After you'd broken off the engagement and Daniel was in Italy, he called, asking me to forgive him. It was like seven P.M. here, and I figured it had to be one in the morning over there. He'd been drinking—he confessed to a half bottle of French Brenne, but it had to be more than that—and he was in this sad, talking mood. He said he'd tried calling you every day, had sent you letters."

Letting you go is incomprehensible to me, he'd written.

"He was hurting," Robin continued. "The poor guy broke down crying, and then he started reliving everything the three of us did as kids and in college, and then things just the two of you did. He needed to talk . . . and okay, I listened."

"But you didn't just listen," I practically shouted. "You used what you heard. You violated his trust and mine."

The smell of exhaust hung around the car and seeped through the air vents. I folded my arms across the steering wheel, laying my forehead in the crook of my elbow. My eyes welled with tears. I squeezed them shut, then lifted my head and looked at him.

"Do you think I'm unforgiving?" I asked.

"First of all," he replied, "I wrote that about Margaret. Not you."

"Yeah, well, I hate Margaret," I said.

I blotted my eyes with my sleeve, while Robin riffled through the glove compartment for a tissue, coming up with a brown Starbucks napkin.

He handed it to me. "I don't want you to hate me," he said.

"I don't hate you. I hate that you told the truth."

Robin gave me a confused look.

"It was Daniel who ruined things between us," I said. "I'm clear on that. I don't think for a minute his cheating was my fault. But what if you're right? What if I'd forgiven him? People do that. *Married* people do it. Things happen, affairs happen, and people stay together. They work at it. Maybe you're right that what we had was worth fighting for—I don't know. I was so mad and hurt I never even considered forgiving him. If I had, we'd be together now."

"I would've done the same thing you did," Robin said. But he wasn't very convincing.

"Now thanks to your damn book, I have all these questions, and . . . regrets."

"I didn't want that to happen."

"How could you not know that would happen? Did you not care?"

"I guess I didn't think," he said.

We sat for a few moments not saying anything. Robin got out of the car, dismantled the jumper cables, and banged down the hoods. I thought about the pair of turquoise flats I'd seen in the apartment, and for a second, I thought of asking him about the woman who'd left them behind, but I had no energy for it.

Robin came around to my window and rested his arms on top of the car. "I'll pull the book if you want me to. You're more important to me."

"I don't want to be the person who ruins this for you," I told him.

"Think about it. After that, if you still want me to pull it, I will. I'll give back the advance."

I put the car in reverse and backed out of the parking space. "Be careful," I called. "You might be sorry you made that offer."

"We all have to live with our mistakes," he said.

Twelve

$\mathcal{A}$ banner inside the main exhibit hall of the Conservancy proclaimed June the Month of the Manatee. Robin was right—it was Eco-Sunday. The room hummed with parents glad to have a worthwhile outing for the kids, environmental supporters, and vanloads of tourists from area hotels. Perri typically provided transportation for guests from the Hotel of the Muses, and I glanced around to see if Marco might be the driver today, but didn't spot him.

A manatee mascot in a baggy, silver-gray costume mingled with the visitors, posing for photos and peering through two eyeholes cut above the end of a whiskered snout. As I slipped around the edge of the crowd, I wondered which docent had been roped into wearing it. Through the large plate-glass window that stretched along one side of the hall, I could see numerous people launching red and yellow kayaks from the dock, nosing out into the mangrove estuary, where they were likely to see a real manatee.

Passing the touch tank, I paused to watch an exuberant toddler yank a starfish from the water. "Be gentle," one of the new teenage docents begged. *"The starfish are alive."* She pried it from the toddler's fist and placed it back in its habitat. That was me fifteen years ago—a high school volunteer, clocking hours during summers and on weekends, trying to keep small children from shaking the horseshoe crabs to death and reciting my spiel on sharks and local ecosystems to anyone who'd listen.

I peeked inside the small auditorium, where Russell was giving a lecture. "Manatees are gentle, slow-moving creatures, the aquatic relatives of the elephant," he was saying. Peeking out from the sleeve of his white Columbia shirt was the toothy mouth of the University of Florida Gator, a tattoo from his college days, which had to be at least twenty-five years ago. I watched him tuck a shoot of shaggy, golden hair behind his ear as he strode across the small stage in his flip-flops. His stage presence always made me think of a tanned, laid-back Steve Jobs.

Spotting me, he nodded in my direction. I waved.

God bless Russell. Years ago, when he'd hired me, I'd started off assisting with the shark monitoring program in the bays just south of here, known as the gateway to the Ten Thousand Islands. Eventually, I'd taken over the program, and Russell made me associate director of research, then later, director. Whenever I came up with grant money for research trips, he always encouraged me to go, letting John, my associate director, take over the shark monitoring until I returned. I'd had multiple research terms—in the Keys, Belize, Australia, and now Bimini, with Mozambique on the horizon only two months away. It was unusual for me to leave again so soon, but Russell had given his blessing anyway. Studying sharks around the world was the job I'd dreamed of.

Entering my office in the administration wing, I flipped on the fluorescent light, taking in the familiarity and quietness, and heard myself exhale a tiny gale. The space was, as Perri would say, a room of my own. It was one of the larger offices, with three windows overlooking a copse of flamboyantly orange poinciana trees, and beyond that, the parking lot. I twisted the rods to open the blinds, noticing the fine layer of dust that sifted through the light, then walked over and dropped my messenger on my desk.

The desk was really an old oak dining table I'd found in a second-hand store in Miami, something Spanish-mission-looking with carved pedestals. A true find. Maps of Mangrove Bay and the Ten Thousand Islands lined the walls, along with the wooden shelves piled with project files, grant applications, books, professional journals, three shark jaws, a dashboard shark in a hula skirt, and a specimen jar cocooning a baby hammerhead that floated ghostlike in a vat of formaldehyde.

I dialed John, intending to ask for an update on how the monitoring had gone in my absence. What I really wanted to know was if he'd seen any decline in the numbers since the finnings, but he didn't pick up. While my computer booted, I spread out my research, then reached into my bag for the photos Nicholas had given me. Riffling through them, I wondered if he had found the hidden Anaïs Nin quote before he'd left. It was painted on the inside of the wardrobe. "He was in that state of fire that she loved. She wanted to be burnt."

The thought of it caused a small stab of pain, the sensation of loss, or it could have been the jab of loneliness, or even longing. It surprised me, and then it was gone. I pinned the photos of me and Sylvia to a bulletin board and sat on the edge of my desk. Gazing at them, I remembered the uncomplicated happiness of being exactly where I wanted to be. Underwater.

I worked uninterrupted for the next hour or so, taking some pleasure in the quiet absorption of tracking data and recording the behavioral patterns I'd collected on Sylvia and her lemon cohorts. I was so lost in my notes that I didn't hear Russell when he tapped on my open door.

"So, the shark whisperer has returned," he said, grinning from the doorway.

"Come in," I said, getting up to give him a hug. "Your lecture all done?"

"All done. So. Welcome back."

He was holding the backlog of my mail. As he laid it on my desk, his eyes swept over the photos. "Impressive. Is that you swimming beside the lemon?

"Yours truly."

We talked for a while about the research I'd done in Bimini, whether there was anything publishable in it, before he shifted the conversation to the shark finning. "You've heard what happened on Bonnethead Key?"

"God, Russell, I'm having a hard time believing this happened on our doorstep."

"I don't know much more than what I've seen on the news, but then, there hasn't been much of it," he said. "The fins were found on the guy's property. He's probably just some low-level guy hired to store them, which means the finners are still out there."

I thought of my conversation with Marco. His friend Troy believed the ringleaders were still out there, too.

We commiserated for a while, expressing disbelief and outrage, grasping for plausible theories of who was behind it and where the investigation might be.

"I called the Sheriff's Marine Bureau and requested a briefing," Russell said. "They suggested we set up a hotline for illegal marine activity. I've already got someone on it." He moved toward the door. "Whenever you're ready to present on the lemons let me know and I'll get you on the lecture schedule."

When he was gone, I thumbed through the mail, finding a fat envelope from the Indian Ocean Center for Research in Mozambique. It contained an information booklet, forms, and a letter advising me about travel documents and vaccination requirements. Flipping to the page in the booklet on lodging, I came upon pictures of grass-thatched chalets with front stairs leading right onto the beach.

I had no idea whether Nicholas would go now. Once he was face-to-face with Libby, anything could happen. I knew the power that an old bond could hold over two people, and part of me feared

he would never return. Part of me feared he would. I wouldn't allow
myself to dwell on it.

As I stuffed everything back into the envelope, the phone rang.
John, I imagined.

"Maeve, it's me."

"Daniel?" I asked, the awkward moments in the grocery store coming back to me.

"Is this a good time?"

"Fine. It's fine."

"Look, Hazel is going on about the Shark Club. She's dying for
you to see this DVD of hers. So I'm thinking . . . the sous-chef is in
charge of the restaurant on Sundays. My one night off, so why don't
you come for dinner and we'll watch it."

I hesitated long enough for him to add, "I've seen it a few hundred
times. You'll like it."

"I guess I am partly responsible for this club," I said. "Sorry about that."

"Don't be. Seriously, it's given Hazel a new interest. It seems to be
helping her. Plus, I get to be in the club with you—that's another perk."

I fell silent again. For so long he'd been a figment, the subject of
pained nightly remembering, and now we were making dinner plans
like it was the most natural thing in the world.

"How about seven?" he said.

"All right. For Hazel."

I turned off the lamp.

In less than three months I would be underwater again, swimming with giants.

Thirteen

*D*aniel's childhood home was barely visible from the road, even though it was perched on stilts. The tip-top of the roof hovered just above a jungle of tropical foliage, royal and imperial palms and serpentine live oaks. Pulling into the driveway, I was greeted by Aunt Van's smiling dolphin mailbox. It'd been there since forever. Practically the size of a real dolphin, the concrete sculpture stood upright on its tail with the mailbox tucked under its flipper. In October, Van dressed the dolphin in a witch's hat and little black cape. November, a Pilgrim's hat. Christmas, a Santa hat and strands of multicolored lights. In March, the dolphin became a leprechaun with a green bowler, and in July, an American patriot in a star-spangled Uncle Sam top hat. *Only in Florida*, as we were fond of saying about ourselves. I imagined Hazel was going to love it.

I opened my car door into a hedge of plumbago and grabbed the box of cupcakes I'd bought on the way over. One dozen, and twelve different kinds. I'd gone overboard, but I wanted at least one of them to be something Hazel liked. As I climbed the front steps, I remembered Daniel used to keep his bike under the stairs. Parked beneath it now was a Hot Wheels with daisy stickers on the seat.

Cupcakes in hand, Hazel's handmade Shark Club badge pinned at my shoulder, I rang the doorbell. I cleared my throat. I brushed at

the front of my dress. I'd changed clothes three times before settling on a white sundress and sandals, not too casual, not too dressy.
On the porch, I was eye level with the bird-of-paradise plant-turned-
tree that reached up to the first floor window and bloomed in the
shape of Japanese cranes.

I heard footsteps inside and my stomach tipped a little. It crossed
my mind to wonder what I was doing. The last time I'd been here was
for my engagement party.

When Van opened the door, Hazel skated up behind her in socks.
Van hugged me and said, "It's been far too long."

Hazel stood by, waiting, stretching her arms behind her back.

"And how are you?" I asked, handing her the box of cupcakes.

"Good," she said, her voice lilting upward like a slide whistle. "Dad's
in here."

She bounded off toward the kitchen. "Hey, Hazel," I called. When
she turned, I pointed to the shark badge on my dress. Still clutching
the box, she managed to point to hers, then took off.

I didn't miss the polite but perplexed little frown that passed over
Van's face. As if she were trying to calculate what could've changed in
the inner workings of the universe that would allow me to be social-
izing with Daniel and the daughter he'd created with another woman
while engaged to me.

"She's irresistible," I offered.

Van put her hand on my back, patted once, then led me toward the
kitchen. "Hazel has been working on this club meeting all day," she
said. "And Daniel—he's been in the kitchen for the last two hours."

He was bent over the stove, sampling whatever was in the wooden
spoon he held to his lips. The room vibrated with smells I couldn't
identify. Paprika? Saffron?

"Maeve's here! Maeve's here!" Hazel shouted.

He looked up and gave me a grin. "Then I guess the Shark Club
is in session." He picked up the meat pounder from the cutting board

and rapped it playfully on the counter like a gavel. Giving the pot another stir, he said, "Hazel, wanna taste?"

She scrunched up her nose. "Gross."

"Well, what are you going to eat then?" I asked.

Pulling a step stool to a cabinet over the counter, she retrieved a microwavable bowl of macaroni and cheese. She rattled it like a maraca. Daniel shook his head, mumbling under his breath about powdered cheese.

"It kills him that she won't eat his cooking," Van said.

"How about you?" he said, holding the spoon out to me with one hand and cupping his other underneath it.

I walked over to the stove and let him lift the spoon to my lips. I watched his mouth part simultaneously with mine.

She wanted to be burnt.

Tomato, paprika, and olives sizzled on my tongue. "I love the green olives," I said.

"I remember. Spanish chicken marinara. Lots of olives." He set down the spoon and leaned in slightly. "I'm glad you came."

"Me, too."

I retreated across the kitchen without making eye contact with Van.

"Hazel, you wanna get your mac and cheese going?" Daniel said.

She peeled the lid off the bowl.

"Have fun with your club," Van said, sliding her purse onto her arm.

"You're not leaving," I said. The words sounded slightly desperate.

"I have game night at Tweetsy's. Mexican Train."

She took both my hands. "Tell Perri to come see me. You come back, too."

I nodded even though I couldn't imagine letting myself return.

She turned to Hazel and clapped her hands once. "Come here. Give me a kiss." Hazel giggled as her grandmother pelted her face with kisses.

Van was nearly out the back door when she stepped back to the wine rack. "What the hell," she said, grabbing a bottle of red. "It makes game night all the more entertaining."

Daniel shot her a look over the word *hell*. *Sorry*, she mouthed, and slipped out the door while Hazel stood unfazed in front of the microwave, and I tried to adjust to Daniel in the role of father. He seemed naturally suited to it.

The microwave beeped and Hazel popped open the door. Daniel took two plates down from the cabinet.

"Can I do anything?" I asked.

"No, let us. You sit."

I took a chair at the end of the table and watched Daniel arrange Spanish chicken onto the plates along with chorizo, yellow rice, and black beans, while Hazel glided around him in her socks. I hated myself for how much I wished to be part of it.

Hazel set the mac and cheese on the table beside a tube of strawberry yogurt and a banana and came to sit next to me. Daniel, sliding a plate in front of me, sat across the table.

"Smells delicious," I said.

"The other night he cooked a fish and it smelled up the whole house," Hazel announced.

"Pompano. And I don't think Maeve eats seafood, either." He looked at me. "Or is that still the case?"

"You don't like fish?" Hazel asked.

"It would be like eating my friends." I stabbed an olive.

"Wait," Hazel said. "We have to say the blessing."

I put down my fork.

"Go ahead," Daniel told her.

She folded her hands into an earnest little ball under her chin and closed her eyes.

"God is great. God is good. Let us thank him for our food. And bless Mommy and let her find my bottle."

Daniel watched her, too, then shifted his eyes to me.

"Amen," he said.

⌒

After we'd polished off the meal, I told Hazel to grab the cupcakes. "Dad made dessert," she confessed.

I gave him a look of surprise. "But you never used to make dessert."

"I do pie now."

"*You* made a pie?"

"Key lime."

"Can I have a cupcake?" Hazel asked.

He nodded. "You can have a cupcake."

She plucked one from the box and skipped off.

I got up to help with the dishes.

"Leave them," Daniel said. "Let's have dessert."

"I never thought I'd see the day you were baking pies."

"I think my mother never thought she'd see the day you were back in this house," he said, retrieving the key lime from the refrigerator.

"It sort of surprises me, too."

"A good surprise, I hope."

"I see you went nonmeringue," I said.

There was such a thing as the Florida key lime pie controversy, its main point of contention being whether to top with meringue or not. Floridians took a hard line one way or the other. The Hotel of the Muses had always been on the side of meringue. "I've taken a stand," he said. "I'm a purist. No fluffy stuff."

"You'll be starting a revolution at the hotel," I joked.

Sitting side by side at the counter, we ate in silence. Afterward, he stood and leaned against the counter and stuffed his hands into his jeans pockets.

"I guess your friend left?"

"Nicholas. Yeah, he left."

"You two were in Bimini together."

"We were."

He reached across the counter for the shark badge Hazel had made for him and pinned it to his shirt. "We should start the video," he said.

In the living room, Hazel cued the *Swimming with Sea Monsters* DVD, then tapped the space next to her on the sofa. "Sit by me," she said.

Plopping beside her, I noticed the Ziploc bag with her shark tooth inside lying prominently on the coffee table.

Daniel took the club chair, and Hazel scooted forward, a note pad on her lap.

"I have something to read," she said. "A . . ." She looked at Daniel for assistance.

"Ple—" he began.

"Pledge," she said. "Grandma helped me write it." She stood and solemnly held up her right hand, then turned it sideways. "With this fin, I do swear."

She gawked at me and Daniel just sitting there. Clearly, we were supposed to follow her lead. We got to our feet, made our hands into shark fins, and repeated after her:

"With this fin, I do swear. To love sharks even when they bite. When they lose their teeth, I will find them. When I catch one, I will let it go. This is the Shark Club vow."

Turning to me, Hazel stuck out her hand. "Fin shake," she said, and we all slapped "fins."

I reached for the bag with the tooth in it. "Maybe we should pass this around."

She liked that idea, and I took a few seconds to study the tooth through the plastic, then passed it to Hazel, who scrutinized it thoroughly before handing it to Daniel, who gave me a grateful look.

For the next hour we watched Nigel Marven go back in time to swim with prehistoric sea creatures. Hazel glanced at me from time to time to be sure I was paying attention. When Nigel got into a shark cage and the megalodon appeared, she exclaimed, "This is it!"

The mammoth shark swam toward Nigel, jaws open, butting the cage.

"Was it like that when you were bitten?" Hazel asked.

Daniel, who'd been sitting with one leg crossed over the other one, uncrossed it and straightened in his chair.

"No, I never saw it coming," I told her.

"It bumped me first," Daniel said.

"You were *there?*"

I looked at Daniel, surprised he'd decided to divulge this window into our past.

"Yep, I was in the water right beside her when it happened."

Hazel glanced at me for confirmation. "It's true. He pulled me to shore. I would've been in big trouble if your dad hadn't been there."

The way she looked at Daniel—I got the feeling she hadn't seen him in this light before. She seemed astonished that her dad had ventured outside of the kitchen for once in his life and into a real shark encounter.

"Nu-uh," she said, momentarily unbelieving, and Daniel made a cross-your-heart sign over his badge.

～

Shortly after Van arrived back home, she announced it was Hazel's bedtime.

"I don't want to go to bed if Maeve's still here," she said.

"But I'm going home and go to bed, too," I told her, rallying myself off the sofa. "I was just about to leave."

I raised my hand and gave her the shark fin shake.

She walked slowly to the stairs, Van prodding her from behind.

On the second step she turned back to see if I was really leaving, which prompted Daniel to walk with me to the front door. As we stepped outside, I waved to her.

"Goodnight, Bug," Daniel called, and closed the door behind us.

We stood on the front porch taking in the balmy dark. The sky was a van Gogh *Starry Night* poster. The leaves on the bird-of-paradise were as big as elephant ears, swishing against the window screens, and the tree frogs were in full chorus, sounding off like a thousand tiny alarm clocks.

"Come on, let's go sit on the dock," he said.

I didn't want the evening to end either.

Our shoes crunched along the crushed shell walkway behind the house. It would have been impossible to count the hours Daniel and I had spent on the dock behind his house after dusk. Some nights we'd lain on the wooden planks and talked, listening for a dolphin splash. Some nights we'd swum in the inky water to escape the heat.

The areca palm fronds had nearly overtaken the path. Daniel went first, pushing them aside as we passed. In the dark, his white shirt took on a glowing bluish tint. His hand was barely visible as it reached back for mine. I took it. I hadn't touched him in so long. It was impossible to think of anything but his palm and fingers against my skin. They felt warm and heavy, and I had the odd sensation of floating inside my body.

A half moon hung in the sky, a bright, broken shell. Around the edge of the dock, lights shone in puddles on the water, making wavy, iridescent patterns across the surface. We dangled our feet over the side, listening to the water lap in whispers against the pilings. There was nowhere to hide. There was me and Daniel and the night splayed wide open. He'd asked me to marry him right here.

"I'm looking at a house in a few days," he said.

"Hazel mentioned you wanted to buy a house. That's great."

"Staying with Mom was always temporary. Game night is out of control over here," he joked. "The drinking. You heard the language."

"That Tweetsy is a bad influence, huh?"

And just like earlier in the kitchen, being together felt surreal and normal and filled me with longing. I didn't know whether being here was good or bad, whether it was like recovering something precious that I'd lost or falling back into a bad old habit. I just knew it was happening and I was letting it.

"Robin's book," he said. "It's strange seeing all of that on paper."

"I was furious with him when I read it. I still am, really. I thought all this time he was working on his old college novel or something. You didn't know he was writing about us, did you?"

"I had no idea."

"He told me he would pull the book from the publisher if I wanted him to. Can you imagine me taking him up on that? He flails around for years, going from one job to another, and then to everyone's shock he actually writes a book that's getting published! How could I take that away from him?"

I stared out into the bay, at small lights twitching on the opposite shoreline. "I just feel betrayed, and embarrassed. God, I'm so embarrassed. Maybe if he changed the dedication. At least then the book wouldn't seem to broadcast that it's about us."

I could feel Daniel looking at me.

"You're not angry?" I said. "About the book, I mean?"

"Parts of it were hard to read, but no. I'm not angry. It's us. Well, it's us right up until Margaret decides to give Derek another chance."

We were silent then, the air turning thick and uncomfortable and unfairly loaded.

"The other night when I was reading Robin's book, I almost came to see you."

"Really?" His voice sounded genuinely surprised. "So what happened?"

"The car wouldn't start. I decided it must have been divine intervention. It was the middle of the night. I don't know what I was thinking."

"You should've called me. I would have come to you."

"Well, I'm here now."

"Can I ask you something?"

"Okay."

"That day you arrived and I stopped by your room, I saw the osprey feather on your dresser. It's the one, isn't it, the one you went into the water for the day the shark—"

"You mean the one you stuck in my ponytail before I kissed you?"

"Yeah, that one," he said. "Why'd you keep it?"

There were so many old ghosts between us now.

Did he remember I'd planned on putting it into my bridal bouquet? "It was our first kiss. I guess I couldn't part with it."

"What about you and this Nicholas guy? Are you with him?"

I looked away from him and into my lap.

"I'm sorry," he said. "It's none of my business."

"We put things on hold," I told him. "Or we ended it completely. I'm not even sure."

Daniel placed his hand on my knee, and I resisted the urge to close my eyes. His touch resurrected that whole tempest of longing and regret, the what-might-have-been. I felt almost dizzy at how quickly I'd gone from living with the memory of Daniel to eating pie with him. "Have you been okay?" he asked.

Have I been okay?

The question was like a bone in my throat. I scrambled to my feet, wanting, needing, to get my bearings. Daniel stood, too, and I stepped away as he reached for me.

"There is always a sadness in me," I said. "I don't want it to be there, but it is. It sleeps inside of me, and when it wakes there's nothing I can do about it. It takes over, and when that happens nothing else exists. You did that. For the last seven years I've hated you for it."

Daniel's face seemed to collapse. "I tried so many times to fix everything."

"I know. I refused to forgive you, and I live with that, too. Now all of a sudden I doubt whether I made the right decision. It's that stupid book of Robin's—"

"Maeve," he said. He stepped toward me.

"I should go home," I said, pulling away.

Despite the darkness, I found my way along the path, Daniel following behind me. "You don't have to go," he said.

I had invested years in trying to move on. To go down this road with Daniel again would be insane, completely reckless, but when I got to the driveway I didn't really want to leave.

I stopped and turned around. "Dan—"

At that same moment, Hazel jumped out from behind my car. "Boo!"

My feet left the ground.

"Hazel, you're supposed to be in bed," Daniel said. "Does your grandma know you're out here?"

Her voice thinned into a whine. "No, I was looking for you. I couldn't find you." She held out my clutch purse. "Maeve forgot this."

"Well, would you look at that?" I said. "I'll need my keys, now won't I? Thanks." I took the bag and hurried to my car.

I backed down the driveway, then watched them in the rearview mirror until I couldn't see them anymore.

Fourteen

*T*he next few days and nights passed in a tightly coiled blur, as if I'd crawled into the tiny space inside a conch. After that night with Daniel and Hazel, I'd put my head down and worked feverishly on my Bimini research from early morning until well past nine in the evening. The work was enough. That's what I told myself.

On the sixth day of my cloistering—my absentia, as Perri had pointedly referred to it earlier that morning when I'd bumped into her in the lobby—I had nearly finalized my findings on the lemons and drawn up an outline for my Eco-Sunday lecture. It was after ten when I switched off the lights in my office and drove back to the hotel, my brain saturated with the woozy, tired feeling that comes from an overload of reading and writing and thinking, and my stomach screeching with hunger. I usually ate lunch at my desk, whatever pizza the volunteers brought in, then slipped into the hotel kitchen when I got home, after it had closed, foraging for a turkey sandwich or the soup of the day, whatever I could find left over from Daniel's dinner specials.

I hadn't spoken to Daniel since the night of the Shark Club. Not since the Spanish chicken marinara and the meringueless key lime pie. Not since we sat on the dock, his hand on my knee and my throat choked with regret and recklessness. Communication with Nicholas was nil, too, but that was just as well.

The kitchen was dark and cool and smelled like Mr. Clean. The refrigerators were churning out a baritone hum, a surprisingly loud serenade I'd grown accustomed to during my nightly pillage. I set my bag on one of the sparkly stainless steel counters and perused the walk-in cooler. The first things I saw were six of Daniel's key lime pies. Tomorrow's lunch dessert.

I picked up one and removed the lid. The sweet, tangy smell hit my nostrils, sending me back to the barstool in his kitchen. I closed the cooler door, grabbed a fork, and carried the whole pie through the dining room out onto the empty terrace.

A diffuse white glow spilled out from the lobby; spotlights illuminated the pool and the palms. The only sound was the slush of waves. I pulled a chair close to the rail overlooking the Gulf and used my knees as a tabletop. I took a bite and turned the fork over in my mouth.

Twenty minutes later, after I'd eaten almost half the pie, I heard the French doors open behind me. Twisting around, I saw Daniel standing on the terrace, holding my bag and the pie lid.

"I knew you had to be somewhere around here," he said.

"I stole a pie," I told him, and stood up, the graham crumbs falling from my lap.

"I see that." Had the moon been brighter, I might have seen satisfaction in his face. Or was he thinking about the way I'd run away from him a few nights ago?

"Sorry. I just saw it and . . ." I threw up my free hand. "What are you doing here? It's eleven o'clock."

"Couldn't sleep." Daniel laid my bag and the lid on the nearest table. "I usually come back and catch up on paperwork. What about you?"

"I worked late again. I came looking for dinner, but found the pies . . ."

"So you're the pie thief."

"Yeah, that's me."

Daniel looked at the half-empty pie shell and laughed quietly. "*God.* Can I make you something to eat?"

"No, that's okay."

"You sure?"

"I'm sure."

Neither of us spoke, and the lull floated there like something alive and hovering.

Finally he said, "After the other night, I thought I should give you some space—"

"I'm sorry I took off like that," I interrupted.

"I understand." He smiled and turned back toward the kitchen. "Well, I've got an inventory to go over. And I guess I have to make a pie."

"Wait. Daniel."

He turned back, standing in a little slab of shadow, his face lost to me.

"I don't want space," I said. "Not from you."

He walked toward me and didn't stop until he was kissing me.

Everything came back with strange suddenness. Memories, the old feelings, the believing, the wanting. And then a sort of déjà vu. I'd never told Daniel, but the first time we spent the night in the Forster Room, I'd gotten a picture in my head out of nowhere of Victoria Falls, of unfathomable amounts of water falling over a cliff. I'd only seen pictures of the falls in a *National Geographic* when I was a girl, and although it had made no impression on me then, the glossy photograph came back to me on that first night with Daniel. I didn't know why that was, but later I would think how a person could step into the water knowing she might pitch right over the side, drown, and not care. The force of my feelings for Daniel that first night awed me.

Now, given another chance, I wouldn't have stepped away from him for anything in the world. We left the terrace and walked to my room. "It never felt over," he said when we stepped inside.

He kissed me again and, with the scruff and warmth of his skin on my cheek, everything gave way. I'd made a fortress of myself and it caved like one of the sand castles that dotted the beach.

I slipped right over the falls.

Fifteen

I steered the *Sundance* with my bare feet, navigating the Conservancy's twenty-five-foot bay boat through the manatee slow zone, nosing between the mangrove isles surrounding Palermo. Moving at the speed of a very old turtle, barely cracking a wake behind the boat, I kept my eyes peeled for the manatees' big gray noses, which often broke the surface.

I'd cast off around 6:00 P.M. with the crew—John, my associate director, three other biologists at the Conservancy, and a grad student named Olivia—for a late-night shark-monitoring expedition. For the next ten hours or so we would capture and tag as many sharks as possible, obtaining measurements and blood samples, and then safely release them. The mission was completely routine, but since learning about the mass finning, I'd been impatient, nervous really, to see how the population was faring, and I'd pushed the expedition ahead of schedule.

The engine buzzed in my toes and my neck stung with the heat of a late June afternoon. I reached for the milk jug I'd filled with water and drank. The crew sat in the stern poring over the plastic-sleeved pages in our monitoring notebooks. They contained printouts of the hundreds of sharks we'd tagged, listing their names (i.e., Oscar, Wendy, Eloise), photos, dorsal fin profiles, body measurements, blood analyses, field notes, latitude/longitude of capture, and the depth, temperature, and turbidity of the water.

As we left the manatee zone, I grasped the wheel with both hands and opened up the throttle. As the bow lifted, everything pitched into sudden, exhilarating speed, and a box packed with our dinner tipped, sending an orange back to the center console where I sat. I tossed it back to Olivia. It made me think of the breakfasts Daniel sent me on the room-service cart practically every morning. Sometimes a blueberry muffin, homemade granola, a cinnamon scone, but always an orange.

We'd spent almost every night together since that first night almost one week ago. He would arrive at my room late after the dinner shift and leave before dawn in order to be home when Hazel woke. We'd been careful about concealing his visits. Well, except for the room-service cart, which wasn't particularly discreet, but it was hardly a giveaway. Even Robin, who shared part of my living space and who had proved himself all ears and antennas in the past when it came to Daniel and me, hadn't picked up on us. Hazel had to be considered, and as for Robin, Perri, and Van, we weren't ready to announce our . . . what?

This morning, sitting on the edge of the bed, Daniel had said, "What if I tell Hazel about us?"

I rolled onto my side, tugging the sheet around my shoulder. "What would you say?" I felt wide awake all of a sudden, acutely aware of the breathy anticipation in my voice.

As he twisted around to look at me, I watched the knobby bone at the base of his neck disappear. He said, "I don't know. I've never been in this situation before." He stood and crossed the room, then turned back. "What are we doing, Maeve?"

I was glad he was the one to ask the question. At times during the last couple of days it'd felt like we were regressing into the same teenagers who'd sneaked into the Forster Room the summer before I went to college, like we were making up for lost time, not thinking, at least not with our heads. Other times, most of the time in fact, what we were doing felt miraculous, as if we'd lost our way back then, had been blown wildly off course, and were finally rescuing ourselves, rescuing our life together.

Even when I told Daniel about my plans to go to Mozambique in August, he didn't protest, didn't bring up the future. Did he see a future? He only asked how long I would be gone. When I said till Christmas, he merely grew quiet.

What are we doing, Maeve? The question hung between us. It felt slightly dangerous, like some small, feral creature had been accidentally set loose in the room. "You tell me," I said.

"What matters is that we're together, and I love you. I always have. We'll figure the rest out."

Right now his words were enough.

After he left, after the room-service cart arrived, I took a cup of coffee to the balcony. I was sitting there wrapped in my robe blissfully not thinking, just watching the sky blister with light and the gulls descend on the Gulf to feast on minnows, when an osprey landed on the balcony railing less than ten feet away. A small fish was clutched in its talons, flopping helplessly back and forth. As I let out a breath, the osprey cocked its head and turned its sharp yellow eyes toward me. Then dropping the fish, it flew off, its wings churning a rush of air.

I decided to leave the fish where it was. More than likely the osprey would return to finish the poor thing off. After I showered, I peeked onto the balcony and there was nothing left but a fish head and a mess of guts. I tossed them into the trash and, using wads of paper towels, wiped the blood into scarlet streaks. As I scrubbed the floor with Lysol, Daniel's question welled up.

For years, part of me had fantasized about this very thing, Daniel and me together, but I'd never imagined a scenario beyond our reunion. I stared at the bloody paper towels as if reading tea leaves. Nature was both saving and inviolately cruel.

"A roscate spoonbill at eight o'clock," a voice called, jolting me back to the boat and the green rippling breakwater, to the pink-plumed seabird stretched out in the air like a feather boa.

We anchored in Calusa Bay two hours before sunset and began the meticulous process of cutting up mullet for bait and fastening the hunks of flesh onto hooks. Once the hooks and buoys were attached to the lines, we dropped them in the water. While a couple of the guys filled the shark wells, I checked the bilge system. The only thing to do now was wait.

We watched for sunken buoys, listened for the splash of a shark taking a hook, and filled the time with fish tales—the fifteen-foot sawfish that had torn up our gear on the last outing; the enormous dolphin fish John once caught, only to have his boat followed for ten miles by the female dolphin fish who was left behind. "It was enough to make me give up fishing," he said.

After the sun set, night hammered down quickly, a huge well of blackness above and below. We put on our bug shirts and hats, drawing the nets over our faces, but not before the no-see-ums and mosquitoes fell on us like a plague from the Old Testament. They swarmed so loudly, I shushed everyone to be sure I wasn't mistaking them for a distant plane.

I kept my eyes on the buoys, shining my flashlight from one to the other in a kind of timed syncopated rhythm. Overhead the planets flickered and glowed, and talk turned to unexplained configurations of lights, to sworn UFO sightings, then to teasing, then to silence.

Every forty-five minutes, we pulled up the lines, checking the bait and repeating the exercise. Waiting.

Close to ten o'clock, Olivia said, "Where are the sharks?," disappointment heavy in her voice.

"We have nights when they never show at all," John told her, but before his words drifted over the hull and were swallowed by the night, I saw the buoy yanked under.

We pulled in a juvenile bonnethead and shortly afterward, two juvenile bull sharks, all small enough to fit in the shark well. On past trips, I'd used a vinyl kiddie pool, which was easier on the sharks and on us, too, but it had been missing from the boat. We lowered each of them into the shark well, then hitting the boat lights, tagged, photographed, and collected our data.

Near midnight, we hooked the star of the night—a female bull with purple scars between her dorsal fins. I'd not seen scars like these except in textbooks, but I knew instantly I was looking at the trauma caused by a pursuing male during mating season. Breeding between sharks was violent, with the female often sustaining injuries from males. They would be struck, flipped, gouged, and bitten, ending up with raw skin and bite marks. To deal with the harshness of it, female sharks had evolved to be larger than males with rougher and thicker skin. Back in grad school that had stirred up jokes by women in the class, jokes that carried an undertone of seriousness, about how male aggression had ended up honing females into the more superior species, that kind of thing.

"So much for romance," I said, pointing out the marks to the others.

She was so big we left her in the water. I worked over the side of the boat, drawing blood and getting measurements, while Olivia took photos and John logged data in the notebook. "I'm recording her name as Rose—that okay?" he called.

"Fine," I said, moving as fast as I could. I didn't want to subject her to any more stress. Sharks were like people when it came to stress. My fear was that we would release her and she would exhibit none of the fight she'd displayed when we'd pulled her in.

"There you go, Rose," I said, and gave her a pat. She thrust away, disappearing into the black water.

Sixteen

*T*wo nights after the shark monitoring trip, I trekked down the access path from the hotel shortly after 10:00 P.M., feeling the wind pick up and hearing the soft roar of waves intensifying off in the darkness. Tonight, instead of coming to my room, Daniel had proposed that we meet on the beach. He had always loved the Gulf better at night. About now he would be finishing up in the kitchen. He would come late, bearing some sort of food offering.

Looking up, I searched for the moon, which had been visible earlier but had now disappeared into a thick, starless sky. There were no lights on the beach either, a courtesy we offered the sea turtles, the first of which had already begun nesting. When the babies hatch, they use the moonlight as their compass; they become disoriented by artificial light, mistaking it as lunar and wandering off in twenty wrong directions. I was thinking how ridiculously nature seemed arranged against the tiny creatures when I almost stepped on top of a fresh nest.

The mother, probably a loggerhead, had made the long crawl from the water and dug her clutch right at the end of a public access, then turned around and gone back to sea. She would never return to the nest.

I examined the large, bowl-shaped hole where she'd buried her eggs, then followed the distinct, fresh drag she'd left in the sand all the way to the water, wondering if I'd just missed her. I made a mental note to have the nest roped off with yellow caution tape.

Since I'd been home, squares of yellow had dotted the beach as if it were some horrid crime scene. Around mid-August, the islanders would begin "turtle watch," waiting nightly for the hatchlings, hoping to see them break for the water, one of the true wonders of the natural world. It occurred to me that I could bring Hazel, until I remembered I would be leaving for Mozambique around that time. If I wasn't here . . . well, Daniel should take her. She shouldn't miss it.

I watched him emerge suddenly from the opaque stretch of beach. He kissed me, then handed me a canvas bag. Inside, resting on top of his kitchen shoes, his chef's jacket, and a rolled up towel, was a key lime pie. "There should be a fork in there," he said.

"This is our thing now—pie?" I said.

"It's one of our things." He spread the towel on the sand and we sat.

I peeled off the pie shell lid and took a bite. "*One* of them? We have others?"

"Late nights."

"True." I handed him the fork.

"That's my fault," he said. "Chef's schedule."

"And movies. Well . . . used to be."

Daniel set down the fork. "The last one we saw together was—"

"That rocket movie."

"No, it was *Saving Private Ryan*."

"Really? I'm pretty sure it was Jake Gyllenhaal building rockets."

"Yeah, I'm positive. We rented it. 'Every man I kill, the farther away from home I feel,'" he said, doing a pretty good Tom Hanks impersonation.

"I take it you've seen the movie a few times since."

"A few," he said, and laughed. "Lately, it's the animated stuff with Hazel. She was five before she sat through an entire movie."

"What was it?"

"There was a purple elephant."

We sat bundled up in the dark, just out of reach of the tide and the sea foam collecting in the wrack line. The wind died, and for a few minutes the moon poked her head through the curtain of gray clouds, causing light to spangle on top of the water and across the rock jetties.

Quietness rose. "Come here," he said. He grabbed my hands, and as I moved over, he made room between his legs, where I reclined against him. He wound a strand of my hair around his finger.

I asked, "What has your life been like? Since back then, I mean."

"There was the restaurant in Miami. And Hazel. Before her mother died, I would drive up to St. Petersburg twice a month to see her."

"That must have been hard. Not having her all the time."

"It's just the way it was."

"Did you . . . you and Holly . . . did you ever have a relationship?"

I felt him let go of my hair. The moon had withdrawn again, but the waves seemed calmer now, rolling small and lakelike, barely making noise.

"We tried," he said. "Hazel was a year old. It made sense to try."

"How long were you together?"

"Four or five months, that's all. Neither one of us was very happy."

My longest relationship had lasted three months, ending right about the time I realized it was going nowhere. Drawing up my knees, I turned into his body. My chest filled with desire and happiness, and then was marred by a shoot of old hurt pushing up into the center of it like a noxious weed.

"How about you?" he asked.

"I had my share of dates, some memorable, most utterly forgettable."

"I always worried one day Robin would call up and tell me you were getting married."

"Me, too."

"Let's go swimming," he said.

"Now?"

"Come on." He stood and pulled his shirt over his head.

"You don't have to be a marine biologist to know that swimming in the ocean at night is a bad idea."

"We won't go out far." He stepped out of his pants.

I laughed at him standing there in his boxers, and though we were alone, I looked around for passersby, for people far away on the hotel terrace.

"Swim with me," he said.

When I didn't move, he wandered into the water calf deep. "You aren't scared, are you?" he said, reminding me of the way I'd taunted him into the water the day of the shark bite.

I wasn't like him. For him the Gulf was entertainment. A vast water park. I was more like Nicholas. He once told me that when he looked at the water, he saw something dark, relentless, and ancient. And I felt that mystery and its dangers even more so at night. I didn't underestimate its ability to pull me into its depths or pick me up by the neck and toss me to shore, but staring at Daniel, his body striated with shadows, his fingers grazing the water, I began to take off my clothes. I left my bra and underwear on and waded in, thinking of the sea turtle that had lumbered out of the waves, then made her way back to the water.

We swam into the swells and stopped waist deep. Daniel faced me. The lustrous blue of his eyes had disappeared in the darkness. He cupped the tepid water over my shoulders, while I wondered if all those times I'd lain in bed remembering Daniel he'd been imagining this, the two of us swimming in the Gulf.

He said, "Do you remember in high school when you came out here screaming at me and Robin to get out of the water?"

"What I remember is that you two had been drinking and insisted on swimming in the middle of the night. Then you pretended to drown just to scare me."

"Not to scare you. To kiss you. You were the only one who knew CPR."

"I thought you were dead until I started breathing into your mouth."

"That was mean of me," he said. "And juvenile."

Daniel pulled me closer, hooking one arm around my waist, then the other. As I rested my forehead against his cheek, something moved under the soft bottom of my foot, and I shook my leg. In the next second, Daniel plunged under the water taking me with him, then sprang back up still holding on to me, laughing.

I gave him a shove. "You're *still* juvenile!" I said, wiping the water from my eyes.

"I'm sorry," he said, half laughing. "Come here. I'm sorry." He drew me into his arms and whispered, "I'm sorry." Over and over. "I'm sorry."

Seventeen

At the hotel's Fourth of July gathering, every guest seemed clad in red, white, and blue. I watched them mill about the restaurant's terrace, pinging from one high-top table to another, seeking a place to rest their hors d'oeuvres and cocktails. I wore a lavender sundress. My patriotism ended at fashion.

A server strolled by with a tray. "Key lime martini?"

"You're kidding."

"It's good," she said.

Daniel had to be the Frankenstein of this concoction. It was sweet and sour, tasting of vodka, lime, sweetened cream, and vanilla. The rim was coated in graham cracker crumbs, necessitating that I brush off my lips after each sip.

I found a niche near the steps leading to the beach that was devoid of people and leaned back against the low stone wall, listening to Billy strum Dusty Springfield on his guitar. He stretched out the lyrics, turning the song melancholy, making me believe he was singing about some woman he never got over. When he finally, mercifully, got through it, Perri sashayed over in her red capris and crisp white shirt and whispered in his ear. Immediately, he lit into Willie Nelson's "Island in the Sea" and Perri, who was old enough now to genuinely not care what anyone thought, started dancing. She looked like she was practicing a form of yoga, rolling her shoulders, stretching her neck, swaying from her waist, bending her knees. I smiled, watching her.

I hadn't been avoiding Perri, but I hadn't sought her out either. I was still in no hurry to explain that Daniel and I were testing the waters, or catching up, or getting to know each other again, or all of the above. She would naturally ask if we were dating. She would ask about Nicholas. I didn't have any answers.

It was enough of a challenge to keep Robin in the dark. He'd noticed I no longer seemed resentful about his book. "I'm glad you've moved on," he'd said. In truth, I had merely tabled the matter. I hadn't read a word of his manuscript past the line about forgiveness that had so thoroughly upended me.

I spotted Hazel standing by the French doors, the waitstaff buzzing like mosquitoes behind the panes. She was in yellow again, a little cap sleeve tee with a big white star in the middle and yellow shorts. Her field bag was draped across her chest as it had been the day on the beach. There was no telling what was in there. Her club badge, a shark tooth, sunglasses, a ticket to the moon.

Perri abandoned the dance floor, going over to greet her about the same time that Van showed up in a blue skirt and red-and-white polka-dot blouse. Hazel took her grandmother's hand as the women talked. She looked as out of place in her yellow as I was in my purple. I was sipping the last of my key lime martini when they all turned and looked at me. I waved, as they motioned me over.

"Well, as I live and breathe, if it isn't my granddaughter," Perri said as I ambled up. "I think you've been hiding out with the sharks again."

I manufactured a laugh and took a step over to block the sun from Hazel's eyes. As her face relaxed, I caught a flash of Daniel in her expression. Here was his daughter. It was still sinking in.

"I've got something," she said, patting the field bag. "Wanna see?"

"Can't wait," I told her.

She dug around inside the bag and tugged out a sheaf of papers. "I made a comic book."

"She's been working on this since you were over at the house," Van said.

Perri looked at me. "Oh? You were at their house?"

"Why don't you come show it to me," I said to Hazel, and led her to a nearby table while Perri and Van caught up, or, as I suspected, discussed my recent visit to Van's house for dinner and the newly inaugurated Shark Club.

Hazel's cheeks were rouged with sun and excitement as she laid out her comic on the table. She had folded white construction paper in half, punched two holes along the crease, and looped it together with a piece of white yarn. On the front she'd drawn a shark and written the comic's title in plump red letters: *SIR FIN*.

She asked me to read it aloud, and I did, frame by frame. It was the story of a small shark that fought a catfish army and was knighted by a shark king wearing a spiky crown.

There were extra pages in the comic, waiting to be filled in.

"You should keep going," I told her. "I want to read more about Sir Fin."

She squinted at me. "We could do one *together*."

"I would love that," I told her, and I had one of those funny experiences where I was in the moment, but also outside of it, observing myself, and I thought, *I do love it. I love her. I love this.* The same thing had happened in Bimini as I swam beside Sylvia, this same rush of knowing.

Hazel pulled out a handful of colored pencils and crayons from her bag. "What should our story be about?"

"Oh, you want to do it *now*?"

She grinned.

"Okay. Well, let me think." I blankly scanned the crowd, waiting for an idea to strike. Van and Perri, I noticed, had been joined by Robin.

I leaned back in the chair and thought of the scarred female bull shark I'd tagged on our recent shark-monitoring expedition. "I have an idea," I said. "How about a girl shark?"

"Mmmm, okay," she said.

"Rose?"

Hazel handed me a pencil. "Rosie."

"If you want, I'll tell you what I'm thinking and you can write it however you want."

"You do it," she said.

I doodled a lump buried in the sand on the ocean's bottom, then drew a dialogue bubble over it. Inside it I wrote: *Help! Help!* In the next square, I sketched Rosie the Shark, a task I should've been better at. She looked a little like Charlie the Tuna minus the hat and glasses. I sketched a Superwoman cape tied around her and in the bubble I wrote: *Someone is in trouble. Rosie to the rescue!*

In the next box, I drew her plunging toward the lump on the sea bottom, adding fitful dashes around her body, and making whooshing sound effects to sell Rosie's super speed to Hazel.

My effort to illustrate Rosie digging in the sand with her nose was slightly feeble, but Hazel seemed riveted, her eyes wide and glued on the paper.

Hold on, I'm almost there, Rosie cried.

In the final frame, I drew Rosie's mouth wide open, adding dimples and displaying rows of pointy teeth. In the midst of them was the stone crab Nicholas had rescued. Safe and sound.

"Is that a spider?" Hazel asked.

"It's a baby stone crab. He's called the Little Prince."

She found this hilarious. I made the crab's pincers bigger and defined the edges of its shell, then shaded in its body with a purple crayon. In the crab's dialogue bubble, I wrote: *You saved me! I'm free! Thank you, Rosie.*

Hazel studied every square.

"It's not as good as Sir Fin," I said, "but . . ."

Before I could get the rest of the words out, Hazel raised her hand for the Shark Club salute. We smacked our "fins" together, causing a small craving at the back of my rib cage.

Van, Perri, and Robin wandered over and took the empty seats at the table, curious to see what Hazel had drawn. Van oohed and aahed.

From the corner of my eye, I saw Daniel making his way around the terrace, shaking hands with partygoers, accepting compliments for his mini crab cakes and shrimp *alla buonavia*. He slipped up behind Hazel's chair and surprised her with a kiss, then leaned around my chair and kissed me on the lips. I looked at him, dumbfounded, the sensation of his mouth still on mine. My eyes darted from him to Hazel.

"Wait. Are you Dad's *girlfriend?*" she asked.

"You could say that," Daniel told her.

Van, Perri, and Robin looked gobsmacked, the words knocked out of them.

"Well, this is a surprise," Perri finally managed to say.

"It's been a surprise for me, too," I said, looking at Daniel, lifting my eyebrows.

His hand drifted to my shoulder and I reached for it and squeezed while Hazel grinned at us like the mailbox dolphin.

⁓

Later that night, after I'd fallen asleep on the sofa to the eleven o'clock news, Robin wandered in and tossed his keys on the table, waking me. Raising my head off the pillow, I narrowed my eyes in the sharp light from the TV. "Hey," I griped.

"Sorry, I didn't see you there."

I sat up, rubbing the back of my neck, stiff from the oversized sofa pillow. "I should go to bed."

"Wait a sec," he said, turning on a lamp and flipping off the television. *You and Daniel?* This is huge. And neither of you said a word."

"I know. There was so much to figure out, and we didn't want to say anything too soon because of Hazel . . . in case things didn't work out."

"I'm glad they did," he said, obviously pleased.

He walked to the kitchen sink and filled a glass with water while I got to my feet.

"Can you hang on? I need to talk to you." He took a sip from the glass and clinked it onto the counter before turning back to me. I dropped back onto the cushion, and he stood there as if mustering his courage.

"What is it?" I asked.

"Perri can't know about this, okay? You have to promise you won't say anything to her."

"Oh God, Robin. Are you in some sort of trouble?"

"No. But thanks for the vote of confidence."

In the past, whenever our conversations had started out with *Don't tell Perri*, he was predictably in a minor mess—unpaid parking tickets, a hangover, an angry boss, a modest gambling debt.

"Sorry," I said, and I truly was. He hadn't deserved my knee-jerk assumption; he'd had his act together the last few years. I gave him a repentant look.

He came and sat next to me on the sofa, retreating for a few moments into silence. Our reflections stared back at us from the glass sliders, and it crossed my mind how grown up we looked sitting here. Thirty-year-old twins. So alike. So different.

"I'm quitting my job at the hotel," he said.

"*What?* Seriously?"

"I've been thinking about it for a while, for a few months, and then when I found out my novel had been accepted, it felt like a sign. I knew if I couldn't seize the moment after that, I'd probably never leave."

"So you're going to write full time?"

"That's the plan. I didn't set out to manage a hotel, you know."

"I know, but . . ." I was going to say something practical about how he planned to support himself. I stopped myself, but I'd already pricked a nerve.

"But *what*? Why does there always have to be a 'but'? Why can't you just say, hey, that's great, Robin, go for it. You don't know what it's like to do something every day you don't want to do. It's soul sucking. We can't all jet around the world with our jobs, Maeve. Some of us are stuck here."

He closed his eyes and pressed his fingers into his temples, leaving white splotches on his skin. "You can't imagine what I deal with," he went on. "Guest complaints every day—I should write a book about *that*. I had to apologize to a man yesterday because the sun was too bright in his Gulf-front room. This is *Florida*, for Chrissake."

"Sorry," I said for the second time in five minutes.

"No, wait, *I'm* sorry," he said, tempering his tone. "I guess I feel sort of desperate about this. I don't mean to take it out on you. Look, I appreciate that Perri gave me this job, but I can't keep doing it. There's never any time left to write. You don't have to worry—I'm not asking for money. I have the book advance coming. It's not a whopping sum—I mean I'm lucky they're printing the thing at all, but it will support me for a while."

"When are you planning on resigning?" I asked.

"I thought I'd stay through the rest of the summer. I just don't know how to tell Perri. She's counting on me to take over the hotel one day. But I guess you knew that."

I did know. Perri had been so surprised at how good Robin was at managing the property, she'd probably gone overboard in her desire to turn it over to him, as well as in her belief he actually wanted it.

He said, "She's told me more than once how much it means to her that the hotel and her vision for it will stay in the family. I feel like I'm abandoning her."

His anguish over disappointing Perri touched me. "If anybody will understand, it's Perri. Talk to her. Besides, she's going to need time to find someone to take your place."

He nodded, and I felt suddenly proud of him for moving forward with his life in such a momentous way. Declaring his independence and his dedication to writing.

"Well, the timing is good," I said. "When I leave in August, you'll have the whole apartment to yourself to write without me coming and going. You can turn your sitting area into an office."

Robin stared at me as if I'd missed the point.

"Maeve, I'm moving out," he said. "I'm going to find a place somewhere on the island. It's time."

"But you can live here rent free. You'd barely have any expenses. You could make your advance money go a lot further."

"As long as I stay here, I'm stuck," he said. He stretched out his arms and looked around. "This is where we came after . . . everything happened. The memories are still here."

It was the closest he ever came to speaking about Mom and Dad. Talking about them without talking about them.

"There are other memories, too," he was saying. "Sometimes I walk through the lobby or across the courtyard and I think about Rachel and it's like yesterday that I met her. I should've moved out already."

His face tightened, and I actually thought for a second he might cry, for Mom and Dad, and for Rachel, who, it seemed, he'd really loved. But he dabbed on his brilliant smile. "I think getting out of here will free me to write differently, too. Better. With more flow. That probably makes no sense, it's just something I feel."

"It makes sense," I said.

He stood, circling the coffee table. "Let's face it," he said. "I've had a lot of fun and made a lot of mistakes. Everybody knows you're the golden girl and I'm the screwup. But I feel like this is my moment to do what I really want to do. And I'm going to try hard, Maeve."

I felt like he was speaking from that gigantic vacancy within him, the one that came after losing Mom and Dad. We both had that empty place, but we'd tried to fill it in such different ways. For me, it was with sharks and oceans, with Daniel and the dream of a family. For Robin it was writing. I don't know why I hadn't quite understood before now that writing was his way of keeping his connection to Dad alive—Dad, the poet, the English professor. After Robin's writing was rejected over and over and he walked away from it, he turned to other ways of filling the void—parties and drinking and a sort of aimlessness. Perhaps it was pain over Rachel that returned him to his novel three years ago, or maybe it was the same inner hollowness as always, but here he was, trying to embrace his writing even more fully.

And here I was, the golden girl, still wanting to take care of him, wanting his plan to work, and knowing, as usual, I would be there if it didn't.

Eighteen

*T*he next morning, a chime sounded on my office computer and like a good, digitally trained, Pavlovian puppy, I stopped what I was doing and checked my in-box.

Maeve,
    I've been surfing with my brother in Croyde and Saunton for the last two days. I miss you. What's the saying—salt water can cure anything? The divorce papers will be filed. I return to London in the morning to work out the final details. I'm sorry for the way things were left between us. I don't know how you feel now about me going to Mozambique. I hope we can go back to where we left off, but if not, we've been colleagues before. I hope we can be so again.

Nicholas

I clicked back to the document I'd been working on, but it was impossible to concentrate now. I spun my chair toward the bookshelf and stared at the entombed baby hammerhead floating in its jar. I should reply to Nicholas, but I didn't know what to say, especially about him coming to Mozambique. And what should I tell him about Daniel?

Turning back to the computer, I typed "Dear Nicholas." Whole minutes passed.

That was as far as I got. I didn't want to hurt him.

I tried piecing words together on some rehearsal stage in my head: *I bet you're relieved to get the divorce papers signed, if that's what you really want.* But how did I say, *I've moved on—Daniel and I are giving it another try? Did you mean what you said about us being colleagues again?*

A knock landed on my door.

"As of today, key lime pie is the official state pie of Florida," Daniel said as he strode in. "By an act of the state legislature. I just heard it on the radio."

"I'm sure you're thrilled."

"The vote was close," he said, suppressing a smile. "The upper half of the state lobbied for pecan pie, the lower half for key lime. I'm happy to say we won. It seemed like you'd want to know about it right away."

I laughed. "So what are you really doing here?"

"I just dropped Hazel at dance class. I thought I'd stop by."

He pulled up a chair to my desk and sat, his eyes narrowed and worried looking.

"Something on your mind?" I asked, and when he remained quiet, I called his name. "Daniel?"

"It's just . . . I don't know how to do this with Hazel. I leave for work early in the afternoon and don't get home until after she's asleep. We have half a day together, but she'll start school in August and then I won't see her at all. Being a single father and a chef is not exactly conducive to a quality family life."

"You have Van."

"I know, and Mom has been great, but taking care of Hazel almost full time is hard on her. I guess I worry about that, too. She adores Hazel, but we've completely disrupted her life." He sighed. "I'm sorry, I'm just trying to figure things out."

"I'm sorry, too." I reached across the desk.

Beneath Daniel's words I sensed the slight hand of finesse, a bit of maneuvering on his part. Was he playing on my sympathies, nudging me to spend more time with Hazel? Was he reminding me of the ticking clock of motherhood? Drawing me deeper into his life? Surprisingly, I didn't really care. Being alone with Hazel appealed to me as much as being alone with him.

"Unless I find another profession I don't know how I'm going to be there for her, and I don't know how to do anything else. I don't really want to do anything else."

How had Holly done it alone all those years?

"Maybe we need to put our heads together," I said. "I'm sure we can come up with a solution. Maybe talk to Perri about another sous-chef?"

"And you," he said. "I worry about having time with you. Eventually, knocking on your door late at night won't be enough. It's hardly enough now."

He stood. I walked around the desk and wrapped my arms around him, smelling soap on his neck. Often, when Daniel tapped on my door at night he was drenched in the scents of wine reductions and shrimp and cilantro butter.

"Why don't I go over to Van's tonight and see Hazel while you're at work?" I said. "We'll have an unscheduled meeting of the Shark Club."

He let out a breath and held me to him. "You would do that?"

"If you think she'd like it."

"I think she likes you more than she likes me."

His eyes flickered over the top of my desk. "What's that?" he asked, reaching over to pick up the letter that detailed my research term in Mozambique. He studied the letterhead: The Indian Ocean Center for Research and beneath it the image of a manta ray. "You're still going?" he said.

"That's the plan." It didn't seem the time to tell him that unless I could finagle out of it, Nicholas might still be going, too. Even though Daniel didn't know exactly what had happened between Nicholas and me, he knew we'd picnicked on the beach. He could connect the dots.

"As you know, there are lots of sharks in Florida to study. Some kid was just bitten by one up in Port St. Lucie."

"I know, but Mozambique is a really great opportunity for me."

"Mozambique is in *Africa*," he said, dropping the letter onto the desk.

Had he just assumed I would change my mind?

I folded the letter and tucked it into the desk's top drawer, suddenly back in that little aqua house we'd shared in Miami while we were in school and planning our wedding—that day I'd told him I was going to Fiji for my dissertation. It had set in motion the beginning of the end of us. I remembered how he'd lashed out: *I put our relationship first. Would it be so hard for you to do that?*

Were we going to do this all over again?

For a moment, he cupped my face in his hands and smiled at me. "You can't blame me for wanting you to stay close to home."

Anger flared in me. *No, I don't blame you for that. It's the assumption you made. The idea that I would drop everything because of you.* I felt a sudden twinge of fear. The beginning of the end. *But that was then*, I told myself. *This is now. We're not the same people.*

I said, "I get it, and believe me, when I think of leaving you . . . I can't even make sense of it. I spent so long thinking of what it would be like to be near you again that to think of leaving . . . It's hard for me, too."

"I'm not asking you *not* to go, but I just got you back. What if I was taking off to China next month?"

"I would miss you terribly. And I would probably say something to you like, *But I just got you back.*"

"See?"

I grabbed his hands. I knew I would miss him. Hazel, too, and for the first time I questioned going.

After he left, I returned to the e-mail I'd been trying to compose.

> Dear Nicholas,
> I'm glad you got some surfing in. "The cure for anything is salt water—sweat, tears or the sea." Isak Dinesen said that or more accurately, as Perri would insist on saying, Karen Blixen said it. (I looked this up by the way.)
> A lot has happened here. I hate trying to explain it in an e-mail. After you get home, we should talk.
>   Maeve

I hit the send button.

Nineteen

ater that same day, I arrived at Van's, lugging Perri's tackle box stuffed with art supplies. My plan was to show Hazel how to make a necklace with the shark tooth she'd found. "She's in her room," Van said, giving me a quick hug. "The old guest room."

I climbed the stairs and tiptoed along the hall, wanting to surprise her. Pausing at the door to Daniel's room, I clipped on my shark badge, then lingered a moment, nudging open his door for a glimpse, grimacing as it emitted a loud, whining plea to be oiled. The bed was made. A hamper sat empty in the corner. A few unpacked boxes had been pushed under the window. There was a small television on the chest of drawers, a book on the bedside table—*The Omnivore's Dilemma*, and a photograph of him and Hazel. That was all.

Hazel's door was ajar, and peeking inside I saw her sitting on the floor gazing into a Victorian dollhouse and clutching a small plastic giraffe. She studied the rooms with intensity, her lips pursed out like a tiny radish. She was still wearing her black ballet leotard and pink tights.

Her room looked freshly painted, a cheerful cerulean blue. Butterfly-print curtains were drawn back at the window revealing the bay that lapped up behind the house, copper dark in the evening light.

"Knock, knock," I said.

She leaped up, surprise breaking over her face. "Maeve!" she cried, and ran to me, grabbing me around the waist. Her shark badge was pinned to her leotard, and I wondered if she'd worn it to class.

"Are you busy? I thought we could have a Shark Club meeting," I said.

"I'm just working on my dollhouse. Dad gave it to me for Christmas." It was overrun with wild animals: a cheetah in a claw-foot bathtub; a zebra, a camel, a bear, and a hippo at the dining table; a buffalo in the bedroom lying on a little brass bed; monkeys on the roof; lions in the kitchen; an elephant in the nursery. A stiff family of five humans in 1890s dress were lined up in the living room along with a gorilla. A kind of Victorian zoo bacchanalia.

"What's all this?" I asked.

She shrugged. "Dad said a cheetah can run seventy miles an hour."

"Do they take baths in a tub, too?"

She giggled.

I handed her the tackle box and told her my shark-tooth necklace idea. As she pulled everything out of the box, creating a mound of multicolored ribbons, buttons, pipe cleaners, mini pliers, felt squares, hot-glue gun, sequins, and wire, I wandered around her room, curious about the photos that were clothespinned to a line that ran the full length of the back wall. Up close, I noticed that all of them were of Hazel and her mother. I'd never laid eyes on Holly until now. She had that porcelain, corn-silk look about her, her skin and hair lighter than Hazel's, her beauty unquestionable. I could see what Daniel had been drawn to, and the thought made me wince.

There she was pregnant. Rocking an infant Hazel. Standing with Daniel at the christening. Posing by the Christmas tree, by a birthday cake. Nuzzling Hazel in a hammock. In one picture, looking particularly radiant, she sat beneath the white-and-green awning of the Café de Flore in Paris holding Hazel on her lap, a chic apple-red scarf wound about her neck in the sort of elaborate knot you might see in *Vogue*. Hazel gripped the hem of the scarf in her small fist. *That should've been me.* It was a ludicrous thought, petty and illogical and shameful, but it came nonetheless. I should have been the one holding Daniel's little girl on my lap.

"That's Mom," Hazel said, coming up behind me.

"She took you to Paris? How old were you?"

"Four. I had a sailboat that I carried everywhere."

"Oh yeah?"

"I put it in the fountains. They have a million fountains." Her eyes swept along the row of photos. "Mom sang to me in French."

"Do you know any French words?"

"I know *boeuf bourguignon, poulet,* and *gâteau.*"

"That's really good."

"Mom called it *gâteau* when she baked cakes."

Had Holly been a French chef, a pastry chef, maybe a Francophile? If Hazel had lost her father, would Holly have scraped crème-filled crepes into the trash on her sleepless nights instead of eggs?

As we settled on the floor beside the art pile, facing each other, I pulled my shark-tooth necklace out from my shirt collar. The inch-long tooth was strung onto a long, white satin ribbon, which, I noticed, had grown dingy over the years.

I slid it over my head and handed it to her. "It's from the shark that bit me. I made the necklace when I was twelve."

She rubbed her finger over the smooth white tooth, then pressed the point into the soft pad of her thumb.

"You didn't put any sparklies on it," she said.

"No, but you can do whatever you want with yours."

"It's so crazy the tooth was in your leg," she said. "I guess there's a shark out there swimming around with a big hole in its teeth."

"Probably looking for a dentist."

⌒

After my shark *incident*—I rarely called it an attack—our own little Jaws-like panic had broken out on the island. Reporters had camped out at the hospital and later in the hotel lobby, hoping Perri would allow them to speak with me. Finding her impervious to their pleas, they'd solicited quotes from nurses, a doctor, one of the hotel housekeepers, several local fishermen, and one of my friends, who reported that I was a well-liked orphan who made all A's.

Within a week of my coming home from the hospital, shark-fishing tournaments sprung up at both marinas on Palermo. Weekly issues of the *Palermo Times* featured photos of dead sharks strung up by their tails or straddled by the men who'd caught them. A television reporter from Fox 4 News called my room while I was still bedridden with stitches and asked if I felt better about going back into the Gulf given that the tournaments were pulling in a dozen sharks every weekend.

"I don't mind going back in the water," I told him, "but not because they're killing sharks. I never wanted anybody to do that." My throat tightened as if I might cry.

Hearing a tremble in my voice, and perhaps not hearing what he expected me to say, the reporter wished me well and ended the interview.

"The shark that bit me was just being a shark," I told Perri, shoving tears off my cheeks. "If it'd wanted to have me for breakfast it would have!"

I began clipping out the pictures of the sharks caught in the tournaments and hiding them in my pajama drawer. When a blacktip turned up, I became inconsolable. "This is the one. I know it. Look at its eye," I sobbed to Perri.

I wrote it an obituary, which I taped on my mirror: *After a life of swimming in the Gulf, this blacktip bit Maeve Donnelly and paid the price. He had a strong body and a curious black eye. Rest in peace.*

⌒

"I keep *my* shark tooth in my jewelry box," Hazel announced, retrieving it from her dresser. As she opened the box, a tiny ballerina popped up and the ting, ting, tinging melody from the *Nutcracker Suite* danced out. The shark tooth lay on the felt lining amid a ragged collection of shells and rocks and bits of coral.

I plopped a bird's nest of ribbons beside her.

"First, we should do the pledge," she said.

"You might have to help me remember how it goes."

Hazel gave the fin salute and I followed suit as we repeated the lines, Hazel doing so from pure memory, and me a beat behind her.

As we tapped our fins together, Hazel fought back a smile by sucking in her cheeks. Shark Club was serious business.

I cut a short piece of wire and gave it to her to wrap around her tooth, but after several minutes of unsuccessful trying, she handed it to me with an exasperated exhalation.

"Small teeth are always harder to wrap," I said.

"I guess we need to find a bigger tooth," she said.

As I wrangled the wire around it, finding it far more of a challenge than I remembered, I asked, "What do you want to be when you grow up?"

Hazel pondered for a full minute, her eyes roaming the ceiling. "A paleontologist like Nigel Marven," she said. "Or a chef."

"A chef? Like a chicken nugget chef?"

"Cakes," she said.

"Was that your mom's job?"

She nodded and pulled a purple ribbon from the cluster. As I began shaping a loop atop the wire, she said, "Before she . . . you know, died, we were gonna go to Disney World. Just me and her. Now Grandma is taking me. Dad, too. You should come." She tilted her head and looked at me. "Since you're Dad's *girlfriend*."

"Do you like that I'm his girlfriend?" I was pretty sure she did, or else I never would've asked. Hearing her say no would have flattened me.

"I like it," she said in a quiet voice almost like we might be overheard, and I saw her cast the smallest glance at the photos on the clothesline.

After an obstinate silence, she said, "Are you gonna come with us?"

Daniel had mentioned the Disney trip to me, but her invitation had caught me off guard. "Maybe," I said. "Let's see what your dad says." Then I told her about the time Robin and I went to Disney World when we were little kids and how I was so scared of Tigger I hid behind Perri.

"Who's afraid of Tigger?" she asked.

"Exactly."

When I finished the loop, Hazel informed me she'd decided to skip the sparkly adornments.

"In that case, you can thread the ribbon through the loop."

When she was done, she grasped the ends of the purple ribbon and held them behind her neck.

"Tie it for me?" she asked.

I took the ends and held the necklace at various positions over her chest until she settled on the spot over her breastbone, then I tied a sailor's knot.

"Take a look," I said.

She smiled into the mirror over her dresser, then turned around. "Now what do you want to do?" she asked.

"Anything you want."

Twenty

*P*erri and I boarded a sailing catamaran at the Palermo Marina along with twelve pink-nosed, pink-shouldered tourists headed to Shell Point Key for what the brochure called a "sun-sational sea-shell tour." By the time we showed up, on the late side of the boarding window, the first mate had engaged the tourists in a deafening game of shouting "Susie sells seashells by the sea shore" as fast as possible.

"Good Lord," Perri muttered from behind her big Tommy Bahama sunglasses. "I wish they would just go buy their shells from Susie and leave us in peace."

It was Saturday, July 22, one of the busier days at the hotel, but at my instigation, Perri had agreed to come on the "sun-sational" tour anyway. She kept a small pirate's treasure chest beside the checkout desk in the lobby filled with shells for the under-twelve guests. The kids would stand there digging through the jumble for the perfect parting treasure to take home until a parent finally dragged them off. Robin kept the chest stocked with shells from the Shell Factory in Fort Myers, but long ago Perri and I filled the coffers by going out on these shell tours. When I'd asked if she wanted to revive the custom, she'd hugged me. I'm sure we both knew the outing wasn't about filling the pirate chest as much as the two of us reconnecting. I'd avoided being alone with her for weeks, worrying if she disapproved of Daniel and me. But then, why would she? She wanted me to be happy. I'd decided I was being ridiculous.

It wasn't all avoidance on my part, though. I'd been exceptionally busy, too, spending long hours at the Conservancy compiling the Bimini research, working on my lemon shark lecture, and escalating the shark-tagging expeditions. I was sure the shark numbers had decreased, and I worried they would get worse if the black market finning wasn't shut down. Despite repeated calls, Russell had heard little from the Sheriff's Marine Bureau. The investigation seemed to have stalled and local news markets had long since moved on. If it had been dolphins or whales, the whole world would be up in arms. But it was sharks.

The catamaran chugged past dock pilings lined with loons drying their wings, opening and closing them like a flasher's overcoat. Out in the open, the sails went up, striped red and yellow, snapping in the bright wind, and the boat picked up speed. Two dolphins immediately emerged in the wake. The other passengers squealed and photographed and applauded as if a herd of unicorns had shown up. As envious as I was of the love heaped on dolphins, I didn't begrudge them an ounce of it. They were the rock stars of the sea, and I never tired of seeing them either. They accompanied us for miles, vaulting out of the water, enjoying the human attention, not unlike Nicholas's stingrays who slid up against human hands in the touch tank as if wanting to be petted.

～

Earlier, when I'd stopped by Perri's room, I found her sitting cross-legged on the rug bent over a slew of papers—a register of names and addresses, room diagram, calendar, budget spreadsheet, checklists. She was all furrowed brow and studious concentration, her slant-eyed reading glasses resting at the end of her nose as if they might suddenly take off and fly. She barely glanced up, giving her hand a little twirl in the air. *Be with you in a sec.* Robin was situated in the same chair I'd crashed in weeks ago after meeting Hazel for the first time on the beach. He had a binder open on his lap and a pen gripped between his teeth.

I said, "Plotting a government takeover, are we?"

"Worse," Robin said. "The Book Bash."

Perri handed me an emerald green card with elaborate silver script.

Join Us for the 25th Annual Book Bash.
Hotel of the Muses, Palermo Island
August 5, 7:00 P.M.
Dress as your favorite author or literary character

Oh God, the annual costume thing again. It was the biggest night of Perri's year. Last year she'd shown up as a hobbit.

"Who are you coming as this time?" I asked her.

"Nice try. Like I'm going to tell."

Her legendary costumes were deeply held secrets right up until the moment she walked into the Bash.

"In case you're interested," Robin said, "I'm wearing a white suit, red-and-white striped vest, black bow tie, and saddle shoes."

"So you're what, Gatsby?" I asked.

"Like the party will need another Hemingway," he said. "Half a dozen men will show up dressed as Hemingway." A wicked, mocking light appeared in his eyes. "And what about *you?*"

I gave him a vicious thanks-a-lot face.

Perri pounced. "You could be Daisy to Robin's Gatsby. I know where we can get a great flapper dress."

"I think you know who I'll be going as," I said.

She sighed. "Maeve, for heaven's sake, you can't be George Sand *every year.*"

"I don't know why not. The top hat is still in my closet. I paid a fortune for it."

She uncoiled herself and sprang nimbly to her feet as though she were still twenty years old. "Well, do you like the invitation?" she asked, twisting the red beads around her neck.

"I like," I told her, and offered it back.

"Keep it. Mark your calendar." She looked at her watch. "I need to go over the menu with Daniel."

"Did you forget you're supposed to go shelling with me this morning?"

"Of course not," she said, and disappeared into her bedroom, un-fastening the red beads as she went.

Robin got up and gave me a peck on the cheek. "We're good, right?"

He was still worrying about my reaction to his book. After banishing his manuscript under my bed for a while, I'd begun reading it again. In the pages, longing and regret were Margaret's companions, not mine. At least not anymore.

"I held onto my anger with Daniel for a long time. I don't want to do it with you," I told him.

"Boy, you're getting off easy," Perri said from the doorway. "I'd freeze you out a lot longer if it were me."

Robin laughed. "That's the benefit of being twins. We shared a womb; I've known her since before birth."

"Don't play the twin card—I still can't believe you did what you did," I said.

"There it is," Perri said.

"I didn't say I wasn't angry. I'm still pissed. I'm just not going to hang onto it for years."

"Let's go to Spoonbills this weekend," he said. "Me, you, and Dan-iel. Like we used to. We haven't talked about anything except my book since you got home. We have a lot of catching up to do."

"I'd like that." As he started to leave, I caught his arm. "Maybe you should bring someone. Someone who wears turquoise shoes?"

The woman's shoes I'd seen in our living room the day I returned were long gone, but I hadn't forgotten about them.

Brushing past me, he whispered. "Like I said, we have a lot of catching up to do."

~

As the catamaran banked on Shell Point Key, Perri rolled her pants to her knees. The island was two miles of deserted wildness. Disembarking, we stepped into ankle-deep water, where the guide passed out mesh bags for collecting our finds.

While the others remained near the boat, moving like a single organism across the dry flats, their eyes peeled to the sandy bottom, Perri and I struck out down the beach to a deserted neck of sand with decaying brown pen shells cracking beneath our river shoes. We raked up handfuls of shells, mostly cockles and scallops and Florida fighting conchs, not bothering to examine them for blemishes.

"Have you talked to Nicholas?" she asked, as I knew she would.

"He's in London. He e-mailed once to say his divorce papers were being filed."

"I was surprised about you and Daniel—I have to say. I thought you and Nicholas were—"

"Well, when you hear 'I'm in love with you' along with 'my wife wants a reconciliation,' it doesn't have the impact you hope for."

"I could tell by looking at him he was in love with you," she said.

"I told him things with us couldn't go anywhere, that he had to sort out his marriage situation first. But I haven't told him about Daniel. I feel terrible about it. I tried e-mailing, but it felt so cowardly to do it electronically. I keep thinking I should do it in person."

"Well, of course you should do it in person." She used that matter-of-fact, reassuring tone she always did when she was trying to take care of me, but I knew she wasn't pandering—she meant it.

I said, "To be totally honest, I guess I was afraid he'd go back to London and they'd get back together. I know he said he loved me, but he loved her once, too. And she's the one who asked for the divorce, not Nicholas. I just didn't want to get hurt."

"And then there's Daniel," she added. "He figured into it."

"Well, yeah, I suppose I would've had to come to terms with my feelings for Daniel even if this situation between Libby and Nicholas hadn't happened. Daniel would eventually have figured into it. He always has."

I thought she would let it be after that.

As we moved along the corridor of sand, I found a little patch of sunray Venuses and then a plump lightning whelk. Along with the shells, we picked up a plastic hot dog bag, an empty bottle of Corona with a rotten lime slice inside, the top of a Styrofoam cooler, knotted fishing line, and a flip-flop.

"You don't think you could get hurt with Daniel?" Perri asked. "Is it me, or is history repeating itself? Just because you've forgiven Daniel doesn't mean you should necessarily pick up where you left off." She stopped walking and looked at me, her bag bulging with shells and washed-up rubbish. "Oh honey, I want you to be sure, that's all."

I didn't respond at first. I stared at the light squeezing through the dense mangrove leaves, thinking what a struggle everything was, my heart laboring. It dismayed me to see that Perri had doubts. I didn't want to hear them. I said, "What happened to not hiding from him and facing the past?"

"I'm sorry," she said. "You're a grown woman. I'm being intrusive."

"It's just that . . . it's *Daniel*."

"I know," she said. "I know."

We circled the island, filled our bags, our pockets, even the plastic hot dog bag. Perri found a cat's paw, the biggest one I'd ever seen. I gave it too much attention, not wanting to think of what she'd stirred up in me. Her words dragged me back to the day of Daniel's confession, to the clink of my engagement ring as I'd dropped it in the bowl on my way out. All that anger and hurt and mistrust. I'd felt them recede to some faraway place, and I wouldn't let Perri dredge them up. I'd forgiven him. I trusted him. We were together. It was what I'd always wanted.

In the distance a whistle blared, the captain's ten-minute boarding signal. Perri and I had just started back to the catamaran when I spotted a bottle lodged in the sand. I picked it up. It was an olive oil bottle. *Giacomo's. Extra Virgin.* A teaspoon of dark gold liquid pooled in the bottom beneath a rolled up piece of paper.

For a strange, transfixing moment, I couldn't move or even breathe. Almost anything flung from the south beach would end up here, but even as I held the bottle, knowing it was the same one I'd helped Hazel toss into the waves, my mind wanted to reject it because that meant I, of all people, had come across it.

Perri looked at my face. "What? What is it?"

"It's Hazel's," I said, surprised at the sprouting of grief that came over me, how it pushed up against the inside of my chest.

I wiped my hands across my shorts and with effort twisted off the cap. Tilting the bottle, I reached my finger inside, digging for the paper, feeling a shard of guilt at breaching her privacy. Whatever was in there wasn't for me, it was for her mother, but I wriggled it out anyway. Perri didn't say a word.

I smoothed the paper open. At the top, she'd drawn two small figures in crayon.

A woman and a girl with yellow hair. They stood on top of a five-tiered cake.

Beneath it she'd written in cramped letters:

Mom,

I wish we could bake cakes again. I made one with Daddy and he says I take after you. I take Grandma

Van's ballet class. I can do a leap. I miss you and cry but not like before. Daddy tells me stories and puts us in them. I live at Grandma Van's and I learned the address. 523 Laurel Ave. Palermo Island, Florida.

I love you.

Hazel

She'd linked double *H*'s across the bottom of the page. H~H. Hazel and Holly.

I handed the letter to Perri. As she read, I felt tears fringe my eyes.

Her face was somber when she handed the note back to me. I rolled the letter tight like a cigarette, popped it back into the bottle, and screwed on the cap.

Then I threw it as far as I could.

Twenty-one

Spoonbills was a breezy, open-air, cabana-style restaurant with year-round Christmas lights strung around the bar and a mounted sailfish on the wall. The owner was a former running back at the University of Florida, who'd been a buddy of Russell's. And whenever some poor fool inadvertently uttered the words Florida State, Seminoles, or Bobby Bowden, a bell was rung behind the bar. If you were unfortunate enough to say the blasphemous words, you were required to buy a round of drinks for everyone occupying a barstool. Newcomers to Spoonbills were innocently lured into the rookie mistake, but you only made it once.

From where Daniel and I sat with Robin, I had a clear view of a bonfire that was burning out on the inlet beach. It was a welcome distraction from the discussion going on at the table about the hotel's upcoming Book Bash, endless talk about the guest count, the band, the hors d'oeuvres, the liquor order, the staff. I turned my attention to the tiny flame on the votive at our table, the liquid wax threatening to swallow it, and then back again to the beach, where a small crowd had gathered around the fire. Orange embers spit into the air.

⌒

Last New Year's Eve in Bimini, there'd been a bonfire on the beach. There'd been champagne and a countdown and a few midnight kisses despite the policy forbidding workplace romance. Shortly after midnight, I'd left my colleagues around the fire and strolled back inside the community house for a glass of water. Not that I was drunk; I was tipsy, and I hoped the water would ward off the headache I feared would plague me the next day.

From the kitchen, I noticed light flashing into the hallway from the rec room. White, blue, white. Curious, I roamed down the hall and peered into the room. It was empty except for Dr. Nicholas Ridley sprawled on the sofa, his bare feet propped on a coffee table. I'd met him only once before, the day I'd arrived, and in the week since, I'd heard others speak about his expertise and his passion. It surprised me to see him here alone in the dark watching television, its light flickering across his face.

I wandered in, edging around the ping-pong table, drawn by the rhythmic drumming coming from the TV, or possibly by Nicholas himself, and noticed for the first time what was on the screen. Half-naked bodies with elaborate designs painted on their white faces and torsos danced hypnotically, many of them carrying torches. Lush green vines were wound around their arms and legs, the leaves curling off their fingertips. They looked wild, primeval, beautiful.

Turning to leave, I jarred the ping-pong table, sending a ball bouncing across the floor in hollow clacks.

"It's the Beltane Fire Festival," he said.

"Oh. And what might that be exactly?"

"The earth fertility rituals of my ancestors."

"So, kind of a family reunion."

He laughed. "Come watch. It's a documentary on Celtic customs."

"There happens to be a real-life custom called New Year's Eve happening on the beach," I said.

"I was out there earlier, but New Year's Eve parties have never been my thing."

Leaving my glass of water on the ping-pong table, I retrieved the ball, then dropped onto the cushion next to him. "We met in the hall the other day," I said, as if I were the most forgettable person he'd ever met.

"I remember. You're Maeve Donnelly and you have a nasty scar on your leg."

"It's Nicholas, right?"

"Hello, again," he said, and I thought, *I will not be one of those daffy women who swoon over British accents.*

"So what's going on with the dancing people? Who's she?" A tall, gorgeous woman was being escorted down a hill by women clad in flowy white dresses. Her skin was painted a ghostly white, her lips poppy red. On her head, she wore an elaborate wreath of roses and lilies, spritzed with baby's breath.

"That's the May Queen." He spoke with his arms folded and lifted one finger. "She has to find the Green Man and then summer can start."

"Like the Hulk?"

"What? No," he said, and grinned. "Green as in vital and new. See, the May Queen is the earth . . . its fertility, and in order for summer to come round she and the Green Man must . . . How shall I put this? Join together." He clasped his hands into a big fist, which he then released and reached for the champagne bottle on the floor.

"Here," he said.

To hell with the headache. I took the bottle and drank. The champagne was cool and effervesced over my tongue.

"*Maeve!*" he said, as if some ingenious realization had just dawned on him. "Your name. *You're* the May Queen."

"*I'm* the May Queen?"

"Maeve is an Irish name. It means May Eve. As in the eve of May when the Beltane fire ritual takes place to mark the arrival of summer."

We stared at the TV, where dancers wearing antlers howled and gyrated with the drums. The spectacle was like a gathering in Narnia.

We passed the champagne back and forth as the May Queen finally found the Green Man. Hooray—life and fertility would prevail.

I said, "My parents went to Ireland before I was born, but I'm not sure they had any of this in mind when they named me. In fact, from what I knew of my mother, her giving me a name that had anything to do with an earth fertility ritual would have been"—I blew a dismissive puff of air from my lips—"outlandish."

"I don't know. Sometimes people surprise you," he said.

A fire began to burn from inside the abundant arrangement of flowers on the May Queen's head, crowning her face with light. I wasn't sure what trick they'd used to keep her from catching on fire. My own head grew hot and all the edges in the room had turned soft. I went over to the ping-pong table and gulped down my water, then picked up a paddle.

"You wanna play?"

"All right," he said, lumbering over and flipping on the overhead light.

Up close in the brightness, I could see the dark stubble that covered his face.

"What shall we play for?" he asked.

"Oh, you're *that* kind of guy," I said, bouncing the ball off the table and tapping it with the paddle.

"If you mean the betting kind, then yes."

"You're not a table tennis champion, are you?" I asked.

He laughed. "No. You?"

"No."

"So we're evenly matched. How about this?" he said. "If I win, you be my dive partner and assist me with my research for the duration of the term, and if you win, I'll assist with yours. Fair?"

"Deal."

I lost the first game 7–11 and immediately called for the best two out of three. Nicholas, amused, agreed to a second game. With the score 8–8, I tried slamming the ball, but it missed the table and soared over Nicholas's shoulder.

"My point," he exclaimed. "Come on, May Queen."

We volleyed, him hitting the ball slow and steady and me sending it right back. The quieter I was, the more he talked.

"Have you done any remote underwater video surveying?" he asked.

"What?"

"It's noninvasive for the sharks."

"I know what it is. I mean, why are you asking?" I said, and put the ball right into the net. "Oh, you're trying to distract me."

"I'm not," he said, but he couldn't say it without laughing. "Okay. I won't talk. Promise."

We played in silence for several minutes. He won the final point and the game. He laid down the paddle with fanfare, an uncontrollable smile on his face, but he didn't say a word.

"You can talk now," I told him.

"Oh thank God. But I'm not going to gloat."

"It's okay. You can gloat. You beat me."

"No, no. I wouldn't think of it, but we should definitely talk about you brushing up on stingrays."

I walked over and extended my hand. "Congratulations."

He took my hand. "Thank you. The stingrays thank you. I look forward to your assistance."

"Well, you're lucky to have me."

Nicholas went on holding my hand. I expected him to continue the back and forth, the flirting. That's what we'd been doing, wasn't it? Sharing champagne and flirting on New Year's Eve. But he turned quiet, studying me, and the handshake turned into something else. He pulled my hand to his chest and held it there.

Down the hall, the screen door creaked open, then slammed. A stampede of flip-flops and hoots of laughter shattered the moment. Nicholas let go and stepped back.

"We'll meet after breakfast?" he said.

"Sure."

"Look, I'm happy to have your help, but not at the expense of your work. Honestly, that would take all the fun out it."

"I'll see you in the morning."

For the next six months, I saw Nicholas every day. We turned out to be remarkably compatible dive partners, taking equal turns assisting one another's research. We didn't speak again about New Year's Eve. Not the May Queen, or ping-pong, or the protracted, wordless moment with my hand in his. We filed it away, surrendering to the policy on workplace romance. At least until that last night on the beach.

A breeze swept through Spoonbills, rippling the strands of colored lights, giving me the sense of unloosed fireflies. I glanced out to where the bonfire still blazed on the beach. Robin's and Daniel's voices had become indistinguishable murmurs.

Robin nudged my hand with his beer bottle. "I can't believe you're going to Africa," he said. "Where is Mozambique anyway?"

"The east coast, near South Africa," I said.

Daniel's face tightened. "All I know is, it's a *long* way away."

There was an unmistakable edge to his words. What had he said in my office? *There are lots of sharks in Florida.* I resisted a retort.

He pushed back from the table. "I'm getting another beer. Anybody want one?"

"What was that all about?" Robin asked when he'd left.

"He's not totally on board with me leaving."

"I guess you can't blame him. You're finally back together after all this time and suddenly you're moving to Africa for four months."

"I know. The timing sucks. I get it."

"You know Daniel," Robin said. "He's an all-or-nothing kind of guy."

"Yeah, but it would be nice if he didn't make me feel bad for wanting to pursue my own life."

Robin offered me a neutral shrug and shoveled a glob of guacamole out of the bowl with a chip.

After I'd broken our engagement, it had seemed possible to me that my going off to Fiji right before our wedding had hit a little too close to home for Daniel—maybe there'd been a semblance in it of his father leaving him. During those first terrible months after his dad left, Daniel used to call his mom at the hotel to be sure that she was still at work, that, while he was in school, she hadn't disappeared on him, too. It used to kill me. *When people leave, they don't always come back*, he'd told me once.

His father had left him. Then I'd left him. As irrational as it sounded I had to figure out how to make him understand that my research trips weren't the same thing as his father's abandonment or our broken engagement. I had to figure out how to make him understand Mozambique wasn't Fiji all over again.

I reached for my Sierra Nevada, thinking of Hazel. I dreaded telling her I would be leaving. It was as if some unlived part of me had awakened during these past weeks. I was just now realizing that my world felt more complete with Hazel in it. I was going to miss her.

At the bar, Daniel was talking with a woman. "Who's that?"

Robin turned, craning, and his face sort of lit up. "That's Mindy. She teaches at Van's studio."

"She's a dance teacher?"

"Yeah. She used to be Cinderella at Disney World."

"You're joking," I said, looking back at her. Cinderella had risen onto her toes and was poised there effortlessly like a long and slender calla lily. She was wearing turquoise flats.

My mind drifted back to Rachel Gregory and the summer fling that had left Robin in such disarray. For months, he'd refused to give up on her, unable to believe all those declarations of love she'd made were anything other than genuine. I'd sat with him late into the nights during that awful time, listening to his desperate attempts to convince himself it wasn't over. I had to repeatedly talk him out of getting on a plane and flying to Vermont. Instead, he besieged her with unanswered phone calls and e-mails. The last of his denial had been shattered when Rachel's husband sent him a letter through an attorney ordering him to cease and desist.

After that, embarrassed and defeated, he turned back to his work at the hotel, started his novel, and seemed to carry on, but a faint aura of darkness lingered about him, as if he'd decided life would inevitably be his enemy; it would fight him tooth and nail, and this knowledge only seemed to make him cockier and more impulsive, determined to get the outcome he wanted.

I thought of his decision to leave the hotel and strike out on his own. Perri had been a champ about it. I suspected, like me, she might have had her concerns, but she'd given him her blessing and begun advertising for a new manager.

Turning back to Robin, I saw him watching Mindy. How different she looked from Rachel, all light and lithe, while Rachel was small and brunette. Had Robin and Mindy's been a seismic meeting, too?

"She's lovely," I told Robin.

"I asked her here," he said.

When Daniel returned to the table, she lingered at the bar.

"You know about Robin and Cinderella?" I asked Daniel. "They're a thing."

Daniel looked across the table at Robin. "I introduced them. I thought they'd hit it off."

"Well, she left her shoes in his bedroom, so yeah, I'd say they hit it off." I elbowed Robin. "Well, are you dating or what?"

"Yeah, we're kind of dating," he said. "Come meet her."

"Robin tells me you've been in Bimini," Mindy said after we'd been introduced. She lifted herself onto her toes again. A dancer's natural inclination, I guessed.

"Maeve is the best shark expert in the world," Daniel said, placing his hand at the small of my back. I felt like he was trying to make up for his earlier comment, and I took a side step closer to him.

Robin joked, "Yeah, as we all know, Maeve got all the IQ points and I got all the charm."

"I understand you teach at Van's studio," I said to Mindy. "Hazel must be one of your students then."

"Hazel is a little doll. One of my best students. Gets her talent from her grandmother. Van's a natural. Such a gift to Palermo. To have an instructor like her on the island . . ."

She talked on and on in short staccato phrases, trailing her arms gracefully through the air as if to counteract it. I tried to picture her with her blond hair pulled up, wearing a blue dress and a black velvet ribbon around her throat, having her photo made with little Disney princess girls. After the devastation of Rachel, I hoped Mindy was helping Robin piece himself back together.

Spying Marco in a booth across the restaurant, I asked to be excused for a moment and hurried over, winding through the maze of tables. He was leaning forward, elbows plunged onto the tabletop, fingers clasped, engaged in what appeared to be an intense exchange with his friend Troy. The conversation that Marco and I'd had about the shark finning the day I'd returned from Bimini came back to me. *Troy knew the guy who'd been caught with the fins laid out on tarps in his backyard.*

I slowed for a second, an odd little wave of unease passing over me, and then I dismissed it.

"Oh! Maeve," Marco said, looking startled. "I didn't see you."

"I don't want to interrupt." Then, looking at Troy, I said, "It's been a while. I'm Maeve."

"Of course. Maeve. Long time, no see." He was fiftyish, in need of a shave, wearing a cap that said GOOD TIMES CHARTER. The skin around his eyes and temples bore the outline of his sunglasses.

Sliding over, Marco offered me a seat, and I scooted in beside him. "Troy was just reliving his greatest catch," he said. "A twenty-pound snook. It's not true, but it's a good story."

"All my stories are true," Troy said. "You just need another beer."

We made silly small talk for a few moments, until I abruptly changed the subject.

"I understand you know the person who was caught with the shark fins," I said to Troy.

His eyes shot toward Marco, then back at me. "Well, not person-ally, but I know people who do. From what I understand, he claims he was paid to just store the fins, that he didn't have anything to do with the finning."

"He still hasn't given up the people who hired him?" I asked.

"No, and I doubt he will. If he talks and makes a deal, I doubt these people would look kindly on him. He probably figures he's bet-ter off with a hefty fine and his skull intact."

"You don't think he'll go to jail?" I asked.

"There was a case in the Panhandle about a year ago—you re-member this, Marco. A guy confessed to cutting off the fins and throwing the sharks overboard. Cops found the fins on his boat, and even then he got off with no jail and a fine of eighteen thousand dol-lars. All this guy on Bonnethead did was rent the finners some stor-age space."

I tried to ignore the way he'd trivialized the man's part in it. I looked at Marco. He was so quiet.

"You don't have any idea who these finners could be, then?" I asked Troy, and there was that foreboding feeling again.

"No, and to be honest with you, I don't want to know. It takes a special kind of mean to cut the fin off a live shark, let alone a hun-dred of them."

Troy and Marco turned their attention to the Red Sox highlights on the TV above the bar, and I told them good night.

I started toward the booth where Mindy sat with Robin and Daniel, and then did an about-face, wandering out of the bar onto the beach for a gulp of air. I was being silly about Troy. Marco would never hang out with him if there was a reason to be suspicious.

I took off my sandals and meandered down to the inlet, where the bonfire, deserted now, burned orange and lonely near the water. Standing beside it, I reflexively held out my palms, even though the temperature was at least 80 degrees. The tide rippled peacefully, its cadence sounding as if it were programmed by a machine in a chic waiting room. Behind me Spoonbills was a box of light. Laughter and voices spilled out.

Alone, staring into the fire, I felt an urge to leap over it the way the Beltane festival dancers had done. I don't know why I wanted to do something so crazy, so completely unlike me, but the desire was accompanied by the feeling that if I didn't, something would be lost to me. Something wild and free and mine.

The flames were at least knee high. I backed up to get a running start, glancing at the small group of people farther up the beach, the earlier bonfire crowd. The bell clanged inside Spoonbills, followed by an explosion of laughter, and I knew some Florida State fan was paying dearly.

The photograph of Holly in the apple-red scarf flashed into my head, and my mind was suddenly a blaze of thoughts. Daniel. Mozambique. Key lime pie. Hazel. Shark badges. Shark fins. Nicholas. Baby stone crabs.

I started to run. My feet pounded the sand. At the edge of the fire I jumped. Heat licked at my feet before I landed, skidding, falling backward a little toward the flames before regaining my balance. The thrill of it took my breath.

I waded into the surf and let the water wash over my feet. I thought of the quiet moment with Nicholas on New Year's Eve. Was he home from England?

As I walked back to Spoonbills, I glanced over my shoulder at the tendril of yellow-orange light and a small happiness rose in my chest and levitated there.

Twenty-two

After work on Monday, I took Hazel to the library for Shark Club. We were in search of shark books.

A larger-than-life sea turtle sculpture sat out front, its shell painted a patchwork of hallucinogenic colors. It looked as if it belonged at the Mad Hatter's tea party. Naturally Hazel couldn't resist climbing onto its back. She straddled the turtle in blue jean shorts, her pale hair lit gold with sunlight. I was feeling what I imagined to be parental pride at being the one to get Hazel a library card.

At the desk, I asked for an application and a man handed me a clipboard and said, "Fill this out. Your daughter can print her name at the bottom."

"May we borrow a pen?" I asked, letting his mistake go uncorrected, and Hazel and I exchanged a conspiratorial look.

She took a mango from a bowlful marked FREE.

"You like mangoes?" I asked.

She sniffed it, rolled it between her hands, cupped it under her chin. "I like them. Just not to eat."

I knew where to find the shark books. When I was a child, Perri took Robin and me to the library regularly, giving us each a canvas bag to stuff with books. I'd brought a bag for Hazel, and she dropped in the mango and swung the bag excitedly as if it were an Easter basket and the juvenile book section held a field of dyed eggs.

I said, "Maybe one day your shark cartoons will be in here. *The Adventures of Sir Fin.*"

"And Rosie, too," she added.

The science shelves held a shark goldmine. Whole series on great whites, tigers, bulls, whale sharks, makos, grey reef, silvertips. Hazel plucked several books and slid them into the bag.

"My tooth is from a lemon," she said, slinging her thumb under her necklace. "Do they have a lemon book?"

I found it, finally, misplaced in the Snake section.

After exhausting the children's books, we headed to the adult stacks, the Oceans collection, where we located the shark books on the bottom shelf. Plopping onto the floor, I ticked my finger over the spines, the smell of dust, and old paper, and my childhood welling up. "I checked out some of these when I was kid," I said, engulfed with nostalgia, with the memory of exploring something I wanted to give myself over to, that strange allure and rapture.

"Are there pictures?" she asked.

"In some of them."

"Are they in color?"

We cracked open every book in search of pictures. If she liked the look of them, we shoved the book into her bag. She was especially thrilled by *Sharks of the World*, with its full-page color plates. She flipped out when she saw a goblin shark, its great big mouth open like a train tunnel, and when she came upon a shark spotted like a leopard, she looked up me and said, "I didn't see that coming."

"Let's find a table," I told her, grabbing *Sharks of the South Pacific* for myself.

We spread the books out on a table near the magazines, away from the senior citizen computer class. I opened *Sharks of the South Pacific* and Hazel studied the illustrations, uttering soft little exclamations.

The photographs Nicholas took of me with Sylvia—she would love to see those. I skimmed the pages, lingering over a chapter titled "Shark Ancestors." I read Hazel a fantastical story about people in the Tuamotu atolls who believed their deceased loved ones took the form of the shark god Taputapua and visited them, swimming up into lagoons where the family members waded.

Hazel's eyes widened. "You mean their grandmother or their mom or somebody died and then came back to see them as a shark?"

I nodded. "And listen to this. In Kontu, shark callers use rattles to lure sharks to their canoes."

"Shark callers? We could do that," Hazel said.

"Call sharks?"

"Could we?"

I paused. "Well, we'd need rattles. We could make our own out of coconuts. We should go to Jolly's."

Jolly's flashy neon sign, not to mention the ticky-tacky store itself, was an eyesore for residents, but we understood that tourists shelled out exorbitant amounts of money for trinkets and junk, which helped our small island economy, and we tolerated it. The store carried everything. Rafts, shot glasses, alligator heads, wooden wind chimes, live hermit crabs, boogie boards, culturally outdated towels printed with "I'm Sexy and I Know It." And coconuts. There were coconut halves turned into thumb pianos. Coconut birdhouses. Coconuts outfitted to send through the mail.

Reading further to myself, I discovered that while the sharks were revered among the people of Kontu, once they'd been lured to the canoe by the callers, the sharks would be pulled on board, bludgeoned, and speared, then eaten. I decided against telling Hazel this part. She was six. She had a Shark Club motto in her head: *If I catch one, I will let it go.* It would be hard for her to reconcile her love of sharks with killing them, even among a culture that considered them sacred. I could hardly reconcile it myself.

I looked up from my book to find Hazel staring at me like I was one of the shiny, preposterous hammerheads in her books.

"Are you going to be my new mom?" she asked, her fingers gripping the lip of the table.

"What? Oh . . . Well, you know . . . I don't . . ."

I should have corrected the man at the desk earlier who'd mistaken me for Hazel's mother. I'd reveled a little too much in that.

Seconds passed. Hazel's eyes widened as she waited. Given the librarian's mistake, she'd asked a logical question, and I was, after all, dating her father. Overhead, the fluorescent light sizzled.

"I don't know how to answer that," I said. "You know, I don't think anyone could take your mom's place."

I thought I'd satisfied her.

"But you *could* be my mom," she said.

As much as I wanted to say what was sensible and true and right for her ears, I had nothing. Daniel and I hadn't talked about marriage—it seemed too soon for that. But hadn't we both assumed that's where it was going? Picking up where we left off?

"My dad said he loves you. He told me."

I smiled at her. "Well, I know he loves *you* very much."

"Do you love him?"

"I've loved your dad for a long time."

She dropped her hands in her lap. "How long?"

"Try since I was seven."

"I'll be seven next year."

"I know, and if we sit here any longer you just might *turn* seven. Come on. Let's go to Jolly's and buy some coconuts. I think I know how we can turn them into rattles."

At the car, I turned on the air conditioner, letting the air cool down before helping Hazel with her seat belt. My hair fell into her face and she blew at it, and I noticed a speck of dried toothpaste in the corner of her mouth and the peach fuzz on her cheeks. Did I love Daniel? It was like asking if water was wet. I'd always loved him. Even when I hated him, I loved him. There would be no regrets this time.

I looked at her in the rearview mirror. If she asked me now to go to Disney World, I would say yes. If she knew about Mozambique and asked me to stay, right now I would. Was this what motherhood was like?

Twenty-three

*T*he next morning, July 25, I drove to work unusually early, the sun just beginning to lift its head into the thin, dark sky. At the Conservancy, I made a pot of coffee in the "kitchen cubby," so called because it was the size of a broom closet, barely accommodating a mini fridge and a Mr. Coffee, then took my mug to my office, where I left off the lights and opened the blinds, flooding the room with light.

Doves had convened in the flame trees, cooing loudly enough to be heard through the closed windows. Any minute the pileated woodpecker would begin its morning drilling on the side of the building, a jackhammer to the skull that necessitated earplugs, or iPods, or Zen calisthenics.

I lingered there, sipping my coffee, thinking about Nicholas. Finally, I went to the computer. I typed:

Nicholas,
Are you home?
May Queen

I reread it. *Please.* I had no business being May Queen. It was flirtatious and misleading. I deleted it, typed Maeve, and clicked the send button.

I got busy scanning Nicholas's photographs of me and Sylvia to include in the PowerPoint presentation on lemons that I'd promised Russell. Each photo was becoming as familiar to me as my own reflection. I held the close-up he'd taken of my eyes behind the mask. They spoke of everything at once: elation, grief at saying good-bye, the belonging I felt in the water. Bimini had been my grandest adventure yet. I didn't see how I could give up Mozambique. I didn't want to leave Daniel and Hazel, but I'd be back and our lives would go on together just as they were now.

I heard Russell's flip-flops thudding along the hall, and a couple of seconds later, he rounded the doorway, looking perturbed and breathless, and Russell never looked perturbed and breathless. "A dead shark has washed up on Teawater Key," he said. "It was finned."

I stared at him for a moment, caught in that initial stupefying space where I heard words, but they didn't register. Then came the hard kick of adrenaline.

"A contact of mine in the Sheriff's Office called," he was saying. "They sent someone out there from the Marine Bureau, and Fish and Wildlife is headed there, too."

I grabbed my bag and the keys to the Conservancy pickup and the boat we kept docked on a lift at Palermo Marina. Teawater Key was just south of Palermo, one of the more popular uninhabited islands that made up the Ten Thousand Islands, attracting picnickers and shell seekers.

"I'm on my way!" I said. "What kind of shark was it?"

"He didn't specify." He paused, looking as if he wanted to say more. "What?"

"If a finned shark has washed up, we both know there are fifty more of them that haven't. Just find out what you can. And be careful. Assholes that commit crimes against marine life will commit them against people, too."

I made the twenty-minute drive to the marina in twelve. The

parking lot was a logjam of trucks—local, die-hard fishermen backing their boats down to the water. Unable to get through the maze of traffic, I parked on the grass near the road and jogged to the dock. Maneuvering the skiff out of the slip, I eased it toward open water and hit the throttle.

The last time I'd dealt with a dead shark had been two years before, when a bull had washed up on the public beach with monofilament line wrapped around its head and gills. It had slowly starved from not being able to open its mouth. A washed-up shark is a rarity—usually a dead shark sank—but if the shark died in the shallows or near mangrove isles, if the waves and currents were just right, it might land on shore.

As Teawater came into view, I made out four or five anchored boats and a cluster of people congregated on a tiny strip of beach. Coasting in, I tossed a rope over and jumped off the bow, my feet splashing into ankle-deep water. Recognizing the Conservancy logo on the boat, the Fish and Wildlife guy came over and helped me to glide it up onto the sand.

"Jack Dodd," he said, introducing himself. He was a fit fiftysomething, his short sleeves fitted snugly around his biceps.

"I'm Dr. Donnelly," I said.

I strode toward the knot of people on the beach, which circled what I presumed to be the dead shark. Most were clad in bathing suits, having boated over for amusement and stumbled into a crime drama.

Two years ago, I'd been given the task of disposing of the dead bull. The protocol was to return a washed-up shark to its environment, moving it far enough offshore that it wouldn't wash back. I'd towed it behind the skiff into open water, where I'd removed the tether line and watched it sink slowly like a small, shiny submarine. I'd been struck by the size and power of the creature, the magnificence of it, the horror and banality of its death, and I'd said a prayer under my breath.

Up ahead, a young woman wearing a tan uniform, a pony tail, and a camera strapped over her shoulder was attempting to move the crowd and cordon off the shark with yellow tape.

Officer Dodd trotted by me. "Okay, folks, let's get moving," he told the curiosity seekers.

As they dispersed, I had a sudden clear view of the maimed shark. It jolted me—the carcass hulked there, its six-foot body wreathed in sand flies, its eye frozen into a hard black marble. I'd never seen a finned shark, not a real one, and the sight of it, the violence and atrocity of what had been done to it, punched the breath out of me. It was a lemon.

I dropped down beside it. There was a vicious white gash where the dorsal fin used to be and her tail was missing. The wounds had been cleaned by the saltwater and nibbled at by crabs and gulls. I rested my hands on her round belly.

"She's pregnant," I said, looking up at the uniformed woman who'd paused beside me, the caution tape spooling onto the sand. I judged the shark to be at the end of a gestation that had probably lasted a year.

"Sergeant Alvarez," she said. "I'm with the Sheriff's Marine Bureau."

"Dr. Maeve Donnelly," I responded, hearing the slight tremble in my voice.

I swallowed, forcing back tears, fighting to remain professional, unruffled, but even then wondering why professional had become synonymous with dispassionate. I didn't know how to be dispassionate about sharks, about the ocean, about the things people did to them.

"Maeve?"

I sucked in my breath. The unmistakable accent. A hand floated to my shoulder, and Nicholas crouched next to me in the sand. The sight of him demolished the last scraps of self-control I had. My eyes welled up.

"What are you doing here?" I asked, getting to my feet, trying my best to stay composed.

He glanced at the sergeant, who wore an expression of polite confusion. "Gina . . . Sergeant Alvarez called our lab this morning to let
us know a finned shark had washed up," Nicholas explained. "She's
good about alerting us when there's an incident. She consulted with
us a few years ago on that documentary we did—"

"*Crimes Against Marine Life*," Alvarez volunteered.

"Anyway, I offered to drive down," Nicholas said. "I thought you
might be here."

"When did you get back from England?" I asked.

"Just last night."

"God, you must be jet lagged."

"I'm awake *now*."

"Excuse me," the sergeant said, and Nicholas and I stepped aside
as she finished roping off the area and began photographing the shark
from various angles. She had an aloof way about her. A kind of indif-
ference to what she was photographing that put me off.

"This has to be connected to the hundred shark fins that were found
on Bonnethead Key last month," I said, shadowing her. My eruption of
sadness had worn off, thank God, but had been replaced with a molten
lump of anger in my stomach. "You must have some leads."

"It could be a local operation," Alvarez said. "There were similar
cases in Pensacola and the Keys where local fishermen were providing
fins to traffickers." She worked as she talked, snapping pictures and
making notes. "The fin trade is a highly lucrative practice. Without a
doubt those fins on Bonnethead were meant for the black market."

"Based on the amount of putrefaction, I'm guessing this shark has
been dead only around a week," I said. "Whoever is doing this could
still be in the area."

Alvarez lifted her eyebrows and made a notation. "You would think
after the guy who was storing the fins was arrested they would've shut
the whole thing down, but apparently there's no accounting for greed.

They're nearly impossible to catch and they know it. Our patrols haven't seen anything suspicious, no illegal commercial outfits on the water. I hate to say it, but the odds aren't good. We just don't have any real evidence."

The decaying smell of the shark clogged my nose. I forced myself to look at it again. I remembered the shark killing rampage that had gone on right after I was bitten. Those gruesome photographs in the *Palermo Times*.

We just don't have any real evidence.

"For God's sake, you have a hundred shark fins and this dismembered shark right in front of you," I said, my voice rising. "If that's not evidence, what is?"

She lowered her camera and turned to me. "Yes, the fins are evidence, the shark is evidence. What I meant to say is that they lead nowhere. We have no one to connect them to. Look, to get real evidence we would have to patrol thousands of nautical miles and board hundreds of boats. We don't have those kinds of resources. It's almost impossible. And it would help if the guy who was paid to store the fins would talk. If we can't catch these people in the act, then what we need, Dr. Donnelly, is to find the fins on board a boat, a boat we can trace back to someone."

Listening to this I felt frustrated and discouraged, indignant that she sounded so procedural about it. They would never catch these people. The sergeant didn't seem to believe they even had a chance of catching them. The black market would go on killing the sharks I'd tagged and named and weighed and studied. I'd given my life to sharks and people were killing them faster than they could reproduce. It was pretty clear at this rate most species would be extinct in a matter of decades.

I pointed at the lemon, my finger shaking a little, my anger starting to spill over. "This shark was fished out of the water, Sergeant

Alvarez. Her fin was sliced off, then her tail, and all the while, she was alive. She was thrown overboard where she drowned and bled to death. And who knows how many pups she's carrying."

Alvarez stared at me in that insufferably cool way she had. "I *know* how sharks are finned."

I should have reeled it in right then, but I couldn't help myself. I shouted, "There are probably hundreds of more sharks in the Gulf getting slaughtered but people don't give a shit unless it's a whale. Save the whales. We all love whales; *I* love whales. But humans are torturing sharks for profit and pleasure. For shark fin soup. But who cares? It's just a shark."

"Maeve," Nicholas said. He faced me, putting his hands around my elbows, locking his eyes onto mine. *"Maeve."*

He turned to Alvarez. "When you're finished, we'll take the shark and dispose of it. Unless you need to keep it as evidence."

Ignoring me, she said, "I don't need the body. The photographs are sufficient. You can take it. Just make sure you dump it well off-shore."

Nicholas steered me back along the beach. "Do you have anything in your boat we can wrap the shark in?"

"There's an old plastic tarp."

We sat in the boat, waiting for Alvarez and Dodd to leave. My anger had dissolved now, and I was feeling embarrassed by my outburst.

"You were quite something back there," he said, smiling at me. "I think Gina wanted to Taser you."

As Alvarez and Dodd departed in separate boats, Nicholas and I spread the blue plastic onto the sand and rolled the lemon onto the center of it. Each taking an end, we half carried, half dragged her to the boat, where we laid her in the hull.

"You want me to drive?" he asked, and I realized how tired I felt. I took the passenger seat beside the wheel and gave him the keys.

He drove slowly at first, slowly enough to miss a sea turtle that surfaced in front of the bow. Its shell was heavily barnacled—there was no telling how old it was.

"If you'd hit that turtle, it would've done me in."

"What, you're not done in already?" His hand left the wheel and rested on top of mine. Selfishly, I let it stay there, wanting the weight and heat of his palm, the nearness of him.

"We have a lot to talk about, but let's save it for a better time," I said. The Daniel confession. I breathed in, feeling the twist of dread. I wasn't ready for that. Would I ever be ready? "I'm glad you're here," I told him.

"Me, too."

When we were far enough from shore, Nicholas killed the engine and dropped anchor. I looked over the side of the boat, into the distance. "The shark was probably headed to the estuaries to have her pups when she was caught," I said.

"I thought you'd want to be the one to put her back in the Gulf," he said. "Are you sure you're okay to do this?"

I didn't blame him for asking. I'd had a small meltdown or what I would hereafter try to think of as an outbreak of righteous indignation. Of course he worried that putting this finned, pregnant lemon back into the food chain would upset me.

"I'm okay," I said. "I lost it a little back there, but I'm okay."

As the skiff bobbled on the water, we stood on either side of the shark, preparing to hoist it up.

"Let's get this over with," he said.

He stood there holding his side of the tarp, but I couldn't move.

"Second thoughts?" he asked.

"Are we sure there's no reason to keep her?"

"Keep her? Seriously?" He let go of the plastic. "We don't need to do a necropsy, Maeve. We know why she died. And Alvarez said she didn't need the body to make a case."

"I know it's crazy." Still, I didn't reach for the tarp. I went on standing there, looking at him, wanting to make sense of my reluctance. I said, "I don't know—maybe we should do the necropsy anyway. We might learn something. There must be something to be gained by keeping her. Maybe we could . . ."

"Could what?" he said.

And there it was suddenly, the idea I was fumbling for. "Maybe we could use her in some way. A picture is worth a thousand words, and a finned shark is worth a thousand pictures."

Twenty-four

Inside the lab at the Conservancy, I extracted the shark pups from the lemon. Slicing open the yolk sac, I found six of them between ten and twelve inches long. As suspected, she'd been full term. One by one, I cut the placental cords, thin as yarn, and handed the pups' silvery gray bodies to Nicholas, who injected them with concentrated formaldehyde. We tied identifying labels through their gill slits and carefully slid them into individual jars of dilute formalin. We were gowned, masked, gloved, our eyes walled behind safety glasses, and still the toxic fumes stung my corneas and nostrils. Tears began to leak onto my cheeks.

"Sadness or formaldehyde?" Nicholas said, screwing on the last lid.

"Both," I told him.

As we wrapped the lemon in a blanket, I vowed to call every media outlet I could think of to come see the finned shark for themselves.

I glanced at the wall clock. Three twenty. "We need to get this shark into a freezer, and we have to rush if we're going to make it during the lull between lunch and dinner."

"Wait—we're putting it in a *food* freezer?"

"At the hotel. The kitchen has two big walk-ins."

He shook his head, more in disbelief, it seemed, than opposition,

and thankfully did not argue, and it struck me how patient and toler-
ant he'd been through the whole ordeal. A real ally. It felt familiar
seeing his brown-green eyes behind goggles. We'd logged so many
timeless hours underwater together, in sync with a world we both
reverenced. A professor had told me once not to name the sharks I
studied, that it would personalize them and muddy my objectivity. I
named them anyway, the way Nicholas had named his rays. Both of
us were after more than just probing and measuring sea creatures;
we sensed our kinship with them.

For a moment, I hoped he was still going to Mozambique.

We loaded the shark onto the back of the pickup and drove to the
hotel, parking in the back where the food trucks made deliveries. I
glanced at my watch, hoping the kitchen would be clear. About now
Daniel would be holding a kitchen staff meeting in the dining room
to go over the menu.

We found the delivery door locked, and I was forced to call Robin
to come open it.

"What are you doing in the delivery zone?" he asked.

"Just hurry, okay?"

A few interminable minutes later, he found Nicholas and me on
the landing by the door with a mysterious six-foot bulk concealed
inside a blanket.

"What's going on?" he said.

"I need to get this into the freezer," I said.

"Jesus, you didn't kill anybody, did you?" he said, and laughed.
"What's my sister gotten into?"

"It's a shark," I said. "I need to store it for a while."

"A shark. You have a shark. Are you *crazy*? I can't have that in the
freezer with the food."

"There're dead fish in there already. What's the difference?"

Nicholas suppressed a laugh, and Robin turned to him. "I'm Robin,
Maeve's twin—the older one, the one who's *usually* causing the trouble."

"Nicholas Ridley." Nicholas shook his hand. "We're just looking to store it for a day. Two days max."

"It's been finned," I added.

"Well, why do *you* have it?" Robin asked.

What reason did I have that would make any sense to him? It barely made sense to me. What *was* I doing? Buying time until I could scare up a TV crew from Naples or Fort Myers to come tromp through the kitchen and whip up public opinion against shark finning? The shark's body was proof of a reprehensible act, maybe not enough to convict someone in a court of law, but surely in people's minds. Even if a person hated sharks, like Robin had as a kid, encountering a finned shark in the flesh was still a visceral, wrench-in-the-gut kind of thing. I couldn't dispose of the shark without trying to attract public attention to what was happening right under our noses.

Robin didn't wait for me to postulate an answer. He said, "Look, Maeve, I don't know what's going on, but we aren't putting a dead shark in the freezer."

He'd dug in.

"I'm sure you can understand," Nicholas said. "It's been a long day. We were out on Teawater this morning with the authorities and we've spent the last few hours doing a postmortem and removing six of her pups. I don't think either Maeve or I am up to taking the boat out again today and dropping the shark into the Gulf. What do you say, mate? Give us a break?"

"Robin, you owe me," I said. I gave him a pointed look and he knew exactly what I meant.

He exhaled and unlocked the door. Peering inside, he said, "I don't know how we're going to explain this to Daniel."

"Let me handle that," I said.

Nicholas and I hoisted the shark through the doorway. Holding on to the ends of the blanket, we lugged the shark through the empty kitchen, past Daniel's office, the sinks, the salamander grill, the sanitized stainless steel tables, all the way to the back where the freezers were located.

We set her down, and I scoped out both freezers for a place to deposit her. "There's not a lot of room in either one of them," I said. "We'll have to put her on the floor toward the back."

"Put *what* in the back?" Daniel said, strolling up, his fingers in his jeans pockets, followed by several of his staff. "What's going on?" His eyes darted from me to Robin, then down to the blanket before settling on Nicholas.

Robin, who'd been holding open the freezer door, let it fall shut and I felt a gust of icy air sweep across the back of my calves. We all seemed to have gone mute.

Daniel asked again. "Anyone going to tell me what's going on?" He smiled, but I heard the edge in his voice, thin as a razor.

I said, "I know this is crazy, but hear me out, okay? I'm putting a shark in your freezer. Just for a day or so."

He looked at the ceiling incredulously. "You're joking."

He listened without interrupting while I explained about the finned shark, how bogged down the investigation had been, and my hope to spark publicity for it, perhaps even cause someone to come forward, or at the very least to raise public awareness.

Even to my own ears I sounded like a person hanging on to the most meager of hopes.

"You do realize that having a decomposing shark here probably violates about a hundred different health codes. It's not like the fresh fish that arrive on ice. This thing has been lying in the sun rotting on a beach. If an inspector walked in right now I could be shut down."

"But how likely is that?" I said. "Can't you just go with me on this?"

How was it that Nicholas had gotten on board so easily even though he doubted I would get the kind of media attention I wanted? He saw how important it was to me and overrode his reservations.

Why couldn't Daniel do that, too? But then, I was probably being self-ish. Nicholas didn't have a kitchen to protect.

Daniel looked at Robin. "You're on board with her plan?"

"I'm decidedly not, but I'm going along with it anyway," Robin told him.

Daniel tugged me a few yards over toward the pantry and whis-pered, "Dead shark aside, I don't understand how *he* got involved."

I could see why he wanted an explanation, but the undercurrent of suspicion pissed me off. *Please, don't do this now.* "Someone from the Sheriff's Marine Bureau called Nicholas's lab. He came to help."

"Yeah, I bet he did."

Nicholas, who'd been quietly standing in the background, cleared his throat, making me wonder if he'd overheard. It was the first time I noticed how dirty he was, how dirty both of us were. Our shorts and shirts were smeared with God knows what sort of muck. Sweat had dried on my skin, turning my whole body to flypaper. I watched as Nicholas wiped his forehead.

At that moment, Hazel trailed in with several of Daniel's staff. She was wearing a scuba mask.

"Maeve!" she cried, running over to me, slowing when she saw the large hump inside the blanket. "What's that?"

With her nose inside the mask, her voice came out muffled, like she had a bad cold. As she talked, the mask fogged and her eyes van-ished behind the mist.

Daniel said, "If the staff would head back out into the dining hall—thank you."

As they filed out, glancing over their shoulders, Hazel pulled the mask over her head, taking care not to snag her hair.

"What was the mask for?" I asked.

"Onions," she said. The fish smell hit her then and she pinched her nose. "What's that, a fish?"

I looked at Daniel before answering. "It's a shark. It was hurt very badly."

"Is it dead?"

"Yeah, it is."

"What happened to it?"

Again, I threw Daniel a glance and he gave me a small nod. "There are some people out there who cut the fins off sharks so they can sell them. That's what happened to this one."

"Oh." She blinked and crossed her arms. "Can I see it?"

"Please don't unwrap it here," Daniel said.

"But I've never seen one up close before," she said. "Please, Dad."

"This really is . . . unbelievable," Daniel said. "Okay, just a peek."

Hazel and I knelt beside the shark. She took a breath and seemed to be gathering up her courage. I peeled back the blanket. Hazel's eyes swept over the shark's body. She brushed her finger across the skin above its snout.

"It feels rough," she said. "And smooth, too."

As I tucked the blanket back around the shark, Hazel noticed Nicholas and gave him a bashful wave. "I saw you in the grocery store that time," she said. "You know all about rays."

"And you're the founder of the Shark Club, as I recall."

"Put it in the freezer," Daniel said. "But really, you need to get it out of here tomorrow."

"Thank you," I said.

Robin and Nicholas moved the shark into the freezer and laid it on the floor.

Hazel rubbed her thumb across her index finger where she'd touched the shark. "What's going to happen to it?"

"Tomorrow I'll take it out on the boat and put it into the Gulf," I told her.

"Will there be a funeral?"

No one said anything. Daniel rubbed his hand across the top of his head, messing his brown hair. I imagined he was remembering the last funeral Hazel had attended. Holly's. Of course she expected a funeral after the death of this shark, that's what happened after someone died.

"We can have one, if you want," I told her.

"Can I go, Dad?"

I looked at him. "I can take her with me, I mean, if it's okay with you. We don't have to go out far."

"Okay," he said.

Hazel's whole face lit up. "Can you come, too?" she asked Daniel.

"Sorry, Bug, I have to work."

She turned to Nicholas. "What about you?"

"I'm sure he has to get back," Daniel interjected. "It's Sarasota, right?"

"It's no problem, I'm happy to see this through," Nicholas said.

Daniel walked over to me and put a possessive arm around my shoulder, pulling me to him. I had put off telling Nicholas about me and Daniel; I'd been a coward, and now this would be how he learned we were seeing each other. I watched, ashamed, as the message registered on Nicholas's face, stiffening against Daniel, at his proprietary gesture.

Hazel wedged herself between me and Daniel.

"I'm sure I could manage to leave work for a funeral," he told her.

"He's right," Nicholas said. "I really should get back." He said his good-byes and headed to the double doors that led to the dining room.

"*Daniel*," I said under my breath. "Why would you do that?"

"Why do you care so much?" he answered.

I followed Nicholas into the dining room, where a handful of staff were setting up the tables for dinner. When I called to him, he stopped, but didn't turn around.

"I'm sorry. I was going to tell you. I just wanted to do it in person. I e-mailed you this morning to see if you were back and then the call came in about the shark, and you were there. I still can't believe you were there."

He turned and his face was creased not with anger, but hurt.

"It happened after you left for England," I said.

Nicholas shifted his gaze toward the windows that looked out on the gem-colored Gulf. I waited for him to say something, but he didn't.

"I'm sorry," I said again. "You had an expectation . . . a reasonable expectation that we would . . ."

"Maybe I should've seen this coming—you and Daniel. The way he looked at you at the market that day, the way he looked at me, like I was a threat to him." He broke off. "The three of you, though, you look like a happy family." I heard the bitterness in his voice and I felt ashamed.

Glasses clinked nearby. The snap of a tablecloth.

"Shit," Nicholas said. "My car is at the marina."

"It's getting late and we haven't eaten all day. You stay at the hotel tonight—it's on the house. I'll take you to your car in the morning."

"I'm sure Daniel would be keen on *that*."

"Come on, I'll help you get checked in."

"Maeve. Really, I can find the front desk."

He started to walk away, then turned back. "I could've competed with Daniel," he said. "But not with his little girl."

"Nicholas," I said, then stopped, not knowing how to respond to that. I didn't want to defend how I felt about Hazel. I couldn't help that Daniel had a daughter; I hadn't expected to fall in love with her, too.

He waited there a moment before striding off, leaving me alone in the now empty room. Watching him leave was harder than I wanted it to be.

Twenty-five

*T*he television reporter and cameraman from WINK News in Fort Myers arrived at the hotel the next morning before sunrise, well before the breakfast hour. I met them outside the delivery entrance, while Nicholas and Perri waited in the kitchen, sipping coffee.

I watched through a haze of darkness and humidity as the reporter, Leigh Davis, changed into a pair of on-air heels beside the news van, then clicked across the pavement to the delivery door, trailed by the cameraman, who lugged two cases of equipment. My stomach fluttered with nervous anticipation.

Leigh had once covered Perri's annual costume bash. Out of all the stations I'd called last night, she was the only reporter who'd called me back.

"Thanks for coming so early," I said as they reached the landing. "And I hate to rush this, but we really have to be done before the breakfast staff arrives."

"I think we can do this in twenty minutes," she said.

She had shown up camera ready, her face beautifully airbrushed, not a hair out of place. Despite my efforts with the hair dryer and cosmetic bag, the last twenty-four hours had left me both looking and feeling haggard.

⌒

The night before, I'd called Perri to confess there was a shark in the freezer, relaying the whole gory story. The part about the finning had softened her, but she'd still wanted to hear my plan for "getting the poor thing out of the freezer as soon as possible." She wasn't thrilled about a news crew coming either, but I assured her the reporter had agreed to keep our location a secret. As an added precaution, Perri suggested we hang bedsheets over the freezer shelves to conceal the food.

"By the way, I put Nicholas in the Thoreau Room," she said.

I was glad to know he wasn't steeped in the atmosphere of Romantic poetry. Keats. Shelley. Or worse, Anaïs Nin again. "Thanks for that. See you in the morning."

"Right. I'll be the one with the sheets and the duct tape."

As soon as we'd hung up, I screwed up my courage and called Nicholas. I hated the way things were left between us.

"Hear me out," I said. "You once told me we could go back to being colleagues."

He paused for a long second. "You're using my words against me?"

Relieved, I heard the familiar teasing in his voice. "I guess I am."

"Colleagues it is, then," he said.

"In that case, I've got a news crew coming tomorrow morning—"

"Seriously?"

"And I want you to be there."

After everything he'd done, he deserved to be part of the interview, but I suppose I was also driven by guilt. I hadn't treated him well, and I didn't want our last good-bye to be the angry one in the dining room.

"We're starting very early," I added.

"How early is early?"

"Five A.M."

"Anything at that hour makes me more than a colleague."

After we hung up, I lay in bed exhausted, but unable to close my eyes. My thoughts churned. I repeatedly eyed the clock, incapable of shaking the sight of the mutilated shark or the sound of Nicholas's voice as he'd said my name out on the beach, trying to rein me back from my episode of righteous indignation. I felt the phantom weight of Daniel's arm draped around my shoulder, remembering the look on Nicholas's face, and then how he'd walked away, the finality of it.

I hadn't called Daniel, and apparently he had been too occupied to call me. I did e-mail him, though, to say the shark funeral would start at 8:00 A.M. at the Palermo Marina and offered to pick up Hazel if he wanted to skip it. I didn't mention Nicholas or the TV crew that would be arriving before dawn in his kitchen. I hadn't heard anything back.

I stumbled into the kitchen in the morning to find Perri and Nicholas already there and on their second pot of coffee.

"Remind me again how soon you leave for Mozambique," Perri said, making a joke, but after everything that had happened, I wondered if it was totally in jest.

The corner of Nicholas's mouth lifted slightly, despite the mention of Mozambique.

He'd shown up this morning freshly showered, somehow wearing clean clothes, though his shirtsleeves landed an inch above his wrists and the cuffs of his pants skimmed the top of his ankles.

"Where'd you get the clothes?" I asked.

"Yeah, I know. An atrocious fit. Perri sent them up to me. They might belong to your brother."

More likely Marco, I thought.

He rolled the sleeves to his elbows. "Not much I can do about the pants."

My first thought was to tease him: *maybe they can shoot you from the waist up.* But I refrained. I could feel the tension between us, hovering like one of those giant, rogue waves known to capsize ships.

⌒

In the kitchen, I made introductions. Perri wasted no time in telling Leigh to keep the Hotel of the Muses out of the news. "Health code violations would be very bad for business. I'm sure you can understand."

"I'll say I'm reporting from an undisclosed location. It's more dramatic that way, anyway," Leigh said. "We'll get some B-roll first. You want to show me this shark?"

Inside the freezer, I uncovered the frozen shark and stepped back so the cameraman could get his shots. A few moments later, with the lens and light pointed on me, he counted down with his fingers. Three, two, one.

"What can you tell us about the shark's injury?" Leigh asked.

My voice came out trembly. I wanted to think it wasn't nerves, that the cold inside the freezer was to blame, and maybe that was what Leigh thought. Bending down, I pointed to where the shark's dorsal fin used to be and to the stubbed end of the body, missing its tail, my voice growing strong as I described in grisly detail exactly how the shark had been finned.

"The thing is, there are a lot more sharks just like this. Around eighty million a year are finned for profit."

Leigh resumed the interview with Nicholas and me inside the warmth of the kitchen with our backs to the freezer door. We told her finning sharks was a crime, a multibillion-dollar business, and that the fins often ended up on menus right here in Florida. When I brought up the hotline the Conservancy had set up for people to call and gave out the number, Leigh jumped on it. "We'll get that number on the screen for people, and you're encouraging them to call if they see anything at all suspicious."

I said, "Yes, if you're out on the water and something looks off or feels off, be vigilant. Even if you see people shark fishing, just pay attention. Maybe there's more going on on the boat than meets the eye. We don't want anyone to approach a boat, but take a picture."

Leigh tilted the microphone toward Nicholas. "With an operation like this," he said, "there can be quite a few people involved—there are those doing the actual finning, of course, but also these fins are being dried and stored and transported, so if you know anything about any of this, please call."

I was seized suddenly by a kind of desperation. "The Gulf Marine Conservancy where I work is giving a five-hundred-dollar reward for information that leads to the capture of the people responsible for this." I'd completely made that up of course, but I wanted to give them a reason to call. How many were going to dial the hotline out of a love for sharks? If Russell balked at the reward, I would have to take it out of my own pocket.

"Dr. Donnelly, why do you think people should care? Why do *you* care so much?"

Why do you care so much? It was the same question Daniel had asked me yesterday right before I'd followed Nicholas out of the kitchen.

I looked at him. "I've always cared," I said, then, turning to Leigh, "Sharks matter. Everything swimming in the oceans matters. Dolphins, stingrays, the tiniest sea horses, and the smallest crabs." *The smallest, purplest crabs,* I thought. "The thing is, without sharks our oceans will die, and if the oceans die, we're next, but they don't matter just because they benefit us; they matter simply because they exist."

Leigh waved her hand at the cameraman and the light on the camera flicked off. "Thank you," she said. "We've got some good stuff. We're going out to Teawater to get some footage. I'll call if I have any follow-up questions."

Perri put her arm around me. "Good job. When will it air?"

"It should be on the five and the eleven o'clock news today," Leigh said. "And possibly on the noon news tomorrow."

When they had packed their equipment and left, Nicholas said, "Since when is there a reward?"

I shrugged. "Since five minutes ago."

Perri said, "You managed to get the interview done before a single one of the kitchen staff arrived. Now for the shark."

"It's as good as gone," I told her.

"And me, too," she said, and excused herself.

"Thank you for this," I said, turning to Nicholas. "Especially after what happened yesterday. And don't worry. I'm going to wake Robin up, and he's going to help me move this shark—you've done enough. Anyway, just . . . thanks."

He gazed at me for a moment without speaking. "You're welcome."

"Can I at least take you to the marina to get your car?" I asked.

"Perri reserved the shuttle for me." Nicholas looked down at his feet, then into my eyes. "I did this interview for you and for the shark and because I'd like to help find the miserable piece of shit who cut off its fins, but I hope you can understand that as much as I'd like to spend time with you—in a car or a boat, in Mozambique or here right now—I'm going to do myself a favor and not see you."

There had been no harshness in his voice as he'd said it. Only resolve.

Twenty-six

L ater that morning at the Palermo Marina, I waited at the dock beside the Conservancy skiff, wondering if Daniel and Hazel would show up for the shark funeral. It was 8:20 A.M. I didn't know how much longer I should delay. A couple of workers at the marina had helped me load the shark into the boat's hull, and for the last twenty minutes the skiff had bobbed on the water, gassed and ready to go.

Ten more minutes. I'll wait ten more.

It had barely been light out when Nicholas had taken the hotel's shuttle to his car. He was probably in Sarasota by now. *I'm going to do myself a favor and not see you.*

I had just climbed into the boat and was about to toss the ropes when I saw them hurrying along the dock, Hazel waving her arms almost frantically, shouting "Wait for us!" and Daniel following behind her with his Tampa Bay Rays cap pulled low on his forehead. Hazel was wearing her dinosaur field bag stuffed with who knows what inside of it. What does a person bring to a shark funeral other than a shark?

"Somebody was late," said Hazel, aiming her thumb at Daniel.

He held up his hands in surrender. "Sorry."

"What do you have in your bag?" I asked Hazel, as Daniel lifted her over the side.

"You'll see," she said, and then asked to drive the boat.

I let her steer through the slow zone practically by herself, wishing Daniel and I had broken the ice the night before. He'd barely looked at me when he'd boarded.

When we got out into the Gulf, Daniel called Hazel back to sit with him and watch for dolphins. The skiff bounced across another boat's wake, sending spray over the side, and Hazel, buckled to her chin in a lifejacket, squealed and wiped the lenses of her sunglasses on her lavender terry shorts. *There's the child in the life jacket, the one who shakes oranges loose from the tree. There's the man who waits for us in the kitchen.* It was what I'd always wanted, wasn't it? It should have been the perfect picture. Except for the tension. Except for the shrouded dead shark at our feet.

I slowed the speed and turned off the engine, which created a sudden vacuous quiet. We were nearly a mile off shore, far enough out that we wouldn't be overrun by Jet Skis, and more important, the shark wouldn't get pushed to shore again by waves.

The water was full of chop from the wind. The boat swayed on the surface. How did one begin a shark funeral?

"Where's Nicholas?" Hazel asked, so out of the blue it startled me.

Daniel tugged on the brim of his cap, then moved his arm from behind Hazel's shoulders.

"He went back to Sarasota this morning," I told her.

"Oh," she said. "I like him—he sounds like a Wiggle."

"A *what*?" I asked.

"The Wiggles," Daniel said. "They're a group of guys in Australia who sing kids' songs." He shook his head as if marveling he possessed knowledge such as this.

"Is Nicholas from Australia?" Hazel asked.

"England," I told her, hoping Daniel didn't detect how uncomfortable I was becoming at all this talk about Nicholas.

"Like the Pilgrims," she said. "*Wait.*" A tiny gasp escaped her mouth. "Is Nigel Marven from England?"

"Yes, probably," I said.

I could almost see Nicholas ticking even further upward in her estimation. "Why did Nicholas leave?"

Daniel sighed. So loud I heard it over the wind.

"He had stingray work to do," I said. "So, let's talk about how we want to do the funeral."

"Good idea," Daniel said.

"Are you ready to see what's in my bag?" Hazel asked.

"Ready."

She emptied it onto the seat beside her. Binoculars, rolled up sun hat, apple juice box, and a hibiscus blossom with a paper towel wrapped around the stem. She picked up the flower and studied it. The petals were a bit wilted, but still vibrantly orange. At its center, a blood-red stain.

"It's very pretty," I told her.

"There were flowers at Mom's funeral. I took one home and Grandma Van put it in a book."

"She pressed it," Daniel said.

"Yeah, she pressed it," Hazel whispered.

I shot Daniel a look, worried suddenly that holding a shark funeral had been a colossal mistake, afraid that a funeral of any sort might throw her into a tailspin of grief for her mother. Seriously, how many funerals did one six-year-old need to attend?

Seeing my concern, Daniel said, "We talked about it last night." He looked at his daughter. "We said it was like the shark was going . . . where?"

"Going home," she said, filling in the blank.

"That's a good way to think of it. It *is* going home, isn't it?" I offered, wanting to say the right thing, but unsure really what that was.

"Yeah, so we don't have to be sad," she said.

"And you know what? You're actually doing an important task by helping me return the shark to the Gulf. You're kind of like a biologist in training."

Hazel liked that and looked up at her dad with a goofy grin.

The three of us gathered self-consciously around the shark, wobbling a little on our feet as the boat undulated. Hazel poked at the blanket with her index finger and grimaced as it hit against the hard, bloated body beneath the blanket. Just visible in the high V of her life jacket was her shark tooth necklace.

"I would like to say we're honored to send this shark home," I said, and for want of anything better to do, held out my hand like a fin, the way we did for the Shark Club motto. Hazel's fin went up, and lastly, Daniel's.

Hazel added, "We're sorry you're dead and we hope the guys that killed you will be put in jail."

Hazel and I turned to Daniel.

"My turn, huh? Okay. Well, I'm sure this was a good shark. Good-bye, shark."

Hazel laughed, a little knowingly, as if Daniel was a token member of Shark Club, not a full-fledged one like she and I were. Whatever the reason, I was grateful for the laughter.

"Daniel, you want to take that end of the blanket?" I asked.

"Wait, what about the pledge?" Hazel said. "Let's do the pledge."

Water slapped hard against the side of the boat as she led us, Daniel reciting a split second behind us so Hazel wouldn't think he didn't know the words.

Daniel and I each took an end of the blanket and lifted the shark over the side. Its ravaged body rolled out of the blanket into the water with a galumphing splash and started to sink. Hazel hung over the side of the boat and peered through her binoculars at the spot where the shark had disappeared, then she tossed in the hibiscus.

We stood there a few seconds and watched it float.

As Hazel lifted the binoculars back to her cheeks, Daniel took my hand and held the back of it to his lips. The way his hair stuck out from under his hat, the sheen of his ultrablue eyes, just the way he stood, reminded me of the thirteen-year-old he used to be. The face that looked back at me the first time I said I loved him. I saw the nineteen-year-old who'd kissed me in the elevator, a kiss filled with hunger and release. It was difficult to separate our history from who he was now. Was it hard for him, too? Did he look at me and see who I was instead of the girl he'd hurt, the girl who'd stormed out of his life, the girl he'd begged to forgive him, but who couldn't?

I turned my hand over and opened it across his warm cheek. What would happen if neither of us ever mentioned yesterday, if I never mentioned the scene with Nicholas? I realized how much I didn't want to talk about it, as if confronting it could change everything. And, if I knew Daniel, he wouldn't want to lift up the stone and look underneath it either. He would let it rest.

I heard a plop in the water. *"My binoculars!"* Hazel yelled. "They went in the water!"

Daniel was saying, "They're only binoculars, we can get another pair," when I stepped over the rail of the boat and dived in after them.

The water rushed up around me, cool and fizzing. Overhead, and far away it seemed, I heard Daniel and Hazel call my name. Then a hollow noise filled my ears and I heard nothing but the inside of the Gulf.

The water was clear, but not crystal. Nor was it very deep, twelve feet, maybe. I descended quickly, spotting the binoculars right away. The strap floated up as though it were draped around some ghostly neck. I slipped an arm through it and was about to push off the bottom when I saw the dead shark lying nearby on the sea floor. Without its tail or its fin, the chopped-up creature appeared more incongruous in the water than on the boat. By now, other sharks would already have detected its presence. In a short while it would become part of the food chain.

My lungs ached as I ascended from that beautiful graveyard, knowing that one day it would be my graveyard, too. My ashes would be scattered out here, and I wondered for a split second who would do the spreading.

I popped out of the water and gulped for air, holding up the binoculars. Hazel clapped with excitement. Daniel stared at me as though I'd lost my mind.

⌒

That night Daniel and I sat on the edge of the hotel swimming pool and dangled our legs in the water. I held my leg against a water jet, feeling the stream pummel my calf, the skin turn numb, and the muscle soften. As the last of the night swimmers toweled and packed their belongings, Daniel leaned over and kissed my neck.

"I'm going to look at another house tomorrow. I want you to come with me," he said. "Hazel starts school in two and half weeks, and I'd like to get us settled in a place of our own as soon as I can. It's a little two-bedroom on Bay Court. It has a small backyard. A nice kitchen."

"Sounds perfect," I said.

The illumination from the pool glowed across our legs. A stray piece of light fell on Daniel's face like a lightning strike. He was beautiful.

"Maeve, I don't know what Nicholas was doing with you yesterday," he said abruptly. "Is there something I should know?"

I felt ambushed and unprepared, surprised that I'd guessed wrong—he *did* want to talk about it. I pulled my legs out of the water, instantly chilling them, and drew them against my body.

"Come on, Maeve. You know what I mean. I saw how you followed after him when he left the kitchen." He splashed his hand across the water. "Tell me I shouldn't worry."

"You shouldn't," I said. "Nicholas was here because of the finned shark. He ended up helping me with the necropsy. He's a friend." Even as I said those last words, I doubted even that much was true now.

I lay back against the cool tiles and stared up at the palms. The branches swept back and forth in the wind, thrashing like giant brooms. One of the fronds twirled in the wind, hanging by mere fibers.

"We haven't talked much about the future," I said. "Why is that?"

"I'm trying to now," he said, reclining onto his elbows. "Come see the house with me."

"Okay. I'll see the house with you. Russell will be out of the office tomorrow for donor meetings in Tampa. I'll take the afternoon off."

It was a relief another day would go by before I had to face Russell about the reward I'd impulsively offered. I rolled my head to the side and looked at Daniel. The light was gone from his face.

Suddenly, the suspended palm frond crashed onto the pool tiles near our heads. I jumped, and all the breath left me.

"God," I said, seeing how close it had come, gazing past Daniel's startled face into the capacious, unreliable dark.

Twenty-seven

*T*he house on Bay Court was a lime green Key West cottage with white shutters and a glass-paned front door that creaked when the Realtor opened it. She was sporting black-and-white-checked capris, red sandals, and sunglasses cocked on her head, holding back a torrent of gray corkscrew hair. She'd introduced herself to me in the driveway as Alex.

Stepping inside, my heart began to pound a little. The vacant house brimmed with light and windows and shining wood floors. I couldn't quite decide what I was feeling. Exhilaration, fear, caution, certainty—it was some of everything.

I turned a full circle in the living room, taking it in. The room had built-in bookshelves and sliding doors that opened onto a back screened porch.

"The yard is small, but it's fenced," Alex said, peeling back the sliding door so we could peer out. "There's no pool, but I don't think you specified a pool, because if you specified a pool—"

"Right, that's fine," Daniel said. "Where's the kitchen?"

It was as big as the living room, with white cabinets and glossy cobalt counters and backsplash. Daniel began to tinker with the stove, turning the burners off and on. He opened the oven, the refrigerator, the pantry, each and every cabinet and drawer. He turned on the little flat-screen TV affixed beneath one of the cabinets, surprised to find the cable still turned on.

I said, "You can heat up a lot of chicken nuggets in that oven."

He gave me a look of pure happiness, lifting his eyebrows into a question. *Wanna live here?*

"I don't suppose there's an orange tree outside," I asked Alex, half joking.

"Lemon," she said.

I stepped over to the empty breakfast nook and gazed out the bay window. The lemon tree was sculpted like a lollipop.

Alex guided us through the rest of the house. The bedrooms were small, but there were two of them. One was blue. I thought how much Hazel loved her blue room at Van's, because, she said, it was the color of the sea, and it made me wish she was here to claim it for herself. Daniel hadn't wanted her to see the house, though, until he was certain about it. We'd slipped away this afternoon while Hazel was at her dance class.

After we'd scrutinized each room and Daniel had asked umpteen questions about copper pipes and hurricane shutters, we wandered back into the living room, where Alex announced she needed to return several phone calls and stepped outside, giving us privacy to talk.

Daniel and I wandered onto the back porch, where he stretched out on a La Siesta net hammock that hung in the corner. "Well?" he said.

"I like it. And Hazel would love the blue room, don't you think? And the yard. You could get her a swing set or maybe just one swing to hang on a branch. And I'm sure you realize the plain, black mailbox out front will never do. Hazel is going to insist on a dolphin mailbox like Van's so she can dress it up during holidays."

"Come here," he said.

I went to him, and he pulled me down into the hammock beside him. The net splayed beneath us and the hammock pitched, threatening to topple us, making me grab for him, laughing. When it settled, we stared at the ceiling, which was painted a cloudy pastel blue.

He said, "You know, you could go to Mozambique and live with the mosquitoes and the malaria for four months, or you could move in here with us now."

I clumsily sat up and swung my legs over the side of the hammock, my back to him. "Daniel, why do you make this so hard for me? You know it's going to be awful to leave you and Hazel."

He reached for my hand. "It's settled then? You're definitely going?"

"It's been settled. I've been clear about that."

His hand on mine went a little rigid, but he didn't move it away. He said, "I guess I thought you might change your mind."

Looking back at him, I felt the hard, irritated edge inside of me soften. "For a while, I thought I might, too. But going to Africa is a big deal for me."

"So is me asking you to live with us," he said stiffly, getting to his feet.

"I can still live with you when I get back," I told him, feeling a brush of fear about where this was leading. "I mean, you're not giving me some kind of ultimatum, are you? You're not saying now or never?"

"I'm not saying that. I would just like to think I mattered to you as much as some shark in Africa."

Gazing through the porch screen, I spotted another lemon tree. Beneath it, a spray of lemons lay in the grass like bright, golden orbs. I wanted to smash them.

Daniel whirled toward me, eyes flashing. "Is this about Nicholas? Is fucking Lord Nelson going to Mozambique?"

"I asked him to go when we were in Bimini, but I doubt he's going now," I shouted.

"What is it with you and this guy? What happened in Bimini? Did you sleep with him?"

"Jesus, Daniel."

He stared at me, and I had the feeling he was sorry for what he'd said, but I was too angry now to care. I said, "So what if Nicholas did go to Africa? You trust me, right? *Right?*"

"I trust you. I don't trust him."

I headed toward the sliding doors, noticing every smudge and fingerprint on the glass, every dead moth on the floor, every ringed rust stain left by leaky old planters.

"You haven't answered my question," Daniel said.

"What? Whether or not I slept with Nicholas in Bimini *before* I came home and found you here? No! I didn't. There. Feel better? If anybody should be questioned about trust it shouldn't be *me.*"

Daniel drew back, then charged into the yard through a screen door in the corner that I hadn't even noticed. I regretted saying it, and I regretted nothing at all. I watched him pick up a lemon from the grass and hurl it at the side of the house.

In the living room, I followed the sound of the TV into the kitchen, where I found Alex with her elbows propped on the counter, watching the little TV.

I tried to look unruffled. "We're all done."

She squinted at me, as if trying to get my face to come into focus, then pointed at the television. "I *thought* this was you! You're on CNN."

And there I was, standing in front of a white sheet inside the freezer in Daniel's kitchen, pointing to the grisly gash on the shark's back. The CNN news caption projected across the bottom of the screen: MARINE BIOLOGISTS SPEAK OUT ABOUT SHARK FINNING IN FLORIDA.

My God. *CNN.* They had picked up the story.

At that moment, Daniel walked into the kitchen to find us spellbound before the TV. He stared at the screen, at Nicholas and me standing in front of his freezer. "I've always cared. Sharks matter," I was saying into the microphone.

"What the hell?" said Daniel.

"You're famous," Alex said to me.

I turned to Daniel, taking a deep breath. *I should've told him about the interview. I should've told him.*

He strode out of the kitchen, my voice on the TV trailing after him. "Everything swimming in the oceans matters. Dolphins, sting-rays, the tiniest sea horses, and the smallest crabs."

Twenty-eight

*T*he morning after the disastrous house showing, I showed up at Perri's office before leaving for work, resolved to tell her what an absolute mess Daniel and I had made of things. I was furious at him for his jealousy and possessiveness, his antediluvian attitude toward my career, and at the same time I was filled with remorse over my retaliation. I'd dredged up Daniel's old betrayal and thrown it in his face. I felt like I'd crossed some dangerous line, and I didn't know how to undo it. I hoped Perri might know. I'd spent a sleepless night reliving the awful pain that had come from losing him before, and I'd wakened desperate to repair the breach.

Perri was always in her office early. I spotted her through the half-open door seated at her desk, and barreled right in, not bothering to knock, speaking before she looked up. "Do you have a minute? I *really* need to talk—"

I stopped abruptly. She had company. Daniel and Robin sat across from her, clipboards and pens in hand. I'd interrupted a meeting.

"Oh, sorry," I said. "You're busy."

"We're going over details for the Book Bash," Perri said, waving me in. "The food orders have to go out this morning, and I've even dragged Daniel in here during his off-hours."

He glanced at me, then away, staring blankly through the window behind Perri's desk, where an osprey hovered like a flyaway grocery bag.

I said, "I'll go. We'll talk later; it can keep."

"You'll do no such thing," Perri said. "Not until we talk about you being on CNN. Who would've thought! Everybody I know has called me about it. I saw the interview last night. You were spectacular. Wasn't she spectacular?"

"Absolutely you were," said Robin. "Our own CNN superstar."

Daniel offered Perri a small, perfunctory smile.

Yesterday, after seeing the interview, neither Daniel nor I had even told the Realtor good-bye. I'd simply followed him out of the kitchen, out of the perfect house with the lemon tree, and we'd driven back to the hotel in an almost smothering silence.

Daniel stood. "So if we're done discussing the menu, I'll just go place the food orders."

Perri cut her eyes at me. "Sure, I think we've talked the menu half to death."

As he passed me, he said quietly so that I barely heard, "Maybe we can talk, too?"

When he was gone, I said, "Okay, I'll let you get back to work." As if the whole awkward scene hadn't occurred.

Perri was not so good at pretending. "Maeve, honey, is everything okay?"

"No, but it'll all work out. Let's not talk about it now, okay?" I said and changed the subject, forcing a lilt into my voice that I didn't feel. "So, the Book Bash is coming right up."

"But—" Perri said, giving me a reluctant, worried look.

"Yep, coming right up," Robin said, coming to my rescue. I don't think I could've borne talking about it to them right then, and somehow he knew it. Our twin thing. "Get your George Sand costume ready," he went on. "I told Mindy to come as Cinderella, which would be perfect, right? She told me Hazel's coming as a mouse. Some dancing mouse."

"Angelina Ballerina," I said.

"Right." Robin sounded surprised.

"I know because Hazel loves the Angelina Ballerina books."

It was taking enormous energy to make small talk about costumes and dancing mice.

∼

The lobby at the Conservancy was empty of people except for the gift shop attendant, who was smashing rolls of coins against the cash drawer. I peeked into the touch tank, as I always did before heading to my office. Despite all the racket, the orange and magenta urchins sat undisturbed. A starfish crept along the bottom on tiny tubular feet. I stood there watching, a bit mesmerized by the scene.

I was stalling. Not only did I have to apologize to Russell for promising a sizable and unauthorized reward from the Conservancy to the viewing public, I had to somehow ask him for the funds.

His door was open, but I knocked lightly before he waved me in. Before he could say a word, I started my speech. "I'm sure you've heard about the interview. I spoke without thinking when I offered the reward. I was in the moment, and it suddenly seemed like a way to get some information. It just came out of my mouth. I shouldn't have put that on the Conservancy. If we can't drum up the funds, then I'll pay it myself."

Russell sat there as still as one of the tank urchins. "Okay. Have a seat," he said.

Taking the chair in front of his desk, I said, "I'm sorry."

"First of all, I saw the interview. I'm proud of you. And I think the

Board will be willing to give you a pass for giving away their money in exchange for the free publicity. But just in case, let's offer for you to pay up to half of it and see where that gets us."

I nodded.

"Second, I've just had a chance to go over the calls to the hotline, and since the interview aired, we've gotten over eighty of them. Most are worthless, but a couple of them might actually be useful to the investigation."

I sat straight up. *"Really?"*

"I said *might* be useful, so don't get your hopes up too high." He patted a stack of paper on his desk. "These are the transcripts of all the calls."

He handed me the top two pages.

The calls he felt had possibility were highlighted in yellow. The first was from someone reporting an incident of chumming the water with blood, a common practice in attracting sharks. The other was a sighting of several men shark fishing offshore. My heart sank a little—it was not much to go on. I read over them again, noticing for the first time that both calls were likely describing the same boat. According to the first caller, the chumming took place on a white boat around eighteen feet with a dirty white canopy. The shark fishing was on a white boat, sixteen to eighteen feet, with a torn tan canopy.

"I'll take this to Sergeant Alvarez," I said.

"Take all the calls," he said, pushing the rest of the paper toward me. "A few of us have read them, but we're not law enforcement."

I stood, but he waved me back into the chair. "There's something else."

I sat down and waited while Russell fidgeted for a moment with the glass motorcycle tire paperweight on his desk, then let out a long, worried breath. He picked up one of the hotline call sheets he'd set aside from the rest.

He said, "One of the calls was a threat. A man called it in. It was aimed at you."

I reached over and took the paper from his hands. *Maeve Donnelly, leave this alone or you'll be one sorry bitch.*

A cold, hollow feeling flooded through me. I looked at Russell with a tinge of panic dimming the edges of things.

"I want you to show this threat to Alvarez," he said.

"You're not taking it seriously, are you?" I said, hoping he hadn't noticed how unnerved I was.

"I am, and you should, too. I want you to back off a little now. Just take your foot off the gas where this is concerned."

"But I have a phone interview this afternoon with the *Orlando Sentinel*. And I've been contacted by the *Naples Daily News* and the local NBC station."

"I figured as much. So let Alvarez handle them."

The involuntary reflex of fear was wearing off. Now I just felt indignant. "I can't back off because some nut made a threat that more than likely is completely empty."

"Maeve, hear me out. Whoever called this in knows who you are and where you work. It wouldn't be difficult to find out where you live. I'm not trying to scare you; I'm saying take it seriously."

I walked to the door, holding the bundle of transcripts. "I appreciate your concern, I really do. I'll be careful, but I can't give up on this. Not now."

Inside my office, I dropped the papers on my desk. A mockingbird perched on the windowsill, looking in, quizzically cocking its head at the unfamiliar world beyond the pane.

⌒

That night I flicked off the lights and climbed into bed with the TV remote and leaned back into a mound of pillows. All day my mind had twitched back and forth between Daniel and the words left by the anonymous caller. Wanting a reprieve, I found Alan Alda wooing Ellen Burstyn in *Same Time, Next Year.*

Halfway into the movie, there was a knock on the door. I climbed out of bed and found Daniel in the hallway, holding a pie.

"Key lime?" I asked.

"Lemon meringue." The memory of him hurling the lemon against the side of his would-be house smashed inside my ears. Or was it *our* would-be house?

He handed me the pie with two hands, bowing a little like it was a peace offering. "I'm sorry," he said.

"I'm sorry, too," I told him.

Inside, Daniel slipped off his chef's jacket. His T-shirt was ringed with sweat around the neck and under his arms.

"I said some terrible things . . . ," I started in, but he interrupted me.

"*I* said some terrible things. We don't have to replay it, okay? We're sorry. Let's not dwell on it."

The hurtful things we'd said, the places inside they'd come from, all of it happening when we were jumping off into a life together—it frightened me. It's not that I felt things were hemorrhaging. Just steadily leaking. What had happened between me and Daniel *needed* to be dwelled on.

He kissed me. It was a kind of tourniquet, and I took it.

"I'm going to take a shower," he said. "Do you mind?"

"Go ahead. I'm just finishing this movie."

He undressed in the dark. The light from the TV strobed across his body. He left his shoes and clothes in a pile on the floor, went into the bathroom, and turned on the shower. I heard it spattering against the tiles. I upped the volume on the movie just as Daniel emerged naked from the bathroom.

"I have some clothes here, right?" he asked without a shred of self-consciousness.

I drew up my legs and laughed into my knees. "Bottom drawer," I said.

He grinned. "You're laughing. I'm naked, and you're laughing."

"I'm amused at the confidence it takes to walk around like that," I said, as he retreated to the bathroom and closed the shower door.

How easy it was to return to a sense of lightness. Maybe we didn't need to dissect the fight. Maybe our bond transcended the need to peel back the gauze and look at the wound.

I hopped off the bed and pulled out a clean pair of shorts and a T-shirt for him, then gathered the dirty ones off the floor. They smelled of sweat and smoke and a smorgasbord of Italian and seafood dishes.

He yelled from the bathroom, "How was your day?"

"Pretty good. I did another interview. The Orlando paper. And we may have a small lead on the finnings."

"Oh yeah?"

"Yeah. From the hotline."

I dumped Daniel's dirty clothes onto a chair, then stood in the bathroom doorway and weighed whether or not to tell him about the threat. I knew, though, I'd already kept enough from him.

"There was something else, too," I said, talking to him through the shower door. I watched foam slide down his back as he pushed the last of the shampoo out of his hair. "It's not a big deal, but someone called the hotline and made a threat . . . at me."

Daniel turned off the water and grabbed a towel, wrapping it around his waist. "What kind of threat?"

"Some man called and said I should leave the whole shark finning thing alone or I would be sorry. A sorry bitch, actually."

"Jesus, Maeve." Daniel put his arms around me. His skin was damp and hot, and I was relieved for a moment to feel protected.

I thought of Perri's painting propped on my dresser. Maeve, the shark. The painting imbued me with a fearlessness I wasn't sure I could live up to.

Daniel said, "It's personal. I don't like this."

I stepped back, still holding onto his arm. "Me either. I'm scared, okay? But what am I supposed to do? Stop doing my job? Stop caring because a coward came after me on a hotline, trying to shut me down? I won't do it."

Daniel pulled me closer. "No," he said. "I don't expect you will."

Twenty-nine

On the last Saturday in July, out on the hotel's boat landing, Marco drilled holes through the white and purplish clamshells and hollowed-out coconut halves that Hazel and I had bought a while back at Jolly's, his drill puncturing the air with a high pitched ZZEEEEE ZZEEEEE. Hazel watched through her safety goggles, her hands clamped over her ears.

When I'd called Marco bright and early, asking to borrow the drill, he'd wanted to know what for.

"Hazel and I have a project," I'd told him.

"What sort of project?"

"A . . . um . . . rattle," I told him.

"A *baby* rattle?"

"No, a shark-calling rattle."

"What the hell is a shark-calling rattle?"

"I was telling Hazel about the Kontu people using rattles to call sharks to their boats and she got it in her head to make one. I know, it's . . . it's—"

"Crazy?" Marco offered.

"I was going to say, it's not your average craft. Not like making a pot holder."

He laughed. "No joke."

"Well, she's not your average six-year-old," I said.

"Right. Why don't I drill the holes for you myself?"

Which is how we ended up out here with bits and pieces of coconut flying in all directions. When Marco finished boring the holes, Hazel thanked him by elaborately offering a handshake, and I guessed what was coming next. When we'd bought the shells at Jolly's, the lure of the dollar knickknacks had been too much for her to resist and she'd begged for a hand buzzer to jolt the palms of unsuspecting people. I'd indulged her.

Marco took her hand and yelped while Hazel giggled, and I said I was sorry. He pretended to lunge at her and she ran off along the dock.

"That's like being stuck by a damn catfish," he said.

After he packed his drill and left, Hazel and I sat on the landing alternately stringing clamshells and coconut halves onto a piece of thin rope, which we looped into a circle and secured with a knot.

"It looks like a bracelet for a giant," Hazel proclaimed, giving it a shake.

The clamshells jangled and clanked against the coconuts, making an echoing kind of music. Her eyes widened. "Wow," she said to me. "We should shake hands."

I bit. The small, tinny shock shot to my wrist. I wrangled the awful device from her fingers and chased her with it, asking her to please shake *my* hand.

As we climbed into the hotel's small skiff tied up beside the pontoon, I snapped a picture of Hazel holding up the rattle. I pulled on my khaki Conservancy cap, tugging my ponytail through the back, then battled a light wind as I drove us out into the Gulf and dropped anchor about eighty yards past the channel markers, the hotel's clay-tiled roof still visible. Hazel's hair blew across her eyes. I watched her dig a headband from her dinosaur field bag, push her hair back, and put on her red sunglasses.

"Can I shake the rattle now?" she asked.

"Yep, go for it."

She dropped her arm over the side of the boat and joggled the rattle, while I snapped a few more pictures. The coconuts beat against the side of the boat. The clamshells rapped like hail. The startling commotion traveled across the water, causing me to look back at the beach to see if we'd alarmed the sunbathers.

"You think a shark will come?" she asked.

"Maybe," I said.

I didn't really think a shark would come, but I didn't rule it out either. I mean, stranger things had happened. The library book on the sharks of the South Pacific had pointed out the Kontu people clacked their rattles against the boat and splashed them in the water, mimicking the sounds of a distressed fish. Sharks were biologically built to respond to those vibrations from great distances, so the Kontu were definitely on to something.

Hazel gave the rattle a few more shakes, then rested a few minutes before bending over the side again. "Maybe if I get closer to the water," she said, dipping further.

I gripped the waistband of her shorts while she shook the coconuts and clamshells. A fish jumped nearby, startling her, and she jerked back into the boat.

"It was a ladyfish," I said, laughing.

"What do we do if a shark comes?" she asked.

"We just look at it. From right where we are."

"You try," she said, handing over the rattle.

Dipping it intermittently into the water, I worked it like a marionette while Hazel kept watch for a shark. If one actually showed up, it wouldn't come like a dolphin with the noisy release of air from a blowhole. It would come by stealth. A fin cutting silently across the surface.

"I'm hungry," Hazel announced.

We put the rattle away for peanut butter crackers. Hazel sat at the wheel and nibbled them. I swigged water while the wind, picking up, blew the front of the boat in a semicircle. Cracker crumbs fell onto her shorts, and I watched her with a content, almost lazy feeling drifting through me. She stuffed a whole cracker into her mouth, bulging out her cheeks. Laughing, I pulled an apple juice box from my bag and handed it to her.

"You want to give the shark calling one more shot?" I asked.

Hazel grabbed the rattle and draped herself over the side of the boat.

Gripping the back of her shirt with one hand, I used my other to hold the binoculars to my eyes.

"Do you see a shark yet?" she asked, shouting over the racket she was making.

"Not yet."

I scanned the horizon for fishing vessels. Maybe a boat was out there now pulling in sharks, slashing off their fins, and tossing their bodies overboard.

Hazel said, "If a shark comes, it might be thinking . . . so, *you* called *me*, what do you want?" She set the rattle on one of the boat seats, took off her sunglasses, and frowned at me. "What do we say to it?"

"Good question," I said, at a complete loss how to answer it. I got the sense there was more to her asking than simple curiosity.

"Remember that story you read about the sharks being, you know, *dead* people who come back?" Hazel whispered dead as if the word was too sad or too sacred to speak out loud. "What if the shark that comes is my *mom*?"

I smiled at her. Was this why she'd wanted to make a shark-calling rattle in the first place? Hazel wanted to talk about her mother, that much seemed obvious.

I pieced my words together carefully. "You know, Hazel, I don't think dead family members *really* come back as sharks. It's a kind of myth, or a fairy tale. But if we pretend . . . Let's say it was your mom who came as a shark . . . what would you want to say to her?"

She looked at the sky like she was deciphering the possibilities. "I'd say, Mom, can you see me? Can you see *me and Maeve?* And she'd probably say, Well, *yeesss,* I see you two all the time."

So that's what it was about. Wanting her mother to be okay with the two of us. I said, "How would she feel about seeing us together, I wonder."

"When I'm in bed, I tell her things," Hazel said. "I told her about Shark Club. How you could be my mom. She was okay with it."

She picked up the rattle and began shaking it, more rhythmically now, studying the watery distances.

I listened to the slow drumming sounds pulsing around the boat. All summer I had been summoning ghosts, too—the specter of me and Daniel.

"Do you think my bottle made it to that place you said it would go?" Hazel asked. "Muzum-something?"

It took a moment to remember what I'd told her. "Mozambique?"

"Mozam-*bique*." She enunciated the word with French emphasis the way she did with *gâteau*.

"It's possible," I said, and it suddenly seemed wrong not to tell her. "I'm going there in a few weeks—to Mozambique. I'll let you know if your bottle turns up."

"You're going?" She sank onto the bench, folded her hands in her lap, and stared at me. She looked dejected. I was glad she'd put the sunglasses back on, relieved I couldn't see her eyes.

"Just for a while," I told her.

"What's there, anyway?"

"Whale sharks and big ol' stingrays."

"I wish I could go, too," she said.

"I tell you what. I'll dive with my camera and send you pictures of everything I see. It will be like Shark Club."

"But you'll be back, and then we can have real Shark Club?"

"Promise," I said.

I let her call sharks for a little longer before cranking the boat and starting back toward the hotel landing. We were barely underway when she began shouting. "Shark, shark! Look!"

Turning, I glimpsed a fin, just a flash of one, then it was gone. Whether or not it was a shark, I wasn't sure. It could've been a dolphin. I glanced back again, expecting to see one leaping in our wake. Instead, I spotted a boat trailing forty or fifty yards directly behind us. It was white, sixteen to eighteen feet long. The right front corner of its tan canopy was torn and flapping in the wind.

The boat from the hotline. It was following us.

Leave this alone or you'll be one sorry bitch.

I tightened my grip on the wheel, a quivery feeling at the back of my knees.

Hazel yelled "Shark!" again, jumping up and down, the rattle still in her hand. She was making a deafening noise with it.

I pushed on the throttle, picking up speed, hoping to leave the boat behind, but it accelerated, too, gaining a little, staying menacingly in my wake. I was being given a warning.

I raised the binoculars, catching sight of two men in sunglasses at the bow, but the boat was bouncing too wildly to see much else. I had an irrational urge to swing around and try to get behind them, but Hazel was in the boat and either way it would have been reckless.

Nearing the shore, I slowed down as we came through the channel markers and the white boat peeled off to the right, speeding back out into the Gulf.

I let out a breath.

"Did you see the shark?" squealed Hazel as I eased the skiff alongside the landing. "It came!"

"It came just for you," I said.

Thirty

Before daybreak the following Monday, I was piloting the Conservancy boat back to the marina after a night of shark surveying, when the boat with the torn, tan canopy showed up again.

Olivia, John, and I had gone out the night before at midnight, set the lines, and waited for five and a half hours without sighting a single shark, an utterly fruitless night. I dropped all of them off in the shallow waters behind the Conservancy, watching as they waded to shore in the darkness, then I turned toward the Ten Thousand Islands, heading to the marina to secure the boat.

With a dull ache pulsing behind my eyes, I decided to take a shortcut through the mangrove islands, the floating forests with their tangled exposed roots. Most people stayed away from the canals through the mangroves, but I knew them well. When Robin and I were teenagers, Marco had taught us to navigate them better than most fishing guides.

As I approached Sand Devil Island, the first traces of pink light appeared in the sky. I slowed in an effort not to create a wake along the eroding shoreline where the loggerheads nested. In the 1970s, three houses had been built on Sand Devil before Palermo halted development in favor of preserving the tiny island's pristine environment. As far as I knew, the houses, which were accessible only by boat and mostly obscured now by palms, pines, and inkberry, had been abandoned since the 1980s. It was exactly the kind of place that lent itself to urban legends. It had alternately been a hideaway for Satanists, mobsters, and runaway lovers. Even the Skunk Ape had been spotted here, Florida's smellier, weirder answer to Bigfoot.

Trawling past the southern end of the island, I made out one of the deserted houses through the foliage, a ripped screen hanging from a window, and then suddenly, there it was, tucked in a bend—the white boat with the tan canopy.

It was anchored at a battered dock beside a pontoon boat. I slowed the boat to idle speed, blinking at the name on the pontoon. *Hotel of the Muses.* My heart began to pound.

What was Marco doing here? It made no sense. If he was out fishing, he wouldn't have taken the pontoon—he piloted it strictly for the hotel's sunset cruises—and I couldn't imagine he'd taken a casual spin in the pontoon at dawn. And why was it parked beside the suspicious boat that had followed me and Hazel? My mind refused to believe he could be associated with the men on the boat or mixed up in the shark finnings.

As I tried to order my thoughts and figure out what to do, I cruised past the island, then swung back, cutting the engine before reaching the dock, letting the boat slide in quietly next to the pontoon. Peering over into it, I saw nothing to indicate a problem.

I dug out my phone and dialed Marco's number. When there was no answer, I dialed Sergeant Alvarez, getting her voice mail. "It's Maeve Donnelly. I'm out on Sand Devil Island. The boat that was reported on the hotline, the one I had that encounter with a couple of days ago is tied up at the dock here. Could you come out or send someone?"

I didn't mention the pontoon.

It would've been sensible to leave or to wait in my boat until Alvarez arrived, but that could be hours. I jumped ashore and started up the footpath that led to the interior of the island. It was edged with dense brush, barely wide enough for walking. At a fork, I kept straight, taking out my phone again and dialing Perri.

"I hope I didn't wake you," I said when she picked up. "Have you heard from Marco? Do you know where he is?"

"I haven't spoken with him since yesterday. I assume he's home in bed, like me. Why are you asking?"

"Did he say anything about taking the pontoon out today?"

"No. Where are you?"

"I'm on Sand Devil. It's so weird, the pontoon is docked here."

"Our pontoon? That's odd."

"You think it could've been stolen?" I said, the thought popping into my head for the first time. It brought a small surge of relief— perhaps Marco wasn't here at all.

I could see the back of one of the old houses now. It sat in a clearing about thirty yards away, the paint nearly peeled off, and behind it, some sort of large makeshift tent rigged out of blue tarps.

"Maeve, if you think the boat's been stolen, you shouldn't be there," Perri said.

"True," I said, coming to a halt. The stillness, the hiddenness of the place, the fresh blue tarps—it didn't feel right.

"Would you get out of there?" Perri said.

"Okay, I'm going." I hung up and turned off the ringer.

I slipped from the tree line to the hanging blue tarps, unable to leave without looking inside the tent. As I pulled back the flap, I was hit by the smell of putrefying fish.

Hundreds of shark fins were spread out on a bloodstained oil-cloth. Rows of gray fins lined up neat as gravestones. Peering through the opposite end of the tent, I could see another blue tent on the side of the house. My breathing grew rapid and shallow. *I'm in real danger.*

A door slammed at the house, followed by the sound of voices. Reaching down, I picked up one of the fins, then slipped out of the tent, ducking behind the tarp, gauging whether I could make a dash for the trees without being seen.

The voices belonged to two men, but they were too far away to distinguish the words. As they grew louder, I knew that if I was getting out of here, I had to go now. The place was ground zero for what looked like a huge finning operation, and I didn't want to think what would happen if they found me.

Grasping the shark fin, I bolted into the edge of the woods, where I flattened myself on the ground and listened. The two men were on the opposite side of the tent, out of view, their voices pitched and angry. I struggled to make out what they were saying. If I left without being able to describe them, I would never forgive myself.

I stole along the periphery of the trees, hoping I might get a glimpse of them, feeling for the boat key in my front pocket, keeping my eye on the distance between me and the path.

"This isn't what I signed up for," one of the men said. "Find another guy!"

I knew that voice.

I could say my heart started to beat dangerously fast, or skip beats, or that it stopped altogether. None of that would be true. My heart broke.

Robin. The voice was Robin's.

"You think it's that easy?" the other man said. "You're in it now. You know too much. You think you can just walk away?"

I dropped to the ground as they came into view. The other man was Troy. And there was a third person I'd never seen before. He was young, with blond hair to his shoulders.

"I want out!" Robin shouted.

Still clutching the fin, I crept back toward the path, then broke into a run. Brush and twigs snapped under my shoes. I looked back, afraid I'd made too much noise, but saw no one. As I reached the boat, though, I heard them running, thrashing along the path behind me. I tossed the fin into the stern, yanked the ropes free, and cranked the engine.

As I pulled away, hitting the throttle, I looked back.

Robin and the young guy stood on the crumbling dock, watching me speed away.

When Sand Devil was out of sight, and I was certain neither of the boats was following me, I called Perri and told her I was sorry to have worried her, everything was fine, hoping the unsteadiness in my voice didn't give me away. "Robin and Mindy took the pontoon to Sand Devil for a sunrise picnic," I told her.

I hated lying to Perri, but the truth was too unbearable. There was a pause.

"A sunrise picnic," she said. "Who *does* that?"

⌒

At the marina, I wrapped the shark fin in an old towel I found in the trunk of my car and drove straight to the hotel. In the living room of our apartment, I laid the fin on Robin's *Sports Illustrated* in the middle of the coffee table and waited for him. He would show. Eventually.

I tried his cell over and over. I called the front desk to see if he'd turned up there. I called Mindy's. *Damn it, Robin.* Part of me wanted to go out and look for him, but I had no idea where to start.

I yearned for a shower, but I stood on the balcony watching the guests eating breakfast on the patio, scrutinizing the boats that were rounding the Cape, willing one of them to be the hotel pontoon, and trying to reassure myself that what I'd seen out there wasn't as bad as I thought. But inside I was consumed with shock and churning with anger, confusion, and fear. I wanted to protect Robin and to throw him under the bus at the same time.

At 8:30, my phone went off, the screen flashing *Sergeant Alvarez.*
I let it ring. I *had* to talk with Robin first.

She left a message saying she was sorry for the delay in getting
back to me, and they were heading to Sand Devil now. I could only
hope Robin was long gone by the time she got there.

I paced back and forth from the living room to the kitchen, unable to settle in one spot, and finally wandered into Robin's bedroom,
where I shamelessly poked about for some clue that would make sense
of what had happened. Of course, there was nothing.

When I finally returned to the balcony and peered over the rail, I
spotted the pontoon at the landing. So, where was he?

A half hour later, he came through the door looking shaken and
sweaty, holding a bag from McDonald's. He set it on the coffee table,
peeled back the towel, and glared at the shark fin, drawing back from
the smell before covering it again.

"*You went to McDonald's?*" I said, enraged. "I *saw* you out there
with the fins, and you know I saw you and you still went to McDonald's?" I swung my arm across the table, sending the bag of food onto
the floor. Hash browns littered the carpet. Two McMuffins rolled
out, still bundled in their yellow wrapping.

"You were spying on me!" he yelled. "Why were you following me?"

"I wasn't following you."

"You just happened to be out at Sand Devil?"

"I was coming back from an all-night survey and saw the pontoon.
I thought it'd been stolen."

Robin combed his fingers through his hair.

"You have to turn yourself in," I told him.

"Whoa, whoa. I'm *not* turning myself in."

"Do you get that you could go to jail? The only thing that will save
your ass is telling them everything you know."

"Jesus, Maeve, is there anything you love more than sharks? Not even me? What about Perri? And Daniel? You chose Africa over him. You packed yet?"

He'd been caught. Now he was going to make me pay. I clenched my back teeth, but there was something about his attack that made me observe him coolly and calmly. It was our old pattern at work: someone had to be the grown-up. I was done throwing food. I resented that he got to play the rash, unfiltered child.

"You know," he went on, gesturing at the fin, "I could never understand why you love these god-awful creatures. You almost bled to death because of one, but by all means, let's devote our lives to them. Let's cover the walls with their pictures and put their fucking teeth in jars by the bed."

He walked over and picked up a hash brown off the floor. He took a bite, then walked to the door of my room and peered inside, where the monumental blue shark, the one I'd christened Mona Lisa, glared at him from above my bed.

Needing time to breathe, to restrain myself from slapping his face, I waited while he calmly chewed and swallowed. He seemed to have no awareness that he was drowning and I was the only one here to help.

I said, "Are you ready to talk? Because I need to know how involved you are in all this."

Ignoring me, he stepped into my room. I got up and followed him.

"I don't know how you stand it in here," he said. "Look at this place—a shark over the bed, shark books, shark teeth." His voice had risen, his anger boiling up again, and it frightened me a little. "You've even got Perri painting them," he cried.

He went to my dresser and picked up the little painting she'd created of me with a shark fin growing out of my back.

I reached for it. "Robin, come on."

He slammed the canvas back down, catching it on the corner of the dresser.

"*Stop it!*" I screamed. "*What's wrong with you?*"

I yanked the painting from his hand and stared down at a one-inch rip near the bottom right corner. It seemed like a tiny sinkhole that threatened to swallow me. My eyes filled. Let him go to jail—I didn't care anymore.

Robin stared at me a moment, then blinked incredulously at the torn picture before walking slowly back to the living room.

I ran my finger along the gash, hoping it could be patched, then placed the portrait back on the dresser, my heart hammering through my entire body. I didn't know if our relationship would survive this or if things would ever be the same between us. His novelization of my life was bad enough, but at the moment there were more urgent matters and Robin was being his own worst enemy. I decided that today I would see him through this. Tomorrow . . . I didn't know.

I found him on the sofa. When he saw me, a long exhale streamed from his mouth as if some terrible balloon had burst. He bent over, dropping his forehead to his knees.

"I'm so sorry." He sat up and gave me an imploring and abject look. "It just feels like everything is closing in on me."

I sat down across from him. "Enough, Robin. I need to know one thing. Did you fin those sharks?"

"No, of course not. I had nothing to do with that part of it."

"How did you get mixed up—"

"Troy," he said. "I saw him at Spoonbills a few months ago and he asked if I wanted to make some money, that it wasn't entirely on the up and up. He told me it involved transporting fish. I figured they were illegally caught, that's all, not the worst thing in the world. All I had to do was get them to Savannah. I didn't know the shipment was shark fins. I needed the money, Maeve, and this opportunity was easy money. My book hadn't been accepted at that point. And like I told you, I felt trapped at the hotel. I was trying to come up with enough money so I could leave."

I tried not to react, not to show how sickened and furious I was. "So you found a driver?"

He looked away, unable to meet my eyes. "I drove them myself. But in my defense, I didn't know until the last minute the truck was full of shark fins."

"Illegal trafficking? God, Robin." I stood and paced, needing time to think. "Who did you deliver them to?"

"I can't tell you that," he said.

"Well, who's finning the sharks?"

"Maeve, no."

"Is it Troy and that other guy I saw you with on Sand Devil?"

"Please, Maeve, the less you know the better."

"*Is it them?*"

"Look, I was trying to get out of it," he said, ignoring the question. "Last week right after I saw that shark you put in the freezer, Troy called, telling me there would be another shipment coming up in August and I would have to drive it. I've got no love for sharks, but to see what they did to it . . . it was horrible. I went out there to tell Troy to find somebody else to transport the fins, that I didn't need his money now."

"*But Troy is not letting you out of this,*" I said emphatically. "*I heard him.* Now listen to me, I know someone in the Sheriff's Marine Bureau I can call—"

"No, *you* listen. Troy's not a good guy. He said it would be in my best interest to finish the job and to keep my mouth shut *and my sister's mouth* shut. I think we know what that means."

"He knows it was me out there?" I asked.

"He suspects it was you. By the time he got to the dock, you were nearly out of sight. But the other guy, Harry—he saw it was the Conservancy boat. I told them it was likely somebody was doing a nest count on the beachfront. I doubt they believed that. They're not stupid, Maeve."

"Well, it's only a matter of time before they're caught. I left a message with my contact in the Sheriff's Office. They'll find the fins."

He looked down at his hands, studying them. "No, I don't think they will."

I opened my mouth to ask what he meant, then closed it. "They moved them," I said. "After I left, they moved them. And you helped them."

"I didn't exactly have a choice."

I closed my eyes. All that evidence. "Where? Where are they?"

He sprang to his feet. "I'm trying to protect you and myself. You're going to get us killed."

I didn't know if he was being dramatic, exaggerating out of fear—Troy was a shark finner, not a killer, though it was a fine line—but Robin's panic was contagious.

I said, "The other boat I saw out there—who did it belong to? Is it Troy's?"

"Why?"

"It followed me and Hazel the other day, and someone on that boat threatened me on the Conservancy hotline. You think you're protecting us by not talking, but we're in danger either way. I won't be bullied into doing nothing."

I walked over to him. "Robin, I love you, you know that. But I *have* to call the Marine Bureau and report what I saw out there, and I have to do it now. I don't want to go to them without you, but I will."

He didn't take his eyes from mine. I watched them fill with resignation. He nodded.

"You need a lawyer," I said.

"Yeah," he said. "I'll call Sam."

Sam Lovett had been the hotel attorney for at least two decades. Perri had called on him when Robin was arrested back in high school for peeing behind the Palermo Pub. Later, Sam had even managed to get his record expunged. This time Robin would be lucky to avoid jail time.

While he made the call from his bedroom, I filled the coffeemaker and waited for the drip to start. His words floated through the open door in disjointed pieces competing with the soft grinding sounds from the machine: *Illegal trafficking . . . I didn't know, I swear . . . Sand Devil Island . . . Hundreds of fins . . . His name is Troy Fuller.*

Sam would have his work cut out for him. And Perri would have to know everything.

The call lasted nearly twenty minutes. I sat on a stool at the kitchen counter, leveled by fatigue, and sipped my coffee.

"We should go," he said, emerging with a fresh shirt on and his hair combed. "Sam's meeting us at the Sheriff's Office."

I filled two travel mugs with coffee, handed him one, and found a plastic bag for the shark fin. It was evidence and I was taking it with me. Robin walked to the door, stopped, turned around, and I had a sudden fear he was having second thoughts.

"I didn't mean the things I said to you. The last thing I want to do is hurt you," he said.

I wanted to believe him. I wanted to be magnanimous, but I wasn't capable of it right then.

"I'll drive," I said.

Thirty-one

*T*he Sheriff's Marine Bureau was practically surrounded by water, situated on Palermo Point, the conjunction of two canals and Mangrove Bay. I parked the car in the tiny lot and gazed at the small building with the Mediterranean roof tiles, the freshly planted palms, the American flag fluttering atop the flagpole. The place looked more like a visitor's center than a hub for fighting crime.

We sat there a moment in the quiet without speaking. We were all talked out. Finally, Robin opened the car door and I heard the unmistakable spray from a dolphin's blowhole drift from the canal.

Sam was in the lobby, waiting. I hadn't seen him in years, but he looked the same: the neatly parted white hair, red bow tie, and beat-up briefcase.

He led Robin toward a conference room, while I stood in the corridor holding the bag containing the shark fin, lingering in case Robin looked back. When Sam opened the door, I caught a glimpse of Sergeant Alvarez inside seated at a table. Stepping through, Robin turned and looked at me, as I knew he would, and his face was filled with restrained panic. The sight of it triggered a flash of him at six years old, waking from one of his nightmares with this same pale, frightened expression. I remembered how I had touched his forehead back then and told him he was going to be okay.

"Robin," I called as the door began to close. "It'll be okay."

An hour later, after a Fish and Wildlife official and an assistant DA had come and gone, Alvarez found me in the lobby.

"Your *brother?*" she said, shaking her head. "Unbelievable."

"What's going on in there?" I asked.

"Robin's involvement is limited to interstate commerce trafficking. His lawyer managed to negotiate a plea deal, and in exchange, Robin told us everything: Troy Fuller's role, the names of the other finners, where they moved the fins, the persons receiving the illegal shipments in Savannah."

"It's over, then."

"Your brother will have a hefty fine to pay, maybe probation, but yeah, it looks like it's pretty much over. For him, anyway."

"Here," I said, handing her the bagged shark fin. "I took it from Sand Devil this morning."

"My God," she said. "I don't know if you were being brave or stupid, but you never should've ventured onto the island. It was reckless. But hey . . . thanks," she said, holding up the bag. "Come on, I need to get your statement."

In her office, I watched Alvarez transfer the fin into an evidence bag, then seal and label it.

"There were hundreds of those," I told her.

For the next twenty minutes she took down my account of what had happened on Sand Devil.

She reported that when she'd gotten there, the fins were gone. She'd found nothing but large brown patches where the oilcloths had lain, along with one blue tarp that had been left behind, no doubt in a hurry. Thanks to Robin, though, they now knew where to look for the fins.

"I just hope you catch these guys," I told her.

"We already have deputies searching for Troy. We'll find him, but until we do you and brother watch your backs, okay?"

"Yeah, we will," I said, beleaguered by the last twelve hours.

"Your brother is going to be here a while longer," she said. "Why don't you go home and get some rest. I'll call you when we've wrapped everything up."

Outside, I stood atop a corner of the seawall, letting it sink in: Robin was emerging from this fairly unscathed. Good news for him, but there was little justice in it for the sharks. The current created tiny vortexes that rolled and swirled until they gave out of steam and joined the tidal stream again. I lifted my arms and stretched, letting the sun shine on my face and exhaling loudly like the dolphin had.

⌒

At noon I tapped on Perri's office door, took a breath, a deep one, and walked in, intending to break the news about Robin. To my disappointment *and* my relief, she wasn't there. I stood in the empty room and gazed at the framed photo she'd kept on her desk for the last twenty-three years: Robin and me on our seventh birthday, less than one year after our parents were killed. We were posing beside the hotel pool in wet bathing suits and pirate's hats, holding slices of cake and grinning madly.

I walked to the window and stared at the scene below, the pool fringed in palms, and beyond it, the beach sloping into the Gulf, the same beautiful picture as always, but it felt splintered and muted. I sank into Perri's desk chair and rubbed my thumb across the glass over the photo, then dialed Perri's cell.

"I'm down on the landing," she said. "Marco and I are about to take the pontoon for a spin."

"I see you," I told her. "I'm standing at your office window."

She looked up and waved with both arms. "Marco installed some new speakers on the boat last weekend for his guided tour and wants to test them out on me, but we both know it's just an excuse for him to throw a fishing rod and get me out of the office." She laughed. She sounded so happy and unfettered, so insulated from the truth that was about to land on her. How could I tell her the grandson she'd raised was in trouble, and not for pissing in a parking lot?

"We need to talk," I said.

I could see Marco already on the pontoon, fiddling with the engine. "Wait. I'm coming, too." I hung up before she could ask questions.

When I reached the landing, Marco asked me to untie the boat. I tossed the ropes into the pontoon and hopped in.

We cruised parallel to shore for a short while before he swung toward open water, pushing the engine wide open, creating a wake for hitchhiking dolphins. Perri and I sat in the back as three of them drafted, leaped, and flopped, and then, one by one, veered off. These moments were a kind of balm. I tried to soak them in.

"So, what did you want to talk about?" Perri asked. With the engine revved and the wind rushing past our ears, I'd barely heard her.

When I didn't answer right away, she repeated, louder, "What . . . did . . . you . . . want . . . to . . . talk . . . about?"

I held up a hand, motioning for her to wait until Marco slowed down. Finally, he cut the engine and we drifted to a stop. As he lowered the anchor, I said quietly, "It's Robin."

"Perri, you want a rod?" Marco called, unaware of what he was interrupting.

There was an awful swell of silence as he turned, and seeing her face, how grave and still it was, he laid down the fishing rod and sat beside her.

"Just tell us," she said.

I went through it piece by piece, recounting what I knew, trying to say it in order, as if the chronology mattered. I started with the boat that had been reported on the hotline, how I'd stumbled on it at Sand Devil this morning, and the shock of finding Robin there with Troy and the long-haired guy and hundreds of fins. I told them about my confrontation with Robin at the hotel and the part he'd played in it all. It was like laying out the pieces of some bizarre jigsaw on a table, trying to make sense of them. It occurred to me I was doing it for myself as much as for Perri. She didn't interrupt, not once.

When I explained that Robin was still at the Sheriff's Office, having spilled his guts, and was being punished with a fine and most likely probation, relief flooded her face. I should have started with that.

Perri walked to the rail of the boat, where she stared at the faint line between water and sky, and I felt how strange it all was, sitting on a boat in the Gulf explaining how my brother had been involved with shark finning.

"So stupid," Perri said, shaking her head, then turned back. "What the hell was he thinking?"

Marco, who had been sitting calmly, suddenly stood and walked to the front of the boat. He slammed his fist onto the console. "Troy—that son of a bitch."

The console was still vibrating when Alvarez called. "You can come get your brother," she said. "And Maeve, we got Troy Fuller—he's in custody."

I hung up. "Let's head back. I have to get Robin."

"I'm going with you," Perri said.

When we arrived, Robin was outside, sitting on the seawall. Perri had been subdued on the way over, but now she crossed the parking lot with resolve, so much so, I had to quicken my pace to keep up with her. Robin stood and buried his hands in his pockets. I didn't know what was going on behind his sunglasses, but I imagined he had the same fear-struck look he'd had earlier stepping into the conference room.

"Maeve explained everything," Perri told him. I envisioned him rolling his eyes a little as he considered my version of it.

"If I'd known driving a truck to Savannah would lead to all this I never would've done it," he said, giving her a grin.

"Well, you weren't just taking a road trip, now were you?" she said, not in the mood to be charmed.

He lowered his eyes. "I'm sorry, Perri. I don't know what to say, except I'm sorry."

She wrapped her arms around him, and his face relaxed, but she wasn't finished. "I'm glad you're sorry, but you're thirty years old, Robin. You've got to cut this shit out."

〜

Later that afternoon, in the serenity of my apartment, I showered, lingering under the spray, as the acute shock of what Robin had done began to wear off and settle into a painful reality.

I wrapped my bathrobe around me. Postponing the crushing need for sleep a little longer, I called Daniel, who was down in the kitchen. As I recounted the discovery I'd made on Sand Devil and Robin's involvement, my voice took on a serrated edge, the anger flaring all over again.

Within five minutes, he was at my door. He put his arms around me and I felt the heat of his breath on my cheek. He said, "For God's sake, what were you doing sneaking around on that island?"

I felt a little scolded. Like a child who wanders off from her mother in the store and when she's found is embraced first, then walloped. He was scared, and maybe a little bewildered. He let go of me, and I remembered how flummoxed he'd looked after I'd surfaced from retrieving Hazel's binoculars from the bottom of the Gulf. Like he didn't quite know me. He looked that way now.

I sat on the end of the bed, then lay back and rubbed my eyelids, weighted with fatigue.

"Are you okay?" he asked.

"Just tired. And relieved. I'm glad it's over."

He sank down beside me. "I can't believe you got Robin to turn himself in."

"It wasn't easy, but he came around."

"No, I mean, he's your brother. Your twin."

I sat up. "Are you saying you wouldn't have?"

He hesitated. "I honestly don't know," he said.

"Well, you have no idea what it was like to be in that position," I said. "When I saw the hotel boat docked out there, I called the Marine Bureau, but I didn't know it was Robin. . . . And how could I ignore . . ." I stopped. I didn't have the reserves left inside to defend myself.

Daniel looked past me as if formulating what to say. "You're right, you didn't really have a choice. I know. I'll let you get some sleep."

After he left, I pulled the shades, sealing out the brightness of the Gulf, and lay in the dim light. Robin had accused me of loving sharks above everything else. And maybe that's what Daniel thought, too. It wasn't fair. And yet, a suitcase sat in the closet waiting to be packed. I was leaving Daniel and Hazel. I was leaving for the whale sharks.

Thirty-two

On the afternoon of the hotel's twenty-fifth anniversary party, I lay stretched across the Turkish rug in Perri's room staring at the ceiling, and then at her foot, which bounced near my head as she sat, legs crossed, on her sofa.

It had been almost a week since Robin had turned himself in, and in the immediate aftermath, I'd assumed Perri would cancel the party. That, it turned out, was unthinkable to her. "There has been a Book Bash every year since the hotel opened," she told me. "Even the year your parents died. I'm sure as hell not going to let Robin's troubles spoil it."

His involvement in the shark finning had been a fresh, unquenchable scandal all week, but rather than discouraging guests to attend, Perri insisted it would bring them out in droves just to see if Robin made an appearance.

"Is that a toe ring?" I asked, staring at the thin silver band on her toe.

"I'm trying it out," she said.

"So what are you going to paint on the clamshell this time?" I asked, pointing to a canvas sitting on the easel, blank except for a pencil tracing of the shell.

"I'm not sure yet. You know, it's no surprise I've got my easel out

now, with you heading to Africa. I get very productive when I'm missing you."

I propped on my elbows. "I'll be back before Christmas."

"I know, honey. Have you started packing?"

"A little." The rug scratched at my elbows, turning the skin red. I
got up and sat in the chair beside her.

"Is Nicholas going?" she asked, and I glanced at her sideways, catching something in her voice. As if she were fishing a little about him.

"I think it's safe to say he's not. I haven't heard from him since he
left here."

"Does he know what happened?"

"With the finnings, you mean?"

Perri nodded.

"I don't know. I imagine Sergeant Alvarez called him about it. Or
he caught it on the news."

"I thought maybe *you* might have called him about it," she said.

"He made it clear he couldn't see me. I'm honoring that. It's the
least I can do."

"And Daniel? How is he with your leaving?"

"He doesn't totally understand why I'm going." I curled my legs in
and held my bare feet. For a second I contemplated a toe ring, too,
then dismissed the idea. I wasn't a toe ring person. Maybe when I
was seventy-eight like Perri. "Daniel's birthday is next Saturday,"
I added.

"You planning a party?"

"A small one. It'll be just me and Hazel. Daniel is baking his own
cake for a change."

I thought of all the twelfths of August that we'd been separated,
the mornings I'd wakened and realized what day it was, then wished
I hadn't remembered at all. I would wonder how he was celebrating.
Would he be alone or would there be a dinner out with friends, with

Robin, maybe with a girl? This year he would blow out his candles with me and Hazel there to sing to him. Thinking of him caused me to reach up and touch the shark tooth that hung at my throat, the little white dagger that had once been lodged in my leg.

Perri smacked her hands together, making me jump. "The party's in less than two hours!" she announced. "I've got a ton to do, and you've got to dust off your top hat."

My annual George Sand menswear costume. I didn't know if I could face it.

"You're still not going to tell me what *your* costume is?" I asked, hoping she would leak the big secret.

"You'll see soon enough," she said.

～

I flicked through the hangers in my closet, making a last-ditch effort to go as someone other than George Sand, trying to imaginatively adapt my shorts and sundresses into some sort of costume. Finally, I pulled out the black wet suit at the back of the closet, the one reserved for winter dives.

My diving fins and scuba mask were stored in a plastic Tupperware container beneath the bed. Flattening my face against the carpet, I pulled it out, along with Robin's manuscript. For something that had caused me so much distress, the book looked far less threatening now than when I'd kicked it under the bed. I flipped through the pages, looking for a mention of Margaret and Derek, curious how they'd ended up. I placed it on the bedside table. I would finish reading it, finally.

At 7:30, half an hour late, Robin appeared in the living room looking handsome in his Gatsby tuxedo. Wearing the dive suit, I flapped across the carpet in my fins, positioning the mask over my face.

"Is this some Twenty Thousand Leagues Under the Sea thing?" Robin asked.

"I'm Her Deepness, Sylvia Earle."

Robin couldn't resist laughing as he said, "Never heard of her."

"She's an oceanographer and an author." I held up my battered copy of *Sea Change*.

Robin and I were finding our way. Over these past five days, he'd showed up twice at the Conservancy with mango ices and jerk chicken wraps from the Shrimp Shack. A third time he'd appeared in my office with a small package he'd laid on my desk.

"Open it," he said.

Inside was the birthday painting Perri had given me. The tear was mended; there was a small, neat seam where the gash had been. I'd noticed the painting was missing and suspected he'd taken it to be repaired. He was trying hard to make things right.

"Thank you," I said.

He couldn't take back the hurtful words he'd hurled or unreveal some of his long and deeply held perceptions of me; we could only forgive and move on. I feel like that's what transpired when he brought me the mended painting—a tacit but mutually agreed understanding that we would do just that.

It hit me now, however, that despite our unspoken truce, despite our bond, it wasn't my job to rescue him or show him the way. I would let that go, as I should have done long ago, and just pray writing would bring him satisfaction or, at the very least, keep him out of trouble.

I saw him cast a look of dread at the door. Looping my arm through his, I said, "The first five minutes will be the worst."

"Right. And in no time they'll all be too drunk to whisper about me."

Perri had outdone herself this time. Chandeliers and tea lights threw flecks of light across the dining-room walls and pink roses and faux seaweed cascaded out of giant clamshells on the tables. Costumed characters were everywhere, as if spilled from a bizarro literary piñata. They sipped wine, holding little glass plates, wandering through the French doors onto the terrace where the Hurricane Trio played. Guitar, keyboard, and steel drum. The lead singer, who was known only as Dinah, and who claimed Otis Redding as a distant relation, was singing a calypso version of "Sittin' on the Dock of the Bay."

As we cut through the crowd, my fins slapping the marble floor, I tried to step in time with the music. Robin and I made our best guesses at the costumes: a Nancy Drew, a Poe, Hermione and Harry Potter, Jane Austen, a girl with a dragon tattoo. The philosophers in togas were pretty self-explanatory. The Holden Caulfield required a name tag. Peter Pan was a no-brainer.

Mindy appeared across the room in a silvery ball gown with an enormous hoop skirt. She'd turned up as Cinderella after all. Robin hurried toward her, and I froze, fearing she might turn her back, but she opened her arms. Apparently she was sticking with him.

I pushed the mask to the top of my head and looked around for Perri. Finding her on the terrace, I paused and took in the sight of her. *My God.* She wore a long, tattered, white satin dress, gloves with missing fingers, and strands of garish gray beads around her neck. A disheveled veil the color of yellow beeswax floated around her head, held in place by a wreath of dead, crispy-brown flowers.

I walked over to her. "Miss Havisham?"

"What do you think? Not bad, right?" She hiked the hem of her skirt to reveal she was wearing one white shoe.

"You nailed it," I said. "And before you comment on *my* outfit, I'm not dressed as myself. I'm Sylvia Earle. An oceanographer and a *writer.*"

"It's perfect," she said.

Hazel materialized at my side.

"Look at you, Angelina Ballerina," I said to her. Dressed as the dancing mouse in paper ears, a pink leotard, and a gauzy skirt, with a tail made of rope, she held the tail, twirling it like a lasso.

"Who are *you*?" she asked Perri.

"I'm the jilted old bride in *Great Expectations*," she told her.

Hazel looked at her blankly. "Grandma is Sherlock Holmes. Look at her pipe."

Van trailed Hazel in a real-deal houndstooth deerstalker hat, a sheer brown capelet around her shoulders, pretending to puff on a pipe. We laughed over each other's getups and watched the guests dancing on the terrace. When a waiter came by with a tray of Gruyère-stuffed mushrooms, we each took one, except Hazel, who wrinkled her nose at the brown buttons.

"Why don't we find something for you to eat," I said, leading her to Daniel's buffet table. She wandered past the tenderloin, shrimp, and salmon, past the prosciutto-wrapped asparagus, charcuterie, goat cheese and Stilton blues, past the spinach orzo salad, the crostini, and olives, all the way to the fruit. She stabbed toothpicks into strawberries and watermelon chunks, filling her plate.

We sat at a high-top table on the terrace, where she devoured the lot of them.

Marco wandered up in monochromatic gray, his pants tucked into rain boots, a Cape Cod fisherman's cap on his head. I eyed his name tag. CALL ME ISHMAEL, it said.

"I need to borrow this mouse for a second," he said, and Hazel hopped down and followed him.

Minutes later, Perri's voice came through the band's speakers. "Thank you all for being here. I'm thrilled you came to celebrate the Hotel of the Muses' annual Book Bash."

She stood at the end of the terrace, the Gulf stretched endlessly behind her. She was flanked by two of the rose-filled clamshells on pedestals. In her outlandish Miss Havisham wedding dress, and with the sun turning gaudy colors behind her, the scene was theatrical.

Daniel slid into Hazel's vacated chair. "What's going on?" he whispered, as Hazel and Marco sidled up next to Perri.

I shrugged. "Beats me."

Hazel was holding a sand bucket in one hand, twirling her mouse tail with the other.

"I'm grateful for this place," Perri said. "For twenty-five years it's been a hotel, a book haven, and home. And tonight, it's where Marco and I are getting married."

I gasped. Applause broke out.

"Did you know about this?" Daniel asked.

"Not a clue," I said.

"Maeve and Robin, would you join us?" Perri asked.

I duckwalked over to her, Robin falling in beside me, giving me a stupefied look. The priest from the island's Episcopal Church emerged from the crowd dressed as, of all things, a priest. The wedding was happening, officially and spiritually, and I felt the joy and rightness of it. Almost against my will, I pictured myself at a wedding altar with Daniel promising to love and cherish till death do us part, and I was surprised at the odd hesitation that rose up in me. Glancing back at Daniel, wanting to reassure myself, I saw him watching Hazel with an adoring expression. One of the things that most drew me to him was his love for her, but this time it didn't quiet my anxiety. My flesh spiked with heat and disconcertion under the wet suit. I tried to focus on Perri, who looked cool and ready and content.

I leaned in close to her ear. "You're finally doing it," I whispered.

"What can I say? It's our time."

As the priest led them through their vows, I felt Robin's hand on my shoulder. I reached up and squeezed it. I looked for Daniel, but didn't see him.

When the priest pronounced them husband and wife, Marco

cued Hazel, who stepped forward with the sand bucket, slowly tipping it to create a circle of Gulf sand around Perri and Marco. They shared a kiss then, and Perri gleefully announced, "Reader, I married him." A famous line from *Jane Eyre*. The crowd burst into laughter.

As Marco and Perri danced in the center of the terrace, a small hand slipped into mine. Hazel. She was still holding the sand bucket.

"You did a good job up there," I told her.

"Let's dance," she said.

"Yeah? You want to?"

I set down my champagne flute and pulled off my fins, leaving them under a table. Following suit, Hazel placed the bucket next to my glass and began taking off her ballet slippers.

"You don't have to take your shoes off, too," I told her. "I only did it because there's no way I can dance in fins." But she was already lining them up beside mine.

She skipped out among the other dancers. I took her hands, swinging her arms side to side, not really sure what to do.

"Twirl me," she said.

I spun her around. Again and again. Each time she pivoted more quickly and with more energy, her tissuey skirt floating like a spiderweb. Through the wide French doors, I saw Daniel inspecting the food on the buffet. As he stepped to the edge of the terrace, I waved my hand in the air.

"Hazel, where are your shoes?" he asked, joining us on the dance floor.

"Maeve's barefoot, too," she said.

"But you know where they are?"

She nodded.

"You want to dance with me?" he asked her.

I relinquished her to him and wandered to the sideline, where I observed Hazel on her tiptoes and Daniel doing his best not to step on her feet. Finally, he picked her up. She seemed to enjoy the view from up high, her head twisting right and left, taking in everything. Gazing at them, I was filled with love for her.

It suddenly hurt to keep watching, and I knew what was coming— the terrible thought that had wanted to come for so long. It welled inside of me and this time, I let it. *I'd returned to Daniel. But I'd stayed because of Hazel.*

When the song ended, Daniel put Hazel down and dipped her. I lowered myself into a chair. The wave of heat I'd felt earlier congealed into a sick feeling in the bottom of my stomach. Loss, dread, inevitability, and relief. On the other side of the terrace, Van clapped and Hazel ran to her.

The band broke into "How Deep Is the Ocean," and Daniel came over and led me back onto the dance floor. The sun was gone, the sky had gilded over. Servers moved past us lighting the torches. Inside, beyond the long windowpanes, the chandeliers were dimmed and candlelight flickered.

"Here, take this off," Daniel said, and reached for the mask around my neck. I stretched it over my head, my hair snagging in the rubber strap, and let it hang from my elbow. I looked at his throat, unable to meet his eyes.

Everything between us felt tenuous, threadbare, about to split open. Dinah swayed as she sang, lifting her arms like the wings of a frigate bird. Daniel pulled me closer, and I felt myself pull back the tiniest bit. I think he felt it, too.

Since I was a kid, it had always been Daniel. Even when we were apart, I'd lived with the ghost of him. I'd made a nightly pastime of remembering and imagining him.

Resurrecting what used to be. Idealizing what we might have had. I'd circled back to the place where he'd been severed from my life, trying to graft him back on. What I loved was the memory of him, the hope of him. I loved Daniel, but mostly a Daniel I'd created, one that didn't really exist except inside of me.

In June, when I'd returned from Bimini and found him here, I'd been willing to plunge over the falls, not knowing where we'd land. I'd been hesitant to think much about our future, preferring to luxuriate in single moments: opening the door to him after his workday, coaxed by him into the Gulf late at night, the moments that had made the blood pulse at my wrists. I'd been afraid to ponder a future with Daniel because it would've excavated a truth I wasn't ready for. I couldn't stay with him just to be with Hazel.

"Is this what you want?" I asked.

Daniel stopped moving. He looked at me, and I felt like he knew what I was about to say.

"What if we forget about what we wanted when I was twenty-two and you were twenty-three, and we thought about what we want *now.*" I swallowed. "Maybe it's not the same thing. Daniel, what if it's not the same thing?"

He took a step back. He said, "What are you saying, Maeve?"

"It feels like we're trying to finish something we started years ago. To make it come out right this time."

He frowned, letting the words settle. I watched the skin around his mouth and eyes tighten. We were the only two people not moving on the dance floor. My hands felt like hot rocks in his. He let go of them.

"You can't be serious," he said through clamped teeth, spitting out the words like hard, bitter pits. "You're really doing this . . . *again?*"

"I'm sorry. Please, Daniel, let's just go someplace and talk—"

"Save it," he said, cutting me off.

The song ended abruptly. Applause broke out. His eyes contracted into small, dark beads. They were shining with pain and anger and disbelief. He shifted them from me to Hazel, who was standing off to the side with Van. At that moment, she bit into a strawberry.

He walked away. I watched him scoop up Hazel, her chin bouncing above his shoulder, the white bottoms of her feet dangling at his waist. Turning, I saw my diving fins beneath the table beside her pink ballet slippers.

I gathered them and sat at the table with her shoes in my lap. Robin and Mindy danced. The newlywed couple danced. A waiter came around and offered me champagne that I drank too rapidly. Around me, the torches and music and partygoers swirled in a way that reminded me the world would not slow down for my pain. After an hour or so, the party dwindled, and finally Marco and Perri said good-bye to the last of the guests.

I slipped out of the chair, and holding onto Hazel's shoes, I hugged them both.

"It was wonderful," I told them. "Congratulations."

"Thank you, honey. You okay?" Perri asked.

"Oh, I'm fine. I'm danced out, I think. Just tired." I wouldn't burden her. Not now.

"Well, I don't know about you, but I could sleep for days," Perri said.

Marco kissed her head and gave me the biggest smile. We said good night, and I walked through the quiet dining room to the kitchen.

~

Daniel's staff worked to clean up like lethargic bees, the usual electric energy having given way to fatigue and doing what must be done. I paused inside the doorway, scanning the room for Daniel, when the young woman who had burned the prosciutto all those weeks ago caught my eye. She stared at me and the little shoes I carried and pointed to Daniel's office.

I found him sitting on the edge of his desk looking stiff and stoic in Rodin's *Thinker* pose. Noticing me, he poured a beer into a glass, breaking the stillness. I started to speak, but Daniel held up a hand, downed half the glass, then offered it to me. I shook my head.

"There was no way I wasn't going down this road with you," he said quietly. The anger seemed to have left him.

His eyes turned watery, the way they'd looked the day he'd pulled me from the Gulf when I was twelve. "But you're probably right," he said. "Maybe it needs to be finished."

I wanted to reach out and touch him, but I didn't. "I have no regrets," I told him. It felt overwhelmingly true right then. I would never have finished with Daniel if I hadn't gone down this road. There would always have been the what-if, the what-might-have-been.

"I'll explain it to Hazel," he said.

"I can talk to her, you know. If you want me to."

He shook his head. "No, it should be me."

"What will you tell her?" I asked.

"That we're friends," he said, and shrugged a bit.

I was afraid of pushing too far where she was concerned, but I couldn't seem to help myself. "I would like to keep seeing Hazel . . . if it doesn't confuse her. I don't want her to think I abandoned her."

Daniel exhaled, taking a moment. "I guess you and I can find a way to stay in the Shark Club with her, right? That doesn't have to change."

"Thank you," I said, trying to hide the relief I felt.

"That is, if Hazel wants it," he added.

The idea that she might blame me, that she might not want me in her life anymore had not seemed possible until now. The pressure that had built behind my eyes broke into a tiny stream of tears. I swallowed and wiped them away.

"What about your birthday?" I said, remembering that there were plans for the three of us to celebrate it together.

"I need to think, Maeve. I'll do what's best for her."

I had no doubt he would. I set Hazel's ballet slippers next to him on the desk and left.

Thirty-three

*E*xcept for a stack of bathing suits, my suitcase was empty. The rest of my clothes and a wet suit were spread across the bed, waiting to be folded, rolled, and squeezed into the bag. Only a few days ago Perri had gotten married and I'd ended things with Daniel, and though I didn't leave for Mozambique for another week, the urge to pack had been irrepressible.

I paused before the sliding glass doors, catching the blaze of afternoon light on the panes, and for a moment it felt as though my life existed inside a small golden box. I tugged open the doors and stepped onto the balcony. I gave my arm a rub. I'd gotten the required shots for travel to Mozambique: typhoid and hepatitis A. The two purple bruises had started to yellow, but the tenderness remained.

Standing there with the sound of the Gulf rushing up, I almost missed the knock on my door. Opening it, I found Daniel and Hazel in the hallway. It was unexpected. Since the breakup I hadn't seen either of them.

"I made this," Hazel said sheepishly, handing me a hand-drawn invitation to Daniel's birthday party, a sheet of light blue construction paper with crayoned pictures of sharks in party hats. The celebration would take place Saturday night, August 12. Dinner and cake on Botticelli's terrace. Shark Club members only.

"Can you come?" she asked in a different voice that didn't seem to belong to her.

I hesitated, studying her. Was she taking the breakup well or was Daniel having to scramble eggs for her in the middle of the night? Was she okay or was she putting on a brave face? I looked at Daniel. He nodded. *It's fine. Come to the party.*

I crouched in front of Hazel. "Of course I'll be there."

She threw her arms around my neck and I held her, feeling her small shoulders pressed against mine and her tight, knotted grip. When she turned loose, her mouth twisted a little.

I smoothed the hair from her face. "You don't have to worry about not seeing me, all right?"

"All right," she said.

"There's chocolate ice cream in the kitchen," Daniel told her.

I stood in the corridor and watched them get onto the elevator, waiting to see if she would poke her head out before the doors closed and grin at me as she'd always done in the past, an utterly small thing, but somehow, at that moment it felt like everything. The doors began to close, but then her head popped out, automatically jarring the doors open again. She waved. Her mouth was not quite smiling, but she looked thoroughly pleased. Thoroughly Hazel.

On August 12, when I arrived on the dining terrace, the sun and moon were out at the same time, bookending the sky. The entire terrace was roped off, reserved for just us. Among all the tables, one was adorned with a white tablecloth and set for three.

Hazel was at the far end, leaning over the rail, taking in the beach, while Daniel stood behind her.

"I'm ready for cake," I called, but they didn't hear me over the waves. I was on the verge of saying it again, but the words suddenly seemed awkward and unnatural. I walked up unannounced.

Hazel hugged me while Daniel watched, his face a mask of

reserve and uncertainty. We exchanged stilted hellos, after which Hazel led me to the table for what I imagined would be the most subdued birthday celebration ever.

A pizza delivery guy appeared, stepping apprehensively onto the terrace, no doubt wondering if he'd arrived at the correct address. Daniel met him, retrieving several bills fom his wallet, then took two giant pizza boxes from him.

"Your dad didn't cook?" I said to Hazel. "I can't believe it."

"He made the cake," she said. "But it's a surprise what kind it is."

"Dinner is served," Daniel said, setting the boxes on the table.

Hazel flipped open one of the lids and inspected the pizza. All cheese. Not a vegetable in sight. Daniel's name may have been on the invitation, but this party was for Hazel. I caught his eye and smiled. He managed a smile back before snapping open his napkin and grabbing a slice.

As we ate, we talked about Hazel's school starting next week. Hazel gave me the highlights of her back-to-school shopping. An eraser shaped like a mobile phone, an Angelina Ballerina lunchbox, and rainbow shoelaces.

The sunlight waned and the soft outside lights turned on along with the festive string bulbs. We'd nearly finished off one of the pizzas when Daniel retrieved a covered cake pedestal and lifted off the top to reveal a rather plain, three-layered cake iced white. It didn't rouse much elation from Hazel until he cut into it.

"Chocolate!" she exclaimed.

"Wait," I said. "What about candles?"

"Oh right," Daniel said, reaching in his pocket. "But they'll never stay lit in this wind."

"Let's try," I said.

Hazel and Daniel arbitrarily stuck five candles into the top of the cake, and we huddled around it, trying to block the wind, laughing. Daniel was right, the tiny flames blew out almost as soon as he lit the wicks. When we got one flame to stay put, Hazel and I sang a speedy "Happy Birthday," racing each other to the end.

"Make a wish," Hazel shouted. "Hurry."

A wish. He looked at me, and I had to look away, the awkwardness I'd felt when I'd first arrived returning.

Daniel put big slices onto our plates. After we'd devoured them, Hazel leaned back in her chair, purposely sticking out her belly, and threatened to eat another piece.

"Give it a few minutes," Daniel said.

Voices erupted from the beach, and Hazel wandered to the rail and peered over. "There are lots of people down there," she said.

As the tumult grew, Daniel and I joined her. A crowd was gathered around a loggerhead turtle nest. The babies were hatching.

~

We hurried down to the beach, where the throng was forming a horseshoe around the nest, leaving a wide path to the water. A Fish and Wildlife officer was already there, waving people back, cautioning them not to use flashlights or camera flashes, and kindly bending down to smooth away the mounds and indentations in the baby turtles' runway, anything that would sabotage the hatchlings' break for the water. Only one in a thousand would make it to adulthood.

The wind blew even harder beside the water, and Hazel put on Daniel's hoodie, cinching it around her face. The three of us squeezed through the crowd until we found a spot along the runway. I stood behind Hazel with my hands on her shoulders.

The crowd squealed as four hatchlings crawled from the nest, pushing their flippers against the sand like small, willful oars.

"Maeve, baby turtles. Look!" Hazel yelled. The whole scene felt strangely miraculous.

I cast a glance at Daniel. Where does love like ours go? It had lingered for so long, like the soul that stays behind after the death of a physical body, refusing to depart. Maybe some part of me and Daniel would always remain, orbiting the edges. I only knew my life didn't feel entwined with his anymore, that this time there was more freedom in the loss than pain.

Two more hatchlings emerged and joined the others. Each time one reached the surf the onlookers cheered. When the last turtle had disappeared into the waves, folks hung around inspecting the nest. Hazel ran to the shoreline and stared at the water, as if trying to glimpse some last trace of them.

"She needs you," Daniel said.

I loved him for saying that.

"They're out there *somewhere*," Hazel announced as she sauntered back to us.

Daniel leaned in close to me. "Why don't you take a few minutes with her? I have some cleaning up to do back on the terrace."

"You sure?"

"Yeah. You're leaving soon and I think she would like it. Just bring her back to the kitchen."

"Thanks," I said.

"Be safe where you're going, okay?"

"I will."

Before leaving Daniel informed Hazel she could "hang" with me for a little bit, and she immediately came up with an idea.

"You wanna look for shark teeth?" she asked.

"What, by moonlight? Okay." I pointed at the sky. "But look up there. If that cloud covers the moon, we're in trouble."

"We better hurry," she said.

She took off for the top of the beach where there was a bit more light. I chased behind her. We sat on the bottom step of the hotel access stairs.

"This counts as Shark Club," she said, scooping up a palm full of sand and parsing through it with her index finger.

"Oh, it definitely does," I said. For a few moments we worked in silence. "So. You know I'm going to Africa. To Mozambique. Remember?"

She pulled the big hoodie down over her knees. "Yeah," she said, so quietly I barely heard.

"But when I get back, we can have Shark Club again, if you want to."

"Can we?"

"Of course. We can have our next meeting on whale sharks. I'll have lots of whale shark stories to tell you when I get back."

"Okay," she said. Then, "You're not Dad's girlfriend anymore."

"Not anymore. We're friends, though."

"You won't be my mom."

"No. But I'll always love you."

She looked at me and nodded. "There are no teeth in this sand," she said.

"Come on, your legs are covered in chill bumps."

I took her hands and tugged, and Hazel made an exaggerated leap into the air. "Aunt Maeve," she sang.

Thirty-four

*O*n the way to the research center on Tofo Beach, I stuck my head out of the truck window, letting the wind smack me awake. After thirty straight hours of travel—Fort Myers, Atlanta, Amsterdam, Johannesburg, Maputo, Inhambane—I was dog-tired, relieved to be off the plane, and drinking in all the fresh air my lungs could hold.

I had said my farewells to Perri and Marco at airport security. Perri's parting words were the same as every other time I'd left on one of these shark research terms: *Come home in one piece.* I'd given her and Marco a hug, then watched the newlyweds stroll away, holding hands.

The night before, when I'd told Robin good-bye, I'd handed him back his manuscript. "I finished it," I'd said.

"And? You're okay it?"

"I'm fine with it," I told him. With time I'd come to see the story he'd written wasn't the same as my own. Yes, his character Margaret had plucked an osprey feather from the water before sharing her first kiss with a boy who would eventually become her fiancé. Yes, she would be bitten by a shark. And yes, she would be jilted and left brokenhearted. But the similarities more or less ended there. Margaret ends up inheriting a boutique hotel in Vermont, where she feels trapped in a life she never wanted. In the end, she returns to the island of her youth and reunites with Derek. By giving them a happy ending, perhaps Robin was trying to get the ending he wanted for himself.

"Just one question—you were writing about yourself and Rachel, weren't you?"

"Maybe you're right," he said.

"You think you can still have that ending with Mindy?"

"Hope so. We'll see."

Robin had found a place of his own, a small apartment not too far from the hotel, and Daniel had agreed to help him move. When I returned to the hotel next December, his room would be empty. It would be the first time in our lives we lived apart. But as Robin had said, it was time.

With the balmy African breeze hitting my face and the sun assaulting my eyes, I squinted at women on the roadside in traditional fabrics and headdresses, selling tomatoes and cabbages and exotic-looking fruit—a luminous blur of color. We sped past men on bicycles wearing American baseball caps, boys kicking soccer balls, small stores surrounded by stretches of tawny earth, and the occasional baobab or flame tree.

The driver, a young Mozambican named Carlo, an employee at the research center, downshifted the skinny gearshift and asked if I was okay.

"Are you sick? Do you want me to pull over?"

"No, I just needed some air," I told him, drawing back inside just as he hit a pothole that sent my head bumping against the truck roof.

"*Desculpa*," he said in Portuguese. "Sorry."

Fifteen minutes later, the truck turned onto a dirt lane beside a small wooden sign: INDIAN OCEAN CENTER FOR RESEARCH. A lanky dog with butterscotch fur greeted the truck, barking and wagging his tail.

"That's Bear," Carlo said.

We drove up to a group of thatched-roof bungalows arranged in a crescent in the sand, only steps from the beach. He nodded at one of the huts. "You're in casita nine. Right there."

Like the other casitas, it was constructed entirely of reeds—the walls, floors, and small front porch. The grass roof was held in place by an overlay of mesh wire, but it protruded underneath in thick tufts. It looked like the little house was shaking out its hair.

Bear moseyed over to greet me, trailed by an African man in a pink swim shirt and terrain sandals.

"And that is Dr. Abel Mutola, our director," said Carlo, as he plucked my bags from the back of the truck.

I petted the dog's head. "Hi, Bear," I cooed, which promptly put him on his back in the hope I'd scratch his well-fed belly.

Dr. Mutola welcomed me with a wide smile. "We're glad to have you here. We can do the tour first thing in the morning—the cafeteria, the labs, and whatnot. You must want to get some rest."

"Actually, I'd love to get in the water now, if that's okay. It's great for jet lag."

"Now?" he said. "All right, of course. A team went out a few minutes ago. I'll radio Gloria and let her know you'll be joining them."

"Come on," Carlo said. "You get suited up and I'll take you out to them."

The research boats were moored in a wide inlet behind the casitas. Flying full speed into open water, I was seized by a buoyancy and freedom I hadn't felt since Bimini, not since grad school, when we'd careered into the Atlantic on field observation excursions, my body vibrating with the kind of elation that comes when I've abandoned myself to what I love. Spray misted my face and stuck to my lips. The Indian Ocean. The blueness was profuse. Rolling, blinding azure everywhere.

"You're seeing it for the first time?" Carlo shouted into the wind. "The Indian Ocean?"

I nodded, dumbfounded by the beauty, searching for the perfect words to convey my awe and finding none. "It's so *blue!*" I said.

He laughed.

Within minutes another research vessel came into view—small with a front center console and a dark green stripe with OCEAN RESEARCH painted in white. Carlo pulled alongside as a middle-aged woman with short red hair gave me a wave.

"Dr. Donnelly, I'm Gloria Walker," she called in a thick Australian accent. "Welcome aboard." Her whole body moved when she talked, not so much from the boat rocking on the sloshy surface, but from the energy packed in her small frame.

As I stepped into her boat, she held out a short yellow harpoon rod. "How are you at tagging?"

"Pretty good, but I've never tagged anything as big as a whale shark."

"You'll get the hang."

While we strapped on our dive packs and gear, she filled me in on the whale sharks, showing me several images on her laptop that she'd collected for the database. "Could be some newbies out there today," she said. "Oddly, two thirds of the sharks I've catalogued so far are males. Some have tracking devices already." She planted an enthusiastic pat on my arm. "Okay? All ready? Two members of the team are already down there."

We sat on the edge of the boat and flipped backward into the water. After two seconds of disorienting madness, I kicked my fins and trailed Gloria, descending steadily with the harpoon rod. The blue was just as intense below, only darker, thicker. Reef fish fluttered past like multicolored confetti. A school of devil rays flapped by, spinning off tiny whirlpools. Then suddenly the other two divers materialized like apparitions on the rock-strewn bottom.

I gained a foothold beside a stone and watched the others for signals. Time has always disappeared for me on the ocean bottom, as if mundane hours and minutes didn't exist. We could have been there fifteen minutes or an hour when it came—an enormous, dark mass approaching in the distance. A whale shark.

Some whale sharks reached over forty feet and weighed twenty-plus tons—the size of city buses, and even though this one was less than half of that, its size still shocked me. It approached with its gargantuan mouth open, its eye rotated forward as it moved slowly over the tops of our heads. There was an absence of claspers on its body—a *female.*

Gloria clicked her camera in rapid succession, aiming the lens at the pattern of spots behind the shark's gills, the unique fingerprint we would use to identify it, and signaled me to make the tag. I swam as near to the giant as I dared. My breath stuttered in my ears. *Now or never.* I kicked hard, darting forward and jabbing the tag through her tough skin. She quickened slightly, then cruised on farther into the ocean.

Gloria pumped her fist, and one of the other divers gave me a thumbs-up. I gestured back to him, turning my thumb and fingers into the universal okay sign. The exchange had the keenest sense of familiarity about it—how many times had Nicholas and I communicated that same way? I studied the diver's jaw, his hair. Swimming closer, I searched for his eyes behind the mask. *Nicholas.*

He looked back at me, his mouth stretched over his regulator. *Going up,* he signaled, and I ascended behind him, my heart thudding, forcing myself to take measured breaths.

When I reached the boat, he had already slipped out of his tank straps. Beads of water still dripped off the tip of his nose. He waited for me to remove my mask. "I've been here for two days," he said, eyes gleaming. "I thought you'd never get here."

I unzipped the neck of my wet suit and laughed. There were a dozen appropriate things I could have said. Polite, ordinary words that had nothing to do with how I felt. They crowded into my mind, then fell away. Life seemed so slippery and brief all of a sudden, small and bright like a reef fish you must catch with your hands, and at the same time, large and fated—a whale shark moving toward me.

Now or never.

⁓

That night in casita nine, filaments of light squeezed through the grass roof. Wide awake, with my body on Eastern Standard Time, I slipped from bed, quietly without waking Nicholas, dressed, and walked barefoot onto the beach.

The moon glowed full at the top of the sky, creating a cone of polished light on the water. I waded in, the waves slapping against my thighs. The scar on my leg shone like a long, white shard.

I rarely thought of the blacktip that bit me without feeling the old remnants of mystery and urgency. The shark had let me go, it had simply let me go, and I'd been given a chance to be alive. I didn't want to waste that. I still wanted to try and save a tiny part of the world, to save sharks, just as that one shark had, in the end, saved me.

I tilted back my head and took in the dazzling expanse. I felt returned to myself, but it seemed a different me who stood here now. Before turning thirty, I'd been tormented by the ache for what I didn't have: Daniel; a child; that lost, unlived life. But standing here now, my life felt round and full and enough. The sharks, Nicholas, even being Aunt Maeve—they were enough. More than enough.

I turned and waded through the waves, back to the world above the water, guided by the moon that shone like a bright and blemished pearl.

Acknowledgments

I am deeply grateful to the following: Jennifer Rudolph Walsh, for her encouragement and big heart and for championing my first novel. My agent, Margaret Riley King, for her superb guidance, expertise, and wealth of support. My editor, Laura Tisdel, whose brilliant editing and insights have made the book stronger and whose endless support has made all the difference. Everyone at Viking who has supported the book and worked on its behalf, especially Andrea Schulz and Brian Tart. Amy Sun for reading the manuscript.

Thank you to the following invaluable sources in Florida for taking time to answer my questions: Sergeant Dave Bruening, Marine Bureau Supervisor, Collier County Sheriff's Office for background relating to marine law. Patrick O'Donnell, Fisheries Biologist at Rookery Bay National Estuarine Research Reserve in Naples, Florida, who kindly met with me and welcomed me onto research trips in the Ten Thousand Islands. Theresa and Stuart Unsworth at Sunshine Booksellers and Chef Dennis Friedhoff at Island Café, both on Marco Island, Florida. And thank you to Charles Farmer for the tour of the South Carolina Department of Natural Resources.

Special thanks to the places I visited that helped me with the research for this book: Mote Marine Laboratory and Aquarium in Sarasota, which is home to the pioneering shark research of the late Eugenie Clark, the Shark Lady, and which served as inspiration for the fictional Southwest Florida Aquarium. Rookery Bay Reserve in Naples. The Biltmore Hotel in Coral Gables. And beautiful Marco Island.

I would like to acknowledge the Bimini Biological Field Station in South Bimini, dedicated to the study and conservation of sharks, a place that inspired me to begin the novel with Maeve studying lemon sharks in Bimini.

I would also like to acknowledge the following intrepid women who have made contributions to ocean conservation and whose work has been both an inspiration to me and useful in the writing of this book: Sylvia Earle, "Her Deepness," whose books *The World Is Blue* and *Sea Change*, and whose dedication to research and conservation endlessly inspired me and my character Maeve. She became not only a hero to me, but a presence in the novel. Julia Whitty, writer and environmental correspondent for *Mother Jones*, whose exquisite book *The Fragile Edge* caused me to see my relationships with the ocean and its creatures in profound new ways and sparked the idea for Maeve and Hazel's exchange about the shark god Taputapua in the Tuamotus. Andrea Marshall, "Queen of the Mantas," founder of the Marine Megafauna Foundation in Mozambique, whose actions as a guardian of mantas worldwide inspired me to create a research center set in Mozambique at the end of the novel.

Finally, I would like to thank my family. I'm deeply grateful to my mother, Sue Monk Kidd, who read the manuscript as I wrote. I could not ask for a better reader or a better mother. My wonderful father, Sanford Kidd, whose love and support has always been unwavering. My brother, Bob Kidd, who looked for shark teeth with me when we were kids. My grandparents, Ridley, Leah, and LaVerne, for the constancy of their love and belief in me. My husband, Scott Taylor, for his support, his partnership, and for making a home where the surfing isn't great. Luke and Lily, Hazel and Ty, for being the best of companions. And my son, Ben Taylor, inspiration for Hazel and sun of my life, whom I love more than anything.